Griffin's Cure
Adam and Grace
Book Four

For Ken

With love.
Without whom
This book would not
exist.

Copyright © 2020 J.C. Paulson
All rights reserved

The characters and events portrayed in this book are fictitious. Any similarity to real persons, living or dead, or to any businesses in existence or defunct, or to the specific situations of any organizations, is coincidental and not intended by the author.

No part of this book may be reproduced, or stored in a retrieval system, or transmitted in any form or by any means, electronic, mechanical, photocopying, recording, or otherwise, without express written permission of the publisher.

ISBN: 978-0-9959756-6-8

Chapter One

Near Hafford, Saskatchewan, 1997

Jay Griffin's thigh tingled under the heavy, reeking poultice. He could not recall feeling this precise sensation before, despite having succumbed to his mother's ministrations countless times during his reckless boyhood.

Bumps, bruises and broken bones. Cuts, scrapes and gaping gashes. He couldn't possibly count the number of times he had fallen off his bike, out of trees or onto the playground tarmac at school. Even he was amazed at being alive and more or less in one piece.

No matter the injury, Mom had a cure. Well, maybe that was taking it a bit far: the busted arm and cracked rib required trips to the hospital for casting and taping. Usually, though, Mom whipped up some infection-killing, pain-reducing, fast-healing potion that actually worked. Immediately or fairly quickly, depending on the severity of his injury, he'd feel better.

Inevitably, he'd find another way to open his skin bag.

The tinctures and teas his mother forced him to ingest tasted like shit mixed with mould and a little sugar: unbelievably disgusting. Without fail, though, once he gagged them back, he would fall into a deep sleep and awaken energized, not to mention pain-free.

Her arsenal against Jay's accidental owies also included these stinking, stinging poultices. She'd tuck him up in front of the television — or, if he'd also been bad, in bed — and apply the revolting things. There he was exhorted to stay until she declared the ordeal over.

This time was different. Oh, the poultice still stunk and stung, but this tingling thing — this was new. What the hell had she put in the bag this time? Was it safe? Was it melting the flesh from his bones?

Jay, for the very first time, peeked. Had she known, his mom would have killed him. She gave strict orders never to remove or even lift the poultice until it had completed its healing process. But Jay was fifteen now, and the realization that his mother was no ordinary human began to filter into his maturing brain. That said, he was also slightly less terrified of her. Being a teenager changes one's capacity for following instructions.

It had also occurred to Jay that it might be time to modify the risk-taking behaviour. Maybe wearing a helmet while bike-riding wouldn't be such a bad thing. Leaping off the roof could possibly be abandoned as an activity. Swinging from the backyard's massive elm trees, tethered only by his sister's cheap skipping rope, may not have been his best idea. Neither, possibly, was diving into the shallow slough out in the pasture.

And so, his brain beginning its struggle toward manhood, curiosity won over incurring the wrath of his mother.

The slash in his thigh this time came from a farming accident, not a wild desire to fly with the birds or swim with the fishes. A massive hook in the barn had swung down and across his leg, leaving a deep and profusely bleeding gash.

Which no longer gushed and was starting to close, just a little. Just an hour later.

Jay replaced the poultice and threw his head back onto the pillow. My mother, he thought, is either a witch or a fucking genius.

Chapter Two

Saskatoon, October 2007
Detective Constable James Weatherall crouched beside the crumpled body and willed himself not to plug his nose.

Shit he could deal with, but the vomit sprayed over a remarkably large area of the floor was sending ominous signals to his roiling stomach. He would have, by miles, preferred blood.

James breathed through his mouth and considered the corpse before him. The scientist splayed out underneath the strange equipment, much of it oddly covered in aluminum foil, had apparently spewed all of his inner fluids upon death. It seemed to James, as he peered at the face, that this man in life would have carried himself with an abstracted dignity. Neatly dressed, lean of body and probably brilliant of mind, death had stolen that dignity along with everything else. Life. Work. Love.

James twisted his neck to look up at the chief executive officer of the Canadian Light Source, standing beside him. Douglas Brennan was renowned for his very Zen demeanour and approach to management. This bizarre occurrence, however, seemed to have completely rattled him. James noted his shaking hands, one of them pressed to nostrils and mouth, and the sweat pouring down his pale cheeks.

Moments ago, just before eleven on a cool autumn night, Brennan had met James at the heavily-locked front doors and led him to the scene. James had toured the synchrotron in the past but experiencing it at night was something else altogether. Overlooking the massive room on arrival, he had the strangest sensation of swirling past twinkling stars to another universe. The massive electron ring dominating the main floor gleamed silver in the gloom, reminiscent of some futuristic oval spacecraft.

"Who found him?" James asked.

"One of the night janitors. He was cleaning the hallway and saw the light on."

"Was that unusual?"

"No." Brennan gave a terrifying burp. "Could we . . .?"

"Go into the hallway?"

A slight nod.

"Sure." James craved fresher air himself and followed his interviewee out the door. "Okay, Dr. Brennan. Go on."

"Our janitor, Derrick, is very friendly," Brennan said, after sucking in a deep breath. "He'll often stop by if a beamline hutch door is open and say hello. I must say I encourage the practice. It's good for people to communicate, and frankly it's helpful to know who else is around."

"Derrick's last name?"

"Jamieson."

James drew down his mask, snapped off his gloves, picked up his notepad and pen and started scribbling.

"Can you please spell the deceased's name for me?"

"Taras Petrenko. PhD." Brennan repeated the name, then spoke the letters slowly, emphatically. "Oh, God," he added, in a little gasp.

"You knew him well?"

"Yes. Very."

"Do you know if he was ill?"

"No. He never mentioned anything, and he certainly seemed very healthy; he took better care of himself than most. Taras was a runner. He often said it cleared and sharpened his mind. Which, as you can imagine, would be helpful around here."

"I suppose it would be. What was he doing here? What was he working on?"

"He was imaging plant matter, presently using spectroscopy."

"Come again?"

"In simple terms, spectroscopy is a form of light that allows a scientist to investigate the structure of nucleic acid molecules. It's one of the many kinds of light generated by our ring."

"Nucleic acid molecules." James cast his mind back to university days. "Like DNA?"

"Exactly." For a second, Brennan looked quite thrilled that this policeman was catching his drift. It was not an easy drift to grasp.

"Could anything have happened in there to cause his death? And the vomiting and . . . other purging?"

"I've been asking myself that question ever since I got here. I can't see it. If he had somehow been hit by the beam, which is next to impossible, he would have at least two serious burns somewhere on his body — where the beam went in, and where it came out. I've had only half an hour to check, but so far there's no indication of malfunction anywhere in the facility."

"I've only done a cursory check of the body, but I saw no burns. Would they be noticeable?"

"Oh, yeah. I don't think you could have missed them. Or the smell."

"I'm not so sure about that," James said, wrinkling his nose at the memory of the reek in the little lab behind them.

"Trust me on this."

"Right. Okay, Dr. Brennan. Please hang around, will you? I'll come and speak to you later, once I've finished checking the body. And also keep the janitor here."

"I'll be in my office," he said, pointing up to the mezzanine. "In the northeast corner."

James watched him climb the red metal staircase with a heavy tread, head bowed. If he knew anything about body language, Douglas Brennan felt considerable pain over the death of Taras Petrenko.

James yanked his gloves back on and replaced his mask — not that it helped alleviate the overwhelming stench. He used it simply to avoid contamination. Attired in a white jumpsuit, which he had pulled on hastily in the parking lot, he plunged back into the room of death.

Steeling himself, he carefully examined the body, seeking potential telltale burn marks. While he couldn't be positive, he was fairly sure there were none; certainly the victim had not been burned in the head, nor shot nor bludgeoned. His clothing was intact. What the hell had happened to him? Was this the scene of a crime, or had the man simply fallen ill?

Brennan had arranged for another janitor to await the crime scene investigators at the front door.

Judging by the tramping noises, they had arrived. James felt incredible relief at turning over responsibility for the body, and the revolting mess around it.

"James," said the lead investigator. "What's happened here?"

"Abby. I don't know. I can't see any wounds, there is no blood, and there are no burn marks."

"Burn marks?"

"If this was an accident with the light beam, he'd be badly burned, as I understand it from the CEO."

"Ah. I see. Okay. Let me take a look."

Abigail Markham affixed her mask and stepped fully into the room, followed by two colleagues. She gave rapid instructions to bag as much of the feces and vomit as possible, while attempting to avoid placing feet in the mess. Leaning over the still-limp body, she opened one of his eyelids, letting it snap shut a second later.

"This man's name, James?"

"Taras Petrenko."

"Honorific?"

"Doctor."

"Thank you."

The investigator silently went on with her work for a few moments, before speaking again.

"Dr. Petrenko appears to be an extremely fit male in perhaps his late thirties or early forties. There is no rigor mortis," she said, checking her watch, "at eleven-forty p.m. When was he found?"

"At about ten-twenty. I arrived about ten to eleven. It took the CEO a minute or two to process what had happened before he called us."

"I would say he was still alive at nine, nine-thirty. He hasn't been gone long, and the evidence — the vomit, and so on — is not old."

"No kidding."

"And he is still in a primary flaccid state," Abby continued, ignoring James's remark. "We will watch carefully for the onset of rigor. That will tell us fairly closely when Dr. Petrenko died."

"Any idea how he died?"

"None. He has not been stabbed, shot, hit with a heavy object or burned. However, I do detect the odour of aldehydes. A very strong odour. Was Dr. Petrenko a heavy drinker?"

"Are you suggesting this is the worst hangover from hell in history?"

"I don't know what to suggest. This man does not look like an abuser of alcohol. There are no broken capillaries that I can see, no drinker's belly, nothing." She carefully lifted the upper lip. "Excellent teeth, as well."

"Dr. Brennan — the CEO — said he was a runner."

"That fits the profile. We must ask Dr. Brennan if his colleague was a drinker, just the same. What was Dr. Petrenko doing here? What was his research topic?"

"He investigated plant matter, I'm told. At the DNA level."

"We must also ask Dr. Brennan if he could have ingested this plant matter, and what exactly it was. Could it have been poisonous?"

Good question, James thought, wishing that possibility had occurred to him.

"I don't suppose you see any needle marks," he suggested.

"No, but they are often very hard to see. We'll have to wait for the autopsy to be sure. I think I can more or less guarantee he was not a junkie, though. At least, not by vein."

"Okay. Thanks, Abby. I'll leave him in your capable hands, and head upstairs to see Dr. Brennan."

"Good."

Abigail Markham, thought James as he approached the mezzanine, was possibly the most deliberate, respectful and somewhat stick-like crime investigator on the planet, but she was also fantastic. The Saskatoon police force was well-served by having her on their side, as well as Jack McDougall, the forensic pathologist who would conduct the autopsy.

When James reached Brennan's door, it was slightly ajar; he could see the big man cradling his silver head in his arms, curled together on the wide desk. A pang of sympathy pierced James's heart, and he had to remind himself that if ever there was a damn good suspect, should this turn out to be a crime, it was Brennan. Even so, James decided against knocking; he crept several paces away from the door and stomped loudly back, giving the man time to collect himself.

Noise had the desired effect. Brennan had lifted his head and was staring at the door when James arrived.

"Dr. Brennan? May I have another minute?"

"Yes, Constable, come in. May I offer you tea or coffee?" he asked, gesturing vaguely at a small brewing machine on a shelf behind him.

"No, thank you, I'm fine. Sir, I have to ask you if Dr. Petrenko was a heavy drinker."

"Taras? God, no. You saw him. He'd have a beer once in a while, maybe a glass of wine at a fancy dinner. Taras would never have sullied his body with more than that."

"You're sure? You knew him well enough to be positive of that?"

"Yes. I'm absolutely certain."

"What about drugs?"

"No. No recreational drugs. And yes, I'm sure."

"About this plant matter he was investigating," James continued. "Would he ever have eaten some of it, for whatever reason? Maybe to experience its effects?"

"You're suggesting it may have been poisonous."

"Yes. Or a serious allergy. You hear of scientists going to extreme lengths sometimes. Maybe that's a stereotype, but I had to ask."

Brennan gave a small snort of laughter.

"Perhaps the stereotype is well-deserved. I'd be surprised if he had not ingested the plant matter at some point. But it was not poisonous. In fact, it was quite the opposite."

"What do you mean, opposite?"

"Taras was investigating a plant that may — or may not — have healing properties. But it's not like this is unusual at the synchrotron."

"It's common to shine lights through plants around here?"

"Yes. For example, we have another group testing a new wheat hybrid for higher anthocyanin levels."

"You've got me on that one. Anthocyanin?"

"It's a flavonoid. I'm sure you've eaten your share of saskatoon berry pie. Saskatoon berries are very high in flavonoids, which are antioxidants. Their dark purple colour is a giveaway that anthocyanins are present."

"And this plant Dr. Petrenko was bombarding with electrons?"

"It's a fungus." Brennan closed his lips.

"Not exactly a plant."

"No."

"Are you going to tell me what this fungus is called?"

"To be honest, I'm not sure it has a name." The CEO paused again. "Listen, Constable. We've kept this research very, very quiet. Again, it may or may not have remarkable properties. There are reasons that would stretch around the electron ring for keeping it hush-hush. Among them, we don't want the public getting too excited about research in its early days."

"I see."

James considered. Did he need to know more about this research? Should he press the point, get a warrant? Or should they wait to find out how Petrenko died? If he was not the victim of a crime, would the research prove important to the case? One way or another, this was a strange and suspicious death.

"We're going to need to know more about it, Dr. Brennan. I'm sorry. We won't share the information with anyone, certainly not the media. But we will have to understand what he was up to."

A deep sigh escaped Brennan. His grey eyes, heavy with sorrow and worry, met James's blue ones with a silent plea. James remained inscrutable.

"All right," Brennan finally said. "I'll speak to his team. I don't personally have the details." Another long pause. "How do you think he died?"

"We have no idea, sir. I'll be back in touch tomorrow. Now, I'd like to speak to the janitor."

"Yes, of course. Derrick is cleaning an office about six doors down, to the right. I'll show you."

"No, that's fine. I'll find him. Thank you, and I'm very sorry for your loss."

The grey eyes dimmed. "Thank you, Constable. Taras is a great loss to all of us, and the scientific community."

James nodded with a small moue of sympathy and left the office.

On his way down the hall, he ruminated over the dreadful scene in the small lab. An abstaining, intelligent and high-profile scientist lay steeped in his own bodily fluids. Allergy attack? It seemed unlikely. Deathly allergies normally caused anaphylaxis.

A stomach virus? Possibly, but why did he reek like alcohol, then? Suicide? No one would commit suicide like that, James thought, his stomach giving another lurch.

No. His intuition said otherwise.

He pulled out his cellphone and texted his boss. Away, again. James had warned Detective Sergeant Adam Davis only a few weeks ago not to ever take holidays. Inevitably, something disastrous happened. Sure enough.

"Sorry, Adam. A death at the synchrotron. About 9 p.m. Thought u should know."

The response came a minute later.

"When u say death?"

"Murder, I think."

Chapter Three

Adam lay on his back, glaring upward in the darkness. He had proposed to Honor Grace Rampling a mere hour and a half earlier, and like an idiot had not turned off his phone before asking the most important question of his life.

He had turned it down, but it still buzzed with startling aggression as it vibrated on top of the wood stove. Grace told him to answer it; he demurred, but she reminded him that his impending promotion would require a considerable amount of twenty-four-seven availability.

And so, he had read James's text, responded, and swept Grace off to bed. Once there, he had no trouble focusing on the love of his life, squirming and moaning under him and making him crazy. But once she had fallen asleep, he couldn't help but turn the news of the death over and over in his mind.

They had become engaged at the Rampling family cabin on Ferguson Lake, four hours northwest of Saskatoon. When Adam whisked Grace away to her own cottage, he had every intention of staying three or four days, making love at every opportunity. Now it seemed they would yet again have to cut their holiday short. First thing in the morning, he would call James and get the details on this possible homicide.

He'd been offered the promotion only days earlier. Inspector Adam Davis. Experienced as he was, Adam couldn't quite envision what this new position would mean for him and Grace, their life together, their future prospects. The hours couldn't possibly be more demanding than they were as detective sergeant, but the responsibilities would be considerable. Adam profoundly didn't give a damn about the higher pay, although it might come in handy if — when? — they had a family.

Adam worried that he wouldn't be able to stay away from the sergeant's role. He wanted to be on the front lines, no matter how dangerous, how bizarre, how frightening. Adam had not become a cop with the intention of rising through the ranks. He wanted to solve crimes. Prevent them, if possible.

He could still back out. With Grace's input, he had decided to accept the promotion only a couple of hours ago; the chief did not yet know of his decision. But if he took on the role, either James Weatherall or Charlotte Warkentin, his two right hands, would likely also be promoted. Hell. There were so many things to consider.

Well, for now he was still a detective sergeant and would behave like one. But sleep continued to elude him. He slipped out of bed, grabbed his jeans and a sweatshirt, and headed for the deck, pausing only to pour himself a short scotch.

These October nights were still and cool, and in the province's north no light pollution obscured the sky. Overhead, bright stars littered the black dome, the incandescent swirl of the Milky Way fully visible among them. Adam, gazing at the heavens, realized he had fallen in love with this place just as he had with its auburn-haired, chocolate-eyed denizen.

"Adam, love. Can't you sleep?"

He hadn't heard her pad up behind him. Grace could prowl like a cat when she chose to. Or crash through the brush like a bear after prey.

"No. I'm sorry I awakened you."

"Don't be. What are you thinking about?" she asked, coming out and settling herself beside him, a blanket draped over her shoulders.

"Everything. The dead scientist. The promotion. James. Not wanting to leave the lake. And you."

"Me?"

"Always. I didn't dream your answer, did I? You are going to marry me?"

"Yes, I am," she said firmly, and took his face between her hands. "Yes." A soft kiss. "Yes."

"Even if I have to go back tomorrow?"

"Even then."

"Thank God."

"Good, that's settled. What were you thinking about the scientist?"

"I was wondering how he died. James thinks he was murdered but has no evidence for that conclusion. Still, I trust his instincts. It's driving me slightly crazy not knowing the circumstances."

"You'll know in the morning. Call James and we'll go from there. And the promotion?"

"It's a big decision. I'll miss being on the street as much as I am."

"You adjusted to detective sergeant from constable. Will it be very different?"

"I think so. Never done it before, so I don't really know."

"You will be amazing. If you have serious doubts, you can change your mind, but know that you were born to it. Come to bed."

"Born to it?" Adam repeated doubtfully.

"Absolutely. Look in the mirror for once, Adam. Really see yourself. If you can't, you'll just have to trust me."

*****

Sleep finally took Adam out of his brain, but he rose in the grey near-dawn knowing decisions had to be made.

Again, he removed himself quietly from the bedroom where Grace still slept, dressed in the hallway and took his phone to the deck. Heavy clouds gathering over the lake threatened rain, dampening his mood.

"Are you up?" he texted James. Not yet seven a.m., and his constable had had a late night.

"Yep," came the response a few seconds later. *"Rather not be."*

"I bet. Can I call?"

"Give me 2 min. Coffee a must."

Adam gave him five before calling.

"Hey. How late were you up?"

"I think I got home about one. Wasn't too bad. I've done worse than six hours' sleep. How are you doing?"

"Fine. Tell me about the dead scientist. Why do you think he was killed?"

"Gut reaction, I guess. Things aren't adding up, so I'm suspicious. I may have learned something about that from you."

Adam felt that in his own gut. "Thanks for that," he said. "I really appreciate it, James. What's not adding up?"

"Abby was my CSI . . ."

"That's good news."

"Yeah. She said our dead guy reeked like aldehydes, and there was puke literally all over the floor. I've never seen anything like it. So I asked, did he drink himself into this gross death? She didn't exactly answer that, but said the man was incredibly fit and showed no other signs of alcohol abuse. No busted capillaries, nothing like that."

"Could it have been just the one major bender?" Adam asked.

"I guess it could have been, but the Light Source CEO, Doug Brennan, said this man had the very occasional beer or glass of wine. His body was a temple. He was a runner. Doesn't make sense, right?"

"Who was he? What was his name?"

"Dr. Taras Petrenko. He was a professor in the Plant Sciences department at the university's ag college."

"What was he doing at the Light Source?"

"Hammering fungi with electrons. Trying to see the DNA."

Adam groaned. "I see research in our futures." He paused, struck with the same thought Abby Markham had. "Did he eat it, maybe? Was it poisonous?"

"He may have eaten it, apparently. But Brennan said it's not poisonous."

"Damn. Okay. Who found him? Was it Brennan?"

"No, one of the night janitors. Name of Derrick Jamieson. I didn't get much from him. He'd knocked on the lab door to say hello and there was Petrenko on the floor, swimming in bodily fluids. Luckily, he had the sense not to clean up the mess."

"He called Brennan? Was he on site?"

"Yeah." James paused. "Okay, is that a bit weird? What was Brennan doing there at ten at night?"

"Good question. He didn't see anything?"

"No."

"We'll have to ask around and see if it was common for him to be there at night. On a Sunday. Was it common for Petrenko, by the way?"

"Yes. He was there at all hours, apparently."

"Anything else that leads you to your murder diagnosis?"

"The mess was spectacular, Adam. There must not have been anything left in his body. What the hell could have caused that in such a healthy man, by all accounts? And here's the other thing. Brennan said the research was being kept very quiet, for a lot of reasons. Maybe that's not unusual, but in this case, the lead scientist is dead."

Another valid point, Adam thought.

"We'll treat it as a suspicious death for now. McDougall has him for autopsy, I assume?"

"Yes. Abby said she'd ask him to watch carefully for needle marks. Which will go over really well."

Adam laughed. "McDougall will love being told how to do his job. Okay. We'll get packed up and I'll be back this afternoon. And thanks, James. You're rocking this."

"Thanks, Adam. Means a lot. See you later."

He *was* rocking it, Adam reflected after hanging up. He always did. James Weatherall would be a great detective sergeant. But so would Charlotte Warkentin.

Hell. There was a dilemma, if ever there was one.

Adam turned to re-enter the cabin and saw Grace on the sectional couch, curled under her blanket with a cup of coffee cradled in both hands.

"Hey, good morning. Did I wake you, again?"

"No. It was time to get up. I'm snuggling with coffee, delaying the inevitable. You talked to James, then. What did he say?"

"He's fairly sure the man was murdered. The evidence is sketchy, but he made a good argument."

Grace sighed. "Here we go, then."

"I'm afraid so. I swear I'll make it up to you. Next time, we'll go to Sumatra, or Scotland, or . . . ah, Senegal. Somewhere so far away, we won't be able to come home. Maybe somewhere we can't even get cell reception."

"Speaking of which. . ."

"I'll turn it off. Which is what I should have done last night," Adam said, doing so. "And now?"

Grace patted the cushion next to her and looked up at Adam with a plea in her eyes. She put down her cup, drew aside the blanket and opened her soft, faded purple robe to expose her breasts.

"Make love with me, Adam. Then we'll go home and start this new life."

Chapter Four

Adam and James stood on the mezzanine level overlooking the electron ring, this time in broad afternoon sunlight. The weather was fine for fall in Saskatoon, very different from the pelting rain that developed earlier in the morning at the lake.

"What kind of light was he using, again?" Adam asked.

"Spectroscopy."

"Right. Okay, show me the lab or beamline or whatever we're supposed to call it."

James led the way down the metal stairs to the probable crime scene, which was considerably less revolting than the night before but still disgusting.

"Ohhh shit," Adam said, surveying the floor from the doorway. "And this is better?"

"Significantly. Crime scene picked up most of it, but obviously it can't be cleaned yet."

They ducked under the police tape and stepped tentatively into the room.

"Prints?" Adam asked, looking around the small space.

"A few. We have identified Petrenko's, of course, and there are others, but we don't yet know who they belong to. I have a list of the people who have security access to this room. They're being printed today. But it's pretty hard to get prints off crumpled aluminum foil."

"What's with that, anyway? Why are all those . . . whatever they are covered in foil?"

"I asked that question but I'm not sure I get it. It's something about preserving a vacuum. The light is created in a vacuum, and they don't want other molecules to contaminate whatever they're doing."

"You're pretty up on your synchrotron science."

"Uh, not really. I'm working on it."

"I'm impressed just the same. But yeah, that foil is not going to help us. So he was lying here?" he asked, pointing to a slightly clearer spot on the floor.

James nodded. "Flat on his stomach."

"He couldn't have pitched forward, though, could he? He would have fallen on this pipe. There's not a lot of room in here. Does that mean he collapsed onto his knees and fell forward from that position?"

"That makes sense. He must've had terrible cramps and realized he was going to be sick. Yeah, maybe it brought him to his knees first."

"What a way to go. Poor guy." Adam continued to look around, peering at the ceiling and examining the equipment. "Is any of the fungus he was researching in here?"

"Only a sliver of it on that slide," James said, pointing. "We couldn't find any more of it, and I'm not sure it works that way. Would he usually have some of it in here, or would it only be on a slide?"

"That's the next question we need answered. Maybe it's kept in a cooler or something nearby."

"Good point. Refrigeration."

"Let's go talk to Brennan. Is he in his office?"

"I hope so. I told him you were coming."

As they climbed the stairs back to the mezzanine, Adam felt rising awe at the massive structure and wondered at the secrets it contained. He knew he'd be spending hours researching synchrotrons and the many kinds of strange, bright lights they created for the pursuit of scientific discovery. For example, what was spectroscopy, and how did that differ from your average X-ray? Daunting, he thought, but it had to be done.

Douglas Brennan indeed awaited them in his office. The door was open, and they saw him get up from his chair to invite them in.

"Hello, Constable," he greeted James.

"Hello again. Dr. Douglas Brennan, this is Detective Sergeant Adam Davis."

"Good to meet you, sir," Adam said, extending his hand. "I'm sorry it's under such difficult circumstances."

"Thank you. And nice to meet you, Sergeant," Brennan said. "Come in. Coffee?"

"No, thank you. James?"

"No, I'm fine."

"Have you learned anything more about Taras's death?"

"No," James said. "We'll have to wait for the autopsy. So far, there's no obvious cause — apart from the purging."

Brennan shook his massive head, reminding Adam of a sorrowful lion.

"How can I help today?" Brennan asked.

"I was wondering where and how the material is stored," Adam said. "Would there be any original stuff in the room?"

"There might be, but normally it's kept in a locked refrigeration unit. We wouldn't want it to spoil, of course;

it's plant matter. Or in this case, more specifically, a fungus."

"Are we talking a mushroom here?"

"Yes."

"How many people were — are — working on this project?"

"Aside from Taras, there are a doctoral candidate, a master's student and an administrative dogsbody."

"What does the dogsbody do, in this case?"

"A bit of everything. Keeps up with the paperwork, helps with writing grants, checks the locks and materials, and so on."

"We have their names?" Adam asked James, who nodded. "What else can you tell us about the project? For example, when did it begin?"

"The group began using the beamline a few months ago, but of course that was preceded by a couple of years of research."

"Just a couple? Don't these things usually take a lot longer?"

"Generally, yes. In this case, there was some unique evidence that they were onto something. Investigating the DNA was a natural early step."

Adam's eyebrows lifted. "What kind of unique evidence?"

"The fungus had been ingested and used topically by one of the students. With interesting results."

"I see. We'll need to speak to him. Or her?"

"Him, yes. He's on your list already. I'd say any questions about the early research would be best asked of Jay."

James pulled the list of potential interviewees from his pocket. "Jay Griffin."

"Yes. I called him late last night to tell him about Taras. They were very close."

"Who else knows of Dr. Petrenko's death?"

"His team. The janitors, of course. I've had to inform the president of the university and the deans of the science colleges."

"And his wife and daughter," James added. "They've been away visiting his wife's parents, but they're on their way back."

Adam considered this information. Was it significant that Taras Petrenko met his death, one way or another, while his family was away?

"We'll want to speak to Mr. Griffin right away. Dr. Brennan, I'd like a tour of the facility as soon as possible after that. Would tomorrow work?"

"Certainly. Say two?"

"Perfect. See you then."

*****

Adam and James tracked down the "dogsbody," a red-eyed Deanna Arlington, at the ag college. No, Jay was not in his office, she said quietly. Would they like her to text him? Yes, they would.

Moments later, she had established that he was out on the edge of the campus, grappling with the death of his professor and mentor. He would be expecting them.

They found the burgeoning scientist sitting on a park bench, perched on the hill overlooking the South Saskatchewan River. An ash blond mop of long, thick hair flew around wide shoulders in the stiffening breeze as he gazed over the water. His spine was straight, not bowed; his hands were clenched in his lap. Jay's posture suggested fury more than grief, Adam thought, but they had not yet seen his face.

"Jay Griffin?" Adam asked as they approached.

He turned his head, displaying flashing green eyes under heavy brows, drawn together so that they almost met. He nodded.

"Detective Sergeant Adam Davis of the Saskatoon Police. This is Constable James Weatherall. We're very sorry for your loss."

Griffin's throat visibly tightened as he swallowed hard and nodded again in acceptance of the condolences.

"Do you mind if we . . .?" Adam indicated the bench.

In answer, Jay slid his long body to the right and cleared his throat. "Please," he finally croaked.

Adam stepped onto the concrete platform and over to the bench, followed by James. He had to admit he didn't know where to start. The fungus? The science? The relationship? Or who might have killed Taras Petrenko?

He decided on none of the above. Instead, he gave his witness wings to fly in whatever direction he chose.

"Tell me what you want me to know."

"I loved Taras Petrenko."

"As a friend? Mentor? Colleague?" Adam did not say lover. He doubted there was a sexual relationship between the student and professor, and considering the latter had been married, he wanted to hold back on such an implication.

"Yes. All of those. And as a genius. As people love Pasteur, Banting and Best, Fleming. With awe and amazement and gratitude."

Adam had not expected that answer. What was this young man's IQ? Not to mention his emotional maturity?

"You viewed him as a great scientist, then. Why is that? What was remarkable about him?"

"Everything. Passion, intelligence — incredible intelligence — and openness. Patience. Speed."

"Passion for what?"

"Humanity."

"And speed?"

"When he decided something was worth exploring, he went for it. He was not just organized scientifically, but administratively. Found the funding. Filed the paperwork. Put together a team. He moved like the world was on fire, and he was the only man to put it out."

Not since Grace Rampling stumbled over the body of a bishop had Adam encountered a witness like this one: insightful, well-spoken, perhaps — no, definitely — brilliant. Adam would marry the former. What would happen with the latter? Would he prove to be the case-solver, the next victim, or the killer? Or something else entirely?

Adam waited quietly, wondering what Jay Griffin would say next.

"If anyone," he finally continued, gravel in his voice, "could have saved the world, it was Taras Petrenko. Along with Pasteur and Banting and the rest, of course. Not everyone wanted that to happen, Sergeant."

"You mean, I assume, this fungal research project had significant potential. For health purposes."

"Yes."

"What, in your opinion, happened to Dr. Petrenko, Mr. Griffin?"

"Someone stopped him. Forever. That's not my opinion, Sergeant Davis. It's a fact."

Chapter Five

Grace rattled around her — no, their — tiny bungalow, trying to focus on sorting laundry and putting away the uneaten food from their short sojourn to the lake.

They'd returned to Saskatoon at two-thirty, and Adam had jumped out of the truck in front of the police station, leaving her with a kiss and an apologetic expression in his navy eyes. Grace completely understood that he had to plunge into this potential murder case. Still, not unlike every woman in history, Grace wanted to talk about their plans, possibly even a wedding date. Did men want that sort of discussion, too? Who knew? It was her first real go at this permanent relationship thing. Apart from the fling with Mick Shaw, but that had proved disastrous.

And so, thoughts like fluttering birds — doves rather than hawks — flitted through her happy but distracted brain.

Where would they live? Would they stay in her — no, their — wee house? Would they have babes? And what about a church wedding? Would Adam prefer to elope?

Grace couldn't even realistically call her sister, which she desperately wanted to do. Hope was in Thailand, eleven hours ahead — the middle of a steamy

Bangkok night. God knew what kind of telecom charges they'd ring up on a call, and Grace didn't know if text messages would work on Hope's burner phone.

Adoption plans for little Lawan had been unexpectedly expedited, spurring Hope into a frenzy of activity. She had flung some clothes in a suitcase, called the airline and taken off in an emotional, confused and terrified state. Grace wished she could have gone with her, but last-minute flights to the other side of the Earth cost a fortune and Grace was embarrassed to realize that her passport would expire in mid-October.

So much for that. Instead, she had become engaged to Adam. And she wanted to tell Hope.

Well, she would be home soon, with Grace's new niece. Hope's daughter. Daughter! Hope had always amazed Grace with her determination and desire to help people. Few were brave enough to challenge Hope's spiky personality and status as an activist social worker. A foreign adoption, despite the paperwork, costs and navigation of international laws, did not faze her. Lawan needed a mother — as indeed too many children did — and that was the end of it.

Except that Hope had fallen utterly in love with the delicate, diminutive, beautiful child after just two meetings. That was an unexpected wrinkle so early on, bringing anxiety into the halls of Hope's heart for perhaps the first time. Grace prayed she was coping, all alone on the other side of the planet.

Hope had emailed a few days ago to say she would, with any luck, return on Wednesday. Only another forty-eight hours and Grace would meet this tiny new person in her life, not to mention hug her sister again.

Grace and Adam had not discussed whom to inform, nor when, about their impending nuptials. She assumed telling Hope of their engagement would be fair game, but what about everyone else? Was it good protocol to call one's parents with such news, or would in-person delivery be more appropriate? Probably the latter, Grace thought.

Which left her alone with her doves, until Adam returned.

Halfway through the second load of laundry, it occurred to her love-drenched brain to wonder when the police would release the news of this scientist's demise. She wanted to cover that story for the StarPhoenix. She'd been sidelined as the main byline on too many stories that year, having been involved as witness, victim and otherwise in too many crimes. This time, she had not found the body. This time, she was going to be the lead reporter on the story.

Grace raced up the stairs, changed into office-worthy clothes and spun her long curls into an untidy chignon. Grabbing her keys, she flew out the door, into her little Honda and headed downtown to work.

Less than fifteen minutes later, she was pushing her computer's on-button, temporarily ignoring the confused expression on the city editor's face.

"Hello, Grace," said Claire Davidson, coming over. "You're early."

"It's four in the afternoon. Hello, Claire."

"Early, as in I wasn't expecting you until Wednesday."

"We had to come back," Grace said, sighing. "I thought I should come in and see what's happening. Any big news today?"

"Not much. A gang stabbing. A fire. The usual. Why? Do you know something I don't know?"

"I might. Then again, I might not. There's been a death, Claire, but I don't know if it's a murder or something else. If it is a murder, I want the story."

"Of course. As long as you didn't find the body again."

"Nope. I wasn't even in the city. As you know."

"That didn't stop you the last time, when you were at the lake. Mere weeks ago."

"This is true."

Grace had been shocked out of sleep by a gunshot, which had barely registered, to see a fire burning across the lake. Flying across the water in a borrowed boat, she and Adam had discovered the body of a veteran soldier — not burned but shot to death. She'd filed the first story on the murder, and the final wrap once the case had been solved. No, she didn't have to be in the city to stumble over crime.

"So?" Claire prompted.

"Adam got a text from James Weatherall late yesterday. It concerned him enough to bring us back here."

"And what did it say?"

"There was a death at the synchrotron. No indication of how the person died, though."

"But?"

"James suspects foul play."

"Really. What a story that would be. When will we know?"

"Not sure. But I had to come in, see if they'd filed a press release to the desk. I gather they haven't."

"No."

"Damn. Well, I'll find out more later. They may be waiting for the autopsy results."

"When will that land, do you think?"

"I don't know. Maybe another day or so? I would think they'd expedite this one, if possible."

"Who died?"

"A scientist. That's all I know."

"Is it possible to call Adam?"

"I can try. I don't want to bother him if he's in the middle of this, though. I could text him . . ."

Claire's eyes suddenly flew open. Grace followed her gaze, and realized the light sparking from her new ring had caught her attention. Claire reached down, snatched Grace's hand and looked into her face, jaw dropping.

"Shhh . . ." said Grace, panicking.

"In the ladies' room. Now."

Claire gripped Grace's arm, pulled her to her feet, and half-dragged her down the hall to relative privacy. After peeking around all corners to establish they were alone, Claire whooped and threw her arms around Grace.

"Oh my God! Congratulations, Grace! This is so wonderful. I'm so, so happy for you. When did it happen? How did it happen?"

"Last night. Right before James texted, actually. It was . . . I can't quite describe it. Emotional, I guess. Incredible," she added, wistfully. "But Claire, no one knows. We haven't had time to tell anyone yet — not even our parents. I shouldn't have worn it, but it didn't occur to me to take it off before I came in."

"I'd never take that thing off. I don't blame you. I won't say anything, but yeah, people are going to notice. This is not a tiny diamond."

Grace thought about Claire's point for a moment, then regretfully slipped the ring off her finger. It seemed unfair to alert her co-workers before her family knew about the engagement. Her face clearly registered her disappointment.

"Oh, Grace. I'm sorry. Don't go by me. I might be wrong."

"No, you're not. You noticed it within three minutes. It'll only be a couple or three days. I can bear it for that long."

*****

No press release appeared by six o'clock. Grace went home and awaited Adam, who had not responded to her messages. The last time that happened, Grace had been deeply shaken with worry, and rightly so; this time, she was fairly sure he was simply busy interviewing people.

Indeed, at seven, Adam finally texted back with an apology and to say he'd be home soon.

Half an hour later, he burst through the door bearing red roses and white chrysanthemums, his bouquet of choice for Grace.

"Babe, I'm so damn sorry about not getting back to you," he said, thrusting the flowers into her arms, then nearly crushing them in an embrace. Grace quickly swept the bouquet out of the way and hugged him back.

"You were busy, methinks," she mumbled into his massive chest.

"I was. Kiss me anyway."

Grace removed her face from his shirt and tipped it up, lips opening to meet his, and lost herself in the sensations his mouth created. They lingered, for a moment, until Grace whispered, "Hungry?"

Adam laughed and admitted he was. After the flowers were arranged in a vase, Grace pulled chicken and vegetables from the fridge, and they started to sauté a stir-fry. As Grace pushed the food around in the skillet,

Adam suddenly took her hand. Bereft of diamond and gold.

"Grace?" he asked, brows coming together.

"Oh! Oh no. Adam, I had to take it off at work. Claire noticed it almost immediately, and I didn't want everyone to know before our family and friends. I'm so sorry. I was lost in thought when I got home and didn't put it back on." She paused. "I'm not used to wearing it yet."

"Thank God. You haven't changed your mind."

"No! Oh, Adam, of course not. We have to decide how and when to tell our people, though. Wait here."

Grace lunged for her purse, opened the little zipper on the side of her wallet, and returned the ring to its rightful finger.

"When does Hope come home?" Adam asked.

"Wednesday. About seven in the evening."

"Can we tell her that evening? I assume we'll get together afterward, to meet Lawan."

"We can. What about your family, though?"

"Right. Good question. I suspect Mom knows already. She knows all, without me having to say a word. But just the same, it would be the right thing to do. And . . . well . . ."

"Well, what?"

"Your father might have an inkling."

Grace's eyes flew open. Dad knew already?

"Why, Adam?"

"I asked for permission to use the cabin, and sort of hinted something might happen. I wanted his blessing, Grace."

"That's awfully old-fashioned of you."

He looked abashed, but not entirely apologetic.

"I know. I felt it was the right thing, somehow. Upbringing being what it is."

It took Grace a moment to absorb this information, and she turned back to the food on the stove, catching it before it burned.

"What did you say?" she finally asked.

"I told him I loved you like no other woman, no other person, on the planet. That I wanted to spend my life with you. And that I hoped he and your mother would be able to accept me, if you did."

"You said that? To Dad?"

"Yes."

"What did he say?"

Adam's eyes suddenly misted.

"He said you were incredibly precious to him, that he loved you too, and whatever made you happy would make him happy. And . . . he shook my hand, at first, but then gave me a bear hug. I took that to mean he would be okay with me in your life. Permanently."

Grace had no words for how loved she felt at that moment by these two men in her life, even if she hadn't been sure at first about Adam's approaching Wallace Rampling. Her hands flew to her chest as she tried to hold back tears, but they came anyway. Adam held her tightly, simultaneously stirring the food behind her back until he finally turned off the burner.

"Are you upset with me, love?" he asked, into her curls.

"Not anymore. How could I be, you with your beautiful words?"

Adam exhaled. "You're beautiful. Babe, let's get some food into us. Then I'll tell you what happened today."

"Okay," she said, snuffled, and gave her lover a crooked smile.

Dinner being served, finally, Adam told Grace about Taras Petrenko, scientist, humanitarian, husband, father and athlete, found dead at the Canadian Light Source. He explained James's reasons for thinking he was likely murdered, and before he could tell her more, she interrupted.

"Do *you* think he was murdered?" she asked between mouthfuls of chicken and bok choy.

"James has an incredible instinct for these things. But I also met a doctoral candidate Petrenko was working with. Jay Griffin is his name. He thinks it was murder, as well."

"Why does he think so?"

"He says Petrenko was the kind of man who felt he was born to put out humanity's fires. In this case, he was researching a mushroom that Griffin claims shows great potential as a pharmaceutical. Or a functional food, at the very least . . ."

"Did he eat the mushroom? Was it poisonous?" Grace interrupted again, rather breathlessly.

"He may have eaten it, but both Griffin and the CEO at the Light Source say it wouldn't have hurt him. No. Griffin says trouble had found Petrenko before, and he believes it found him again. This time, with deadly consequences. Griffin is a very convincing witness. Very intelligent; very intense.

"So do I believe he was murdered? Yes. I do."

Chapter Six

Jack McDougall wielded his scalpel with equal parts precision and fury. A baritone Scottish brogue flew from his tongue with the violence and snap of an attack dog, picked up for posterity on a nearby recorder.

"If you had told me I would ever have Taras Petrenko on my goddamn table, I would have committed you to the psychiatric ward," the forensic pathologist told Adam.

Was there a small catch in his voice? That would be a first, Adam thought.

"I didn't realize you knew him, Jack. I'm very sorry."

"Yes. Well." Jack cleared his throat. "I did. Son Number One studied under Taras. And I'd catch up to him at faculty parties." Jack taught on an irregular basis at the university, Adam knew. "We'd . . . gotten along."

Oh, man, they were friends, despite the three-decade gulf between their ages. Or at least very friendly acquaintances. How hard was this autopsy for Jack to perform? Adam gulped, not knowing what to say.

"Hell," is what came out. "I am really, really sorry. This can't be easy."

"No, it's not. But I'm going to help you find the killer."

"As you always do."

Jack glared at Adam over his glasses. "This one must be found, Sergeant. If anyone did not deserve to die — indeed, should not ever have died, especially this way — it was Taras."

"Does that mean you have determined cause of death?"

Jack sighed. Another first.

"No. Well, not exactly. I'm still waiting for toxicology. That will take some time."

"You think he was poisoned."

"Of course. With what? Alcohol, certainly. But something else."

"But he didn't drink, right?"

"No, he didn't. Well, very little."

"Did you find any needle marks? Could he have been injected with something?"

"Ha. Abby Markham told me to watch for those. The wee brat." But he said it affectionately. "No."

"Okay. What was the cause of death?"

"Ultimately, tachycardia. Heart attack. And he vomited so hard, his esophagus was severely damaged, to the point of rupture; but it wasn't enough for him to have bled out, by the look of it."

"Does that tell you anything? It's a pretty common death from poisoning, isn't it?"

"It is, and we'll have to wait for the tox report. Don't make me guess, Adam. Not with Taras."

"I'm not asking you to. What about the stomach contents?"

"There were no stomach contents, to speak of. Still, we're testing the lining — which was also torn, by the way."

"Right. You'll let me know the minute toxicology comes in, right?"

Jack gave Adam an eye roll that would have felled anyone else's self-esteem, but Adam was used to it. That was a yes, then.

"Jack." Adam held his gaze. "I am truly sorry."

"I am too."

*****

"So we don't know how he died, what he ate, or where he was that night," James summed up an hour later in Adam's office.

"No. We'll have to wait for the tox screen, but we can start tracking his movements," Adam replied. "That shouldn't be too hard. I assume the, ah, dogsbody . . . gah, what is her name? Right. Deanna. She should have his calendar — at least his professional appointments."

"Can we assume his wife is not to blame? Since she was on the other side of the world at the time?"

"Unless she left some dish lurking in the freezer laced with . . . whatever. Our next stop will be his home, and then his office. We'll have to ask about their relationship. Did she do the cooking, for example? Did they share it? We know nothing about them. Also, can we find keys to the home, or will we have to break in?"

"Looks like we'll have to break in. No one I've spoken to so far has admitted to having keys."

"And do we know when his wife is coming home?"

"Tomorrow, I think. I gather it took some time to get a flight."

"We can't wait until then. Let's get over there. We have paperwork?"

"Yep. Let's go."

Taras Petrenko, his wife and daughter lived in one of the smallest homes on University Drive, very near the campus. Presumably, he walked — or ran — to work, Adam thought, as he wiggled his lock-picking device. It didn't take long before they were inside.

He and James stepped carefully from the foyer into the living room, which showed no signs of struggle or illness. Comfortable furniture was arranged around a small fireplace, which was abutted on both sides by floor-to-ceiling shelving crammed with books. Adam stepped around the somewhat-worn sofa and peered briefly at the titles: scientific tomes sat beside modern and classic fiction.

"He, or she, or both, are not the type to live the high life," Adam said. "Fits the profile, so far. Not a mansion, and the furniture has seen some years."

"What would a professor of his standing make, in a year?"

"Not sure. Two-hundred K, maybe?"

"Yeah, so he's definitely living below his means. Nothing fancy here."

"I'd say so. Kitchen next."

There, they immediately saw clean dishes sitting to the side of the sink, at which Adam muttered "damn" under his breath. But advancing into the room, they realized there were more in the sink: a coffee cup, a glass, a plate and a bowl, along with a few pieces of silverware.

James advanced, pulling several large evidence bags from his kit, and began to extract the items with gloved fingers. Adam opened cupboards and drawers, finding nothing unusual apart from a few interesting spices and flavourings. Some of the containers were unlabelled; others were exotic for this part of the world.

"These too," he said to James. "Let's see what's in these bottles. Check them for poisons."

Leaving James to it, Adam turned into the dining room, seeking a liquor cabinet. He found it in the large hutch over the buffet. Two bottles of wine, one of whisky. None were open.

He walked down the hallway toward the private spaces, and noted three bedrooms, one fairly large and two very tiny, before inhaling deeply and entering the bathroom.

A smell assailed his senses. Adam opened the toilet lid and saw . . . nothing. Where was the stench coming from? Not the tub, nor the sink. Reluctantly, and by now certain, he removed the top of the laundry hamper and gingerly, with two gloved fingers, pulled out a towel.

"James!" he called. "Got something. I'm in the main bathroom."

Dried vomit reeked up at Adam — not a lot of it, but the towel was crusty. Unfolding it, he learned it wasn't entirely dry. Not old.

James entered and looked around Adam's arm at what he was holding.

"What does this mean?" he asked, taking the cloth and inserting it into one of the bags. "He came home from somewhere, or ate here, I suppose, then threw up and went to work?"

"Looks like it. What kind of a man pukes and heads back to his office, or lab in this case, at night? A Sunday night?"

"A man with precious beamline time?"

"It's got to be very precious. How rotten must he have been feeling?"

"Pretty awful. But then, some people vomit and then feel better for a while. Possible?"

"Maybe. Let's check the master."

Again, nothing appeared out of place, and there was no sign of illness; but Adam beelined for the clothing hamper, only to find nothing inside.

That sent the two officers into the basement, where the washing machine stood. Full of wet clothes.

"I have to say, I really wish he hadn't done that," Adam said. "I'm going to guess he threw the hamper's contents into the washer, intending to dry the clothes when he returned from the lab. I'd also bet he wouldn't have done that if there wasn't something on his shirt."

"He didn't wash the towel, though."

"It was waiting for laundry round two, maybe? The bathroom hamper is full."

"Could be."

Further examination of the house brought no further clues. Adam had called the crime scene investigators to lift fingerprints, and now heard the doorbell ring.

"Adam?" called one of the investigators.

"Taylor," Adam greeted him, coming into the foyer. "How's it going?"

"Not bad, Sarge. What have you got so far?"

"Dishes, a towel, some condiments and spices. Not much. But the man vomited here. See if you can pick up anything else in the bathroom and print the place."

"Right."

"Can you lock up?"

"Sure." Taylor grinned. Adam knew no door would keep Taylor out, so he could certainly secure the property behind him.

"Thanks. We'll check the yard and garage and be out of here. Stay in touch."

One vehicle stood in the two-car garage, but there was no obvious indication that Taras Petrenko had been ill while in his sedan. The yard itself contained a small deck, patch of grass and a sizeable garden, mostly harvested.

"Well, he either didn't use his car that night, or he managed not to be sick until he got into the house," Adam said. "Obviously, he walked to the Light Source. I wonder where his wife's car is, if she has one?"

"At the airport? Although, that would cost a hell of a lot for parking if she drove herself there. She's been away for ten days or so. I'll check when we get back to the station."

"And I'll call Deanna Arlington." Adam thought about that for a minute. "We should go see her, actually. We're very close. Might as well interview her while we're at it."

The trip from University Drive to the Agriculture College took five minutes. James parked in the loop right out front, and they found themselves a minute later in the soaring atrium of the building. The administrative assistant to Petrenko was, as James had determined, in her office, her sad eyes suggesting that the world had ended.

"Hello, Ms. Arlington," Adam greeted her. "Again, we're very sorry for your loss."

"Thank you."

"We were hoping you had Dr. Petrenko's calendar, or perhaps you know where he was on Sunday?"

"I've been thinking about that," Deanna said slowly. "I don't know where he was most of the day, but he did mention a dinner party or something like that. People were always inviting him over, while his wife was away. He . . . missed her."

"You don't know who invited him that night?"

"He didn't say, no."

"Who else might know?"

"I'm not sure. I've asked Jay, and he didn't know either. Maybe Dr. Brennan would?"

"So it could have been a friend or a colleague, but it wasn't a university event, I assume, if you didn't know about it."

"Yes, right."

"I'm sorry, Ms. Arlington, but I have to ask where you were on Sunday."

"I was home, most of the day. I came in to check on the materials just before dinnertime. Taras said he was coming in at night, and I wanted to make sure everything was in place."

"And was it?"

"Oh, yes."

"Can anyone confirm your whereabouts?"

"My roommate. I don't think anyone saw me at the synchrotron."

"We'll need her phone number, please. What else can you tell us about that day? Did anything unusual happen?"

"I've been wracking my brain, but no, I don't think so. It was like any other Sunday."

"Did you speak to Dr. Petrenko?"

"No. Damn it, no. I wish I had; sometimes we do talk on weekends, but not this time."

"Okay. Could we have a copy of his calendar?"

Deanna Arlington printed off the last month's appointments, along with the next month's, and handed the two sheets of tiny type to Adam. Busy man, he noted. And very organized. His office availability for students, classes, lab times and meetings were carefully marked and, Adam assumed, carefully adhered to.

Even with his almost-perfect eyesight, Adam was forced to peer at the time-slot entries. He was able to make out several names, including Jay Griffin's and Douglas Brennan's, likely because he was already familiar with them.

"Who are these people?" he asked Deanna, pointing to the previous Friday's appointments.

"Some of them are deans, and some are students. He had lunch with the deans of agriculture, pharmacy and biology, and an official with NSERC. That's a granting body."

Adam nodded. He was familiar with the Natural Sciences and Engineering Research Council of Canada. It was often in the local news when university scientists landed funds for their projects; Grace had written a number of stories about them.

"Is the official still in Saskatoon?"

"I don't think so. I think he returned to Ottawa after their meeting."

"Do you have contact information for him?"

"Of course." Deanna returned to her computer and printed his business card. "Anything else you'll need printed off?"

"A list of all Petrenko's students. Sorry."

"No problem. That's easy."

For Deanna, maybe. Good Lord, thought Adam, looking at the lists; it was going to take a very long time to interview three full classes of aspiring plant scientists.

"Did Dr. Petrenko have any problems with any of them?" he asked, hoping for a place to start.

"Sure. Several. But not the kind of issue you're referring to."

"I'll have to be the judge of that, Ms. Arlington. What kinds of issues?"

"Well . . ." she drew out the word, hesitating. "You have to understand, Sergeant, that Taras . . . ah, Dr. Petrenko . . . was, um . . ."

"Attractive?"

"Yes," Deanna said with an exhale, clearly relieved that Adam understood, and she didn't have to say it. "So, yes, there were a couple of students who, ah, expressed interest in more than crop development."

"Please star those names for me."

Deanna complied.

"Any other problems?"

"There were a couple of third years who wanted in on the project, but Taras did not allow it. It would not be protocol to add students to the team upon request, but they didn't see it that way."

"How did he choose team members?"

"Very carefully. They had to be sworn to secrecy, have the right academic background and very good grades. In the case of students, there are only three of us: me, Jay and Livia. They — we — are already on the list I gave Constable Weatherall."

"Did the other students know what the project was about?"

"No. They knew he had launched a new one, but of course there were no details. They just wanted to work with him. As far as I know."

"The project," Adam said, switching gears. "Dr. Brennan said he didn't know if your material, this mushroom, had a name. Does it?"

"Am I allowed to say?" Deanna's brows came together. "It is a secret, sir."

"I know. But Taras Petrenko is dead, Ms. Arlington. We have to figure out why."

She looked a bit wildly from Adam to James, and back again.

"Dr. Brennan suggested we ask you, or Jay."

"Did he?" She mulled this over for a moment. "All right. The shroom doesn't have a scientific name yet. We call it Gryphon."

"Griffin? It's named for Jay?"

"Spelled differently. G-r-y-p-h-o-n, like the mythological creature. It's a lion with an eagle's head, wings and talons."

"Why did you name it that?"

"It was inspired by Jay's name, but we decided to use the alternate spelling. A gryphon was a beast that protected treasures and priceless possessions."

Adam permitted himself a small grin; she was clearly quoting someone, perhaps the dictionary.

"A guardian of the divine."

"Yes. Don't you see, Sergeant? The project and the material are named Gryphon because we are protecting a treasure. Something that could be priceless."

Adam did see.

"Why do you think Taras died, Ms. Arlington?"

Her face crumpled. She turned away before she spoke again.

"Someone wanted to find the treasure. And Taras wouldn't give up the map."

Chapter Seven

"What the hell is going on?" Chief Dan McIvor asked the moment Adam arrived, as requested, in his office.

It was four in the afternoon by that time. Adam and James had toured the synchrotron with Doug Brennan after speaking to Deanna Arlington, interrupted only by an agitated text from McIvor telling Adam to hurry up and get back to the station.

"Was Petrenko murdered? Holy shit, Adam, I've had calls from the president of the university, several deans, the Canada Foundation for Innovation, the mayor . . . I won't go on. Everyone is very upset. How could someone die at our fabulous light source? And I get it. There's a lot at stake, like future funding, prestige, the safety of the people working there, the integrity of the research . . . so give me something. Tell me we're all over this."

"News travels fast," Adam observed. "We think he was murdered, yes. McDougall thinks he was poisoned, although we have no firm evidence of that yet. Who commits suicide like that? No way. Petrenko didn't have some hidden illness that would drive him to suicide. He was, by all accounts, completely committed to this project. He was in love with his wife. Plus, his PhD student and his administrative assistant both think he was killed."

"Could it have been accidental, this poisoning?"

"Anything is possible, but no. If I'm reading the evidence correctly, this man was a genius, and this wasn't just food poisoning. I can't see him accidentally taking a dose of anything so lethal."

"When are we going to get the tox report?"

"Hell, who knows. It may not be conclusive on the first go, either. Depends if they test for the right poisons."

"Did you learn anything on your tour?"

"Security at the CLS is spectacular. Brennan, of course, gave us an elaborate explanation of how hard it is to slip anything past the system. They have emergency shut-down buttons, backup shut-down buttons, screens monitoring every single movement in the radioactive areas, video going back months, you name it. There was no video in Petrenko's lab — they call the beamline labs "hutches" — but he was recorded coming in."

"I gather no one else was on the tape that night."

"No. Except Brennan, the janitors, and two other scientists who came and left before Petrenko arrived."

"Great," McIvor huffed, sarcasm heavy in his voice.

"It couldn't have been that easy, Chief," Adam said, smiling. "It never is."

"Sadly, very true. So, this project he was working on. What do we know about it?"

Adam explained the Gryphon Project was an investigation into the DNA of a certain mushroom, which thus far was otherwise nameless.

"I looked up the project abstract filed to the Light Source, which is the only public document that exists related to Gryphon. Short form, it names Taras Petrenko and Jay Griffin as the lead scientists. It says they're looking at the anti-inflammatory properties of a mushroom related to shaggy manes.

"According to Doug Brennan, there's a lot of research into fungi right now. It's the latest thing. So, the abstract doesn't seem to differentiate this project from others. But Griffin and Arlington say they were keeping it as quiet as possible. There's something unusual going on here."

McIvor's eyes were intent on Adam, growing wider as the explanation went on.

"How much info can we get on this, maybe from this Griffin kid?" McIvor asked.

"I'm talking to him again tomorrow. Chief, when are we going to make this public? Obviously, the entire scientific community knows, most of the university and even city council. It's a suspicious death. What do you think?"

"Get it out there," said McIvor, with a heavy sigh. "It's been two days. We have to show that we're on it. Damn it."

"I think we should position James as media contact. He has comms experience, and he was first on the scene."

Adam held his breath. He hoped Grace would land the story, and not just because she wanted it, but because she was the best reporter in the city. It would be much easier if he could avoid being the media contact, from a conflict standpoint.

"Fine." McIvor paused, and Adam exhaled. "Adam. Are you going to accept the promotion? Or what the hell?"

"Are you sure about this, Chief?"
"I am. You know it, Adam."

"All right. Yes. But can I get through the next week or two on this case first? It's got to be our priority, and it would be hard to get up to speed on the new job at the same time."

McIvor thought about that for a moment.

"Okay. All right. Fine. You have two weeks to solve this case. Two days would be better."

Adam grinned at his boss. "I'll do my best."

He returned to his office, and before calling James to update him, he called Grace.

"Hey, love. I have news."

"I hope you have a news release," she said.

"Should hit your inbox in about an hour. James will be your contact."

"Oooh . . . well done, Adam."

"You're welcome."

Grace hung up the phone and threw her arms in the air, exclaiming "Yes!" Her story, this time. Yes.

*****

The StarPhoenix, online edition
Tuesday, 6:07 p.m.

University professor found dead at Canadian Light Source

By Grace Rampling
of The StarPhoenix

A University of Saskatchewan professor was found dead at the Canadian Light Source (CLS) synchrotron late Sunday night, Saskatoon police said Tuesday.

Taras Petrenko, PhD, full professor in the Department of Crop Science, was found unconscious in his lab by a janitor. He was declared deceased by the coroner before his body was removed from the site and taken in for autopsy.

No cause of death has yet been determined, but police are treating the case as suspicious.

Petrenko was held in high regard by his fellow faculty members, students, research team and other scientists, said Douglas Brennan, CEO of the CLS.

"This is a terrible tragedy. I am shocked and horrified by his death and by the fact that it occurred at our facility," Brennan said in an interview.

"Taras was a brilliant scientist. People say that about researchers all the time, but Taras was truly one of a kind. He was also a great teacher and a good friend. I — we — will miss him very much."

Detective Constable James Weatherall was first on the scene. While he would not say Petrenko had been murdered, he did say foul play is a possibility.

He said the findings of the autopsy are not yet complete. Weatherall would not provide any details about how Petrenko died.

The Canadian Foundation for Innovation, a major funding body for the CLS, said in a statement that it was not reconsidering its financial commitments at this time.

The Canadian Light Source is the only synchrotron in Canada. Scientists from all over the world use its various kinds of light, such as spectroscopy, crystallography and X-ray, to investigate matter at the molecular level. Research projects include investigations into such things as mine tailings and the properties of plants.

Petrenko and his team were researching the DNA structure of a fungus.
More . . .

Chapter Eight

Near Hafford, Saskatchewan, 2001

Jay dropped his backpack with a heavy thud onto the kitchen floor, right next to the massive hockey bag stuffed to the bursting zipper with dirty clothing.

"Yo!" he shouted. "Dad! Mom! I'm home!"

No answer. Unsurprising. In late July, Mom was likely in the yard weeding the colossal garden, and Dad . . . well, he could be anywhere. Spraying the crops. Tending the lambs. Checking the cattle.

He heaved the hockey bag into the basement toward the washer, re-hoisted the backpack and took the stairs two at a time to his room. The city was totally more exciting, but he had to admit he was glad to be home for a few weeks. At nineteen, Jay could still really miss his mom.

Back in the kitchen, he downed a glass of cold water, then burst back out into the farmyard. No sign of either parent, as far as the eye could see. His older sister Christina would almost certainly still be at work; she had a summer job in town. Jay had stayed behind at university to grab a summer school class, a second-year plant biology elective. The faster he completed his undergraduate degree, the better.

He wandered further, still calling for the folks. Finally, Ioan Griffin came into view, emerging from the machine shed as he wiped greasy hands on a filthy cloth.

"Dad!" Jay called. "Hi. What's up? Where's Mom?"

Ioan, now an inch and a half shorter than his enormous kid, grabbed him by the wide shoulders and hugged him.

"Have you grown again, dammit?" he asked.

"A bit. Half an inch, maybe."

"What the hell are they feeding you at that campus?" Ioan regarded the burgeoning body of his younger child with something like awe.

Jay, who lived and ate in residence at the university, laughed. "Whatever the hell they want. And lots of it."

"I hope you're finished with this spurt. We can't have you looming over your father, any more than you already are. Mom's out gathering."

"Oh. Will she be home soon?"

"I think so. She said she'd be back in time to make an enormous dinner. Not that you need another one of those."

"Can I go find her?"

"You'll need your car. She's out in the forest."

"You mean the bush."

"I call it the forest, you call it the bush. Whatever. That's where she went. Go ahead; she'd love the surprise."

"Okay, I will. See you later, Dad."

Jay jumped back into his second-hand Jeep and hit the bumpy dirt road leading to the Twisted Forest, alias Crooked Bush, a well-known and sometimes well-trampled tourist attraction. It had become, to Jay's younger self, so fascinating that it had partly driven his desire to become a plant scientist. The twisted, strange aspens that gave the place its name made him dream of alien influences, of species undiscovered, of elves and fairies. And, of course, his mother loved the place, making it even more alluring.

The trip, only a few minutes long, ended with the discovery of his mother's ancient truck. She was definitely nearby; Crooked Bush was not a big place.

Sofia Griffin apparently heard the Jeep's arrival. Her blonde head emerged from the thick grasses, a smile spreading over her soft features. Her eyes, thought Jay, laughed and danced with even more vitality than her mouth. He loved that about his mother.

"Mom!" he yelled.

"Son!" she yelled back, grinning and crying at the same time. By the time she was hugging him, her tears were flowing freely.

"You're back," she said into his chest, because she only came up to his pectorals.

"I am. For a whole month and a bit. How are you, Mom?"

He pushed her gently away and gazed down into her face. At forty-eight, she looked thirty-five.

"You look fantastic," he said, answering his own question. "What are you picking today?"

"Harvesting, Jay. Harvesting. The usual — saskatoon berries, flowers, mushrooms. Want to help? I'm almost finished here."

Jay followed Sofia back to her enormous woven basket, almost filled to the top.

"What are these?" he asked, pointing to a pale berry.

"They're buffaloberries, dear. You've had those."

"They don't look quite ripe."

"Not yet, but they'll do for my purposes."

"And these mushrooms. They're okay to eat?" he asked, a bit anxiously.

She laughed. "More than okay. Now start harvesting."

"Picking."

"Have it your way."

Half an hour later, they were back at the farmhouse lugging in the laden basket. Once the treasures were unloaded, Sofia began to prepare her famous pot roast with mushroom sauce. As she patted the beef with flour while simultaneously sautéeing onions, she asked her son about university life. Jay answered abstractedly, focused as he was on those odd-looking mushrooms.

"Mom, what are those called?"

"Shaggy manes. You have to eat them quickly after harvesting, before they flake away or the inky parts under the heads begin to exude their stuff. Which is not delicious."

Jay stopped cutting potatoes into quarters and came over to examine them more closely.

"They smell earthy. Almost mouldy."

And it hit him. Why now, and not before?

"You've fed me these. When I've been sick."

"Yes."

"What's so good about them? Health-wise?"

"Most mushrooms are great for fighting inflammation, but they also have other properties. These, though — these particular ones — they're better than most. I have no idea why. The ones my mother used to pick . . ."

"Not harvest?" Jay interrupted, slyly.

"Got me there," Sofia said, laughing. "It's traditional in Ukrainian families, you know. Harvesting from the wild, particularly mushrooms. I learned how to distinguish the good from the poisonous from her."

Jay had occasionally been recruited to help pick mushrooms and berries in his childhood, but once he had grown big enough, his chores revolved around helping his father on the farm in the summer and autumn. He remembered stories about his grandmother, but more as if they were fairy tales. Now he was paying attention.

"Is this what you put into those gross poultices, as well?"

"Yes, among other things."

"Like?"

"Oh, barks and berries and things. All with healing properties. And oats."

"Mom. Remember that time the hook got me in the barn?"

"Yes. That was a bad one." Jay noted Sofia's little shiver. It was a bad one.

"I barely have a scar."

"Let me take a look."

Jay pulled out his shirttails for modesty, unbuttoned and unzipped his jeans, pulled them down and showed his mother the once-afflicted thigh.

"My God," she said, bending over and peering at it. "It's barely noticeable. How long ago was that? Maybe four years?"

"Yes."

Even Sofia, mushroom guru, seemed nonplussed.

"What in the name of all that's holy."

"Right. Maybe don't use all of those shrooms tonight, Mom. Can I take a few back to the city with me?"

"You'd have to do it tomorrow. Like I said, they deteriorate incredibly quickly."

"How long will we be able to pick them, before they stop popping up?"

"Oh, weeks yet. And they freeze fairly well. After harvesting." She winked.

"Right." Jay thought about that for a minute, as he refastened his jeans. "Can I steal a couple and freeze them, just in case?"

"Of course. What are you thinking?"

"I don't know. I guess I want to pull them apart and see what's unique about them. Something like that. I mean, Mom. What's up with these things?"

"Jay, many plants and fungi have healing properties. It's not a secret, and it's not surprising." Sofia pursed her lips. "But you have a point. Where did your scar go? Maybe the wound wasn't as bad as I remember?"

"Nope. It was bad. That was as scared as I ever got."

"Maybe that was a particularly potent crop."

"Maybe." Another pause. "Maybe it was the combination of stuff you put in there. Could it be? Did you do anything differently? Do you remember?"

"I do, because I have a recipe for poultices for open wounds. It was the same. It always is."

"It wasn't that time. It tingled and stung and stuff. More than usual."

"Really?"

"Yes. Is that the only place you, ah, harvest shaggy manes?"

"No. I have several spots. They don't necessarily come up in the exact same locations every year, right? At least not in numbers."

"We have to go pick the rest of them. Tomorrow."

Ioan came in, then, and Christina appeared from work fifteen minutes later. Jay couldn't quite keep his attention on the conversation, although he had little trouble focusing on roast beef, potatoes and mushroom sauce. Apart from that, all he could think about was shaggy manes.

Chapter Nine

Grace was thoroughly beat by the time she got home from work. Filing the Taras Petrenko story was a lot of work late in the day, and she couldn't wait to kick off her shoes, have a shower and sink limply onto the couch.

She unlocked the back door, stepped inside and immediately smelled . . . dinner?

"Adam? Are you home?" she called.

"Wrong question," he said, emerging from the bedroom pulling a clean white Henley shirt over his head. It stretched tightly over his pectoral muscles. "The correct question is, what is that amazing aroma, my chef?"

"Oops. Sorry." Grace laughed and kissed him. "What's the answer?"

"Baked chicken, Italian-style, with spaghetti. What do you think?"

"Sounds fabulous. I'm starving. But how did you get home before me?"

"It's seven-thirty, love."

"Gah, is it? When do we eat?"

"Ten minutes should do it. Go get changed. I'll find you a glass of wine."

"Oh, will you? Thank you. I'll be just a minute."

Grace wandered off to the bedroom, thinking dazedly — not for the first time — that maybe this whole

Adam thing was a little too good to be true. Some kind of euphoric dream? But no, there he was, cooking dinner. Later, he would be in her bed. Someday soon, they'd be walking down a church aisle together. Bizarre.

Grace removed her dress and tugged on a pair of black leggings with a long grey tunic overtop, then returned to the kitchen where the promised glass of wine awaited.

"How was the rest of your day?" she asked Adam, and took a sip.

"Paper-heavy. There were tons of notes from all the interviews today, plus we got into Petrenko's house. In other news . . . Grace, I officially accepted the inspector's job today. You're still okay with that?"

"Of course I am. Adam, whatever you want, but that's fantastic news. I'm so proud of you."

"I won't start until after this case is under control, though."

"That makes sense."

"Let's eat."

The man can really cook, Grace thought after a few bites of tender, juicy chicken breast, a mushroom-and-pepper tomato sauce and slightly al dente spaghetti.

"This is delicious," she said. "What kind of mushrooms did you use? I can't help noticing the things everywhere I go right now, because of the case."

"Yeah, me too. They're crimini browns and shiitakes."

"So good."

"Are all mushrooms good for people, assuming they're not poisonous, do you know?"

"I didn't know, but I looked it up. Many species have anti-inflammatory properties, as the Gryphon abstract says. Yes, I looked it up, too," she said, answering the question evident on Adam's face. "Apparently, and I didn't know this, they also contain antioxidants, and a bunch of vitamins, especially D. Shiitakes are particularly good for immunity, they say. So, well done adding them to the sauce."

"James tells me another research group at the Light Source is looking into anthocyanins, speaking of antioxidants, and whether they can be bred into wheat."

"That's what makes blueberries blue, saskatoons purple and blood oranges red, right? We should have some berries for dessert."

"We still have blueberries from Ferguson Lake?"

"Yes. And raspberries. Would the wheat turn purple or blue or something?" Grace asked, returning to Adam's comment about the wheat research.

"Apparently. Wouldn't that be weird? Blue or purple bread."

"Yeah, kinda," Grace said, making a face. "But I suppose health comes first."

Grace rose, took the plates to the sink, and dove into the freezer to search for her precious little bags of berries. She picked blueberries every chance she got while at Ferguson Lake, and hoarded them like a squirrel hiding nuts for winter.

They thawed quickly, due to their tiny size, as she and Adam washed the dishes. Grace put the mixed wild berries in the microwave for a few seconds, added a drop of vanilla, and brought them to the table, glowing purple-blue and ruby red in the white bowl.

"I wonder if people have used them for dyeing," she mused, licking a blue finger. "I bet they have."

"I was wondering the same thing. Would it stay in fabric, or wash out over time?"

"It probably would wash out. It sure does stain the skin," she said, holding up the finger.

Adam dipped his own finger in the juice that had leaked from the berries, and before Grace could react, drew a blue line down her nose. She gasped, laughed, and reached across the table to draw her own line down the side of Adam's face, from wide cheekbone to jutting jaw.

Grace cocked her head to evaluate the effect on her lover's chiselled face.

"Nice," she said. "You look a little scary. Let's see."

Another dollop of blueberry dye smeared his jawline. Adam watched her with a bemused expression but didn't speak as Grace filled in between the lines. Soon, half his face was indigo.

"You look like the Scots in Braveheart," she breathed.

"That blue warpaint was actually worn by the Picts, generations before the time of William Wallace," Adam said. "And they fought naked. Scared hell out of their enemies. If you're crazy enough to paint yourself blue and wear no armour, or even clothes, what else are you insane enough to do?"

"You would know that, Adam MacAlister Davis."

"You forgot the James."

"Whatever, A.J.," Grace said, by now in a thoroughly goofy mood.

The next warpaint application striped down Adam's neck to his collarbone.

"I like it. Maybe the, um, anthocyanins are hitting your bloodstream by osmosis."

"I think you'd need more than that," Adam said, applying juice liberally to Grace's forehead.

"You should take off your shirt. Do we want to learn that blueberry juice permanently stains white Henleys?"

Adam cocked an eyebrow but said nothing as he pulled the shirt rather carefully over his head.

"Mm. Better." Juice was immediately applied from collarbone to breastbone, in the shape of a lightning bolt that ended at the left nipple.

"Warrior," Grace said, leaning in. "I wonder if it will come off."

Grace dropped to her knees, wondering why a half-blue, although admittedly half-naked, Adam was so arousing. Was there something about a man in warpaint that triggered deep, ancient erotic centres of a woman's brain?

She licked him like a cat, from navel to nipple, soft tongue tasting sticky, sweet juice mingled with the faint salt of Adam's skin.

"You're delicious," Grace panted, drawing her tongue up to his throat. "But I don't think it's coming off."

Adam had thrown his head back; his lips were slightly parted. Now he looked down at Grace, navy eyes narrowing.

"You'd better keep trying, then. I can't very well go to work looking like this."

Grace gave him a wicked smile, reached over to bring the bowl to her lips and took a small sip before rising to meet his mouth. Juice flowed in, followed by Grace's tongue.

"God Almighty," Adam said, moments later. "Play fair, Grace."

He indicated for her to remove her tunic, and she did, wondering what kind of a paint job she was in for.

Nipples, of course. Slowly, he applied sweet dark colour until they were no longer pink. Adam imprisoned her between his legs, and sucked and licked until Grace moaned and writhed and begged him to stop, or to move on.

"You started it," he panted.

"You did," she gasped back. "My nose."

Adam ignored her, and drew his tongue down her belly, trailing blue. Grace thrust her hands in his hair, silently asking him, pushing him for more. Then the fire engulfed them. Grace was suddenly on the table, marvelling at Adam's swift strength; seconds later she was naked, watching him towering over her as he removed his jeans.

Grace stared up at this warrior Adonis adorned with blue lightning, ready to take her on her kitchen table, as if she hadn't seen him before. He leaned over, took her hands and pinned her as if she had surrendered. Which, indeed, she had. Long ago.

*****

The ensuing shower, sluicing down blue faces and bodies, removed the stickiness of the berry encounter but had minor effect on the skin colour.

"You still look like Mel Gibson," Grace said guiltily, looking up into his face.

"It was worth every squashed berry," Adam said. "I won't forget that if I live forever, you sexy, goofy, fucking incredible thing."

He pulled her close, and they stood under the waterfall feeling each other's hearts pounding, remembering the loving.

Grace said, "osmosis."

"What are you saying?"

"Osmosis. It made me wonder. You said Petrenko had no needle marks, as far as the pathologist could tell. Could the poison have been delivered by skin contact?"

"I have no idea. It would have to be fairly long contact. I'd say it's most likely his food or drink was poisoned."

"Then it would have to be tasteless, colourless and odourless."

"Yes. Good point. How many poisons are all of those?" Adam mused.

"I don't know. It's worth looking up, though. Okay, what about inhalation?"

"And another good point. Although if he inhaled . . . whatever it was, how would it have been given to him, and not to anyone else nearby, including the poisoner?"

"Sent to him in a package, maybe, that fluffed out the stuff before he could react?"

"Wouldn't he have gone straight to the hospital, then?"

"Likely. Unless he thought it was something benign, like, I don't know, dust or baby powder. And then, when he got sick, he assumed he had a gastro attack. Unrelated."

"That might work. I'll definitely follow up with Jack on the contents of Taras Petrenko's lungs."

"Meanwhile, how are we getting this blueberry juice off of us? Eek. You're very blue, Adam."

"We could look it up."

"Right."

They turned the shower off, towelled each other down and made it no further than the bed. But later, Grace fired up the computer and moments later gave a little victory whoop.

"Lemon juice, they say."

"Let's give it a try."

It stung somewhat, and helped quite a lot, although Grace privately thought that Adam might be a bit blue the next morning. Which wouldn't help in keeping her hands off him.

Chapter Ten

Adam bought Jay Griffin breakfast the next morning, after a second lemony scrub that reduced the stain on his face to a faint bruise-like remnant.

"How are you holding up?" he asked the PhD candidate.

"Okay, I think," said Jay, between enormous bites of fluffy mushroom omelette and bacon. "I mean, I've been better, but I'm okay. I've been worrying about Emmy."

"Taras's wife?"

Jay nodded, mouth full.

"Tell me about her. When you're ready."

"Emmy. Emmanuelle. She's a French biologist. They met at the Max Planck Institute in Berlin. There's a synchrotron there, as well, and Taras was learning how to investigate the structure of DNA. Molecular genetics."

"You said something had happened to him before. Was it there?"

"Yes. I don't know much about it; Taras was close-mouthed about shit happening. I didn't think it was a big deal, sort of professional jealousy or something like that. Now, though . . . now I wonder."

"Will Emmy be able to tell me about it?"

"Probably."

Adam leaned forward as Jay finished his last bite and pushed the plate away.

"Jay," he began, navy eyes focused intently on the younger man's hazel-green ones. "I need to understand what you are working on. I mean really understand it."

"I know."

"Explain it to me like I'm five."

"This is a secret project, Sergeant. I'm struggling with what to say."

"It won't be a secret much longer; you do realize that, right? And call me Adam. But I'm not going to run around Saskatoon telling everyone the finer details. I need to get this, to find Taras's killer."

Adam could see this brilliant young man's brain churning, through its hazel portal. He waited for a moment, and then said, "You have to trust me, Jay."

Finally, acquiescence.

"Give me your hands," Jay said.

Adam, wondering what would happen next, did so, palms up.

Jay took them in his own hands, and a crooked smile lit his face as he tapped Adam's forefinger.

"Blueberries?"

"Yes," said Adam. "How did you know?"

"The colour. If you had them for dinner last night, the staying power. Okay. You said to explain like you're five, so here we go. A basic thing about human anatomy: your hands are mirror-images of each other. Right?" Jay folded Adam's hands together. "This is not a unique proposition in nature. Are you familiar with mirror-image twins?"

"Yes, but tell me anyway."

"Mirror twins are rare, but occasionally a monozygotic pair — the kind that split from one fertilized egg, to create identical twins — will split later in development. If it happens too late, you get conjoined twins. If it happens in time, you get twins who may have facial features or other characteristics, like cowlicks for example, on opposite sides. One will be right-handed, one left.

"Even more rarely, the twins are opposite internally, as well. The heart or liver in one is on the wrong side."

"I'm with you so far."

"So, other living things also form as opposites. Twisted molecules. A good example of this is Thalidomide. I'm sure you remember the disastrous complications of that drug."

"Yes. I'm not clear on why it caused such terrible birth defects, though."

"Thalidomide, like your hands, is what we call chiral. It contains two molecules: the left-handed molecule in the drug was effective, but the right-handed one was toxic to fetuses. They had no idea at the time; it only came to light after they investigated what went wrong.

"Another example. Sugar molecules digestible by the human body are all right-handed. Most amino acids, which is what we make protein from, are left-handed. So you see, it's important to get it right, and to understand the chirality of molecules. Especially in drugs.

"Shining a light through matter, like we're doing at the synchrotron, to determine the makeup of matter is not new," Jay continued. "Louis Pasteur separated crystals of tartaric acid and its twin, called paratartrate, shone light through both and found that one beam twisted to the left, and the other . . . "

"To the right. They were mirror-image crystals."

"You're on to me." Jay smiled, a little sadly. "Yes."

"So your fungus," Adam prompted.

"My fungus. When I was a kid, my mother used to dose me with all kinds of pretty revolting substances. Flowers and berries, those were okay. But there were also foul-tasting, and smelling, barks and mushrooms and God knows what else.

"One day, when I was fifteen, I had a pretty bad accident in the barn. A hook swung down and slashed my leg. She put a poultice on it, which fucking reeked and stung and tingled like hell. But I barely had a scar there, three, maybe four years later. You can't see it now, although of course it's also covered in hair. Which is also incredible."

The light came on, and Adam didn't need a beamline to see where Jay was going.

"This mushroom. It's a mirror-image twin of another one."

Jay nodded. "We think that's what's up. It's why we needed to do spectroscopy, to see which way the light bends."

"And it has some unique healing properties, then."

"Apparently. Most mushrooms contain antioxidants, right? But some are poisonous, as well. We try not to eat those, and we're not actively trying to use them in drugs."

Jay paused, and his face betrayed the interior struggle of how far to go. Adam waited.

"If Mom's mushrooms pan out," he finally said, "well, they seem to have properties that are antibiotic, antioxidant, and promote cell renewal."

"You're shitting me."

"Nope."

"And not poisonous."

"Right. Look, antibiotic resistance is becoming a problem. A very, very big problem. No one in the pharmaceutical industry is investigating new antibiotics; it's too expensive, and they'd rather produce anti-depressants and other drugs that people have to take all the time. But that's not okay. It has to be done, or people are going to start dying of infections in droves. And so, we're doing it. Or at least, we're trying to."

"So," Adam said, "this mushroom, this Gryphon as you call it, could have significant potential for new drugs that fight infections."

"Yes."

"And improve immunity."

"Yes. But that's not all."

"Cancer treatments."

"Got it in three."

"Holy fuck."

Adam wondered for a second if Jay Griffin was having him on. He thought about what Grace had said last night — that there was a considerable amount of research going into mushrooms, and their prospects for human health. And he remembered the blueberry-slash-anthocyanin experience, which caused a small stirring in his loins.

"Taras was not poisoned with your mushroom, then."

"No. We've eaten those babies countless times, and in high volumes."

"What if they were distilled, or something? Down to their essence? Could that make you sick? For example, if you take two acetaminophen, you're okay, but if you take twenty, your liver might object."

"I see your point. I suppose an overdose is possible, but we haven't found that level yet. Who else would?"

"That would be my question."

"Another scientist, I suppose. But really, Adam, I don't think that's what happened."

"Why not?"

"Well, two things. First of all, none of our material is missing."

"Maybe they could have found their own?"

"I don't think so. As far as we know, Gryphon has only been discovered in one location. I'm sure it exists elsewhere — at least, that would make sense — but we've kept this very quiet. I doubt anyone else could find it."

"And where is it found?"

Jay chewed his lip, hesitating.

"Let me guess," Adam said. "It has to be somewhere near your parents' farm."

"I've never told anyone, Adam. Except Taras. Of course, my mother knows. I also know she has never mentioned this to anyone. The woman is a vault. Besides, she wouldn't want anyone messing with her special little spot."

The beam of understanding exploded into Adam's brain for a second time.

Jay Griffin was next. The only man alive who officially knew where Gryphons grew. But first, the killer would have to persuade him to give up his secret. And how would he do that?

"Jay," Adam said, trying to find the words.

"It's okay, Adam. I know what you're going to say. I know. I'm in deep shit."

*****

The dean of agriculture, James thought, was a pain in the ass.

He met the man in his office on campus, politely shook his hand, and was immediately subjected to a lecture on the importance of discovering Taras Petrenko's killer. Then the dean answered the phone three times, as James attempted to get a word in edgewise.

Finally, when the phone rang a fourth time, James stood up from his chair, leaned across Dr. Grant Stockton's desk, and firmly placed his hand on the receiver.

"Sir," he said, as Stockton looked up at James with anger snapping in his eyes. "This is a police interview as part of a potential murder investigation. I need your full attention. Is there somewhere else we can go, where you will not be interrupted? Or can we unplug the phone?"

James loomed over the smaller, seated man, leaving his hand on the ringing phone. Arrogant as Stockton was, he apparently saw authority and determination in the detective's face and posture.

"Fine," he grumbled, and removed the phone's jack. "What do you want to know?"

"Thank you, Dr. Stockton." James sat back down. "First of all, do you know where Petrenko was on Sunday night, before he arrived at the Light Source? I've been told he may have been out for dinner."

"Yes. He was with us."

James didn't expect his answer. Not boom, like that.

"Who are 'us'?"

"Myself and my wife, Ellen. Dr. Devon Horvath, and his wife, Andrea, also a professor. Dr. Evan Gorsalitz and his partner, Silas."

"And who are they?" Although James knew. He had looked them up on the university's website.

"Horvath is dean of pharmacy. Gorsalitz is dean of biology."

James paused, waiting for the third professor's area of expertise. It didn't come.

"And Andrea Horvath?"

"Oh. Dentistry."

"Anyone else?"

"Not at dinner. My children were home."

"What time did you eat?"

"About six. Early, I know, but it was Sunday and Taras had his obligations."

"What was served?"

"The usual Sunday sort of thing. Roast chicken."

"And?"

"Well, it was stuffed. Ellen made potatoes and salad and green beans."

James wanted to quip, "no mushrooms?" but bit his tongue. Did Stockton know what was going on with the Gryphon Project? He didn't want to show his hand, any more than necessary.

"Was alcohol served, as well?"

"Yes, of course. We had wine with the meal."

"And how did you feel later that night?"

"Perfectly fine."

"And the other guests? The deans and their partners?"

"Also fine, as far as I know. Certainly Ellen was in good health."

"Did you notice if Dr. Petrenko had a glass?"

"Yes, he did. Just the one, if I recall correctly. Perhaps two."

"And when did he leave?"

"About quarter to nine, I think. As you know, he had to run an experiment that night. Beamline time being what it is."

"Did he show any evidence of feeling ill?"

"I'm . . . not sure. He didn't look his best; perhaps a little pale. I didn't really think anything of it. Constable, you are not accusing us of poisoning Taras at dinner, are you? Because of course, that's ridiculous."

"Why, sir, is that ridiculous?"

"Taras was one of us. He brought not just expertise but prestige to the university. Why in the name of God would we try to hurt him, much less kill him? You're barking up the wrong tree."

"Dr. Stockton, he had dinner with you Sunday night and died only hours later. Let's say it's a reasonable avenue of inquiry. Did any of your colleagues have any reason to dislike Dr. Petrenko, or have concerns about his project?"

"Why on Earth would they? Nobody really even knows about what he was up to."

"Do you?"

"Of course. I'm his dean. Was his dean."

"Tell me about it."

"Taras was investigating the anti-inflammatory properties of a fungus. It's fairly new and very exciting research."

"Anything else?"

"Should there be more?"

"I don't know, Dr. Stockton. That's why I'm asking."

"Isn't that enough?"

James stifled a sigh.

"I'm sure it is." James had another thought. "And by the way, where did you have lunch that day?"

"The faculty club. How did you know about that?" Stockton asked, brows lowering.

"Come on, Doctor. It was in Petrenko's calendar. We have a copy."

Stockton, not deigning to respond to James's comment, rose to his feet. "Let me know if you need anything else. Now, I really have to get back to work."

He plugged the phone back in, turned his back and brought his computer to life. James laughed.

"Nice to meet you, too," he said, and left.

Once outside, James texted Adam.

Petrenko was at the ag dean's for dinner.

He waited for several seconds.

Did they have mushrooms?

Ha. No.

Did TP drink?

Yes. 1 or 2 glasses, says Stockton. What next?

Meet me at the station.

K. Got news?

U won't believe it. See u in 10.

*****

James, ensconced in Adam's office with the door closed, stared at his sergeant with the predicted disbelief etched on his face. What Jay Griffin had disclosed blew him away, as it had Adam. Charlotte Warkentin's expression showed she was of the same mind.

"Is that even possible?" James asked. "That a mushroom could cure or at least mitigate disease to that extent?"

"Hell, I don't know. But the Gryphon Project people believe it might. And Taras Petrenko is dead. So someone else believes it, too, I assume."

"Right. But who?" Charlotte asked. "Obviously, it was a huge secret. And if what the dean of ag told James is true, and even he didn't have a full picture of what was going on — which is weird, but whatever — it seems incredible that anyone else would."

"I suppose he could have been killed for another reason," Adam mused. "Unrelated to Gryphon. Jealousy? We haven't met his wife yet, and Deanna Arlington mentioned that some of the young women in the college were fonder of Taras than they needed to be." Adam shook his head. "But would any of them have the technical knowledge to pull off a murder like that? We don't even know what killed him yet."

"I don't know if they would," James said. "Still, this Griffin kid seems like a bit of a genius; maybe there's another Einstein in the crowd?"

"Hell," Adam said. "We need that tox report. Char, can you call McDougall's office and see how far out it is? And here's the other thing."

Charlotte nodded, anticipating the other thing. "Jay Griffin."

"Yes. He's refused any kind of police protection. But that doesn't mean we can't provide a little surveillance. But who? Who won't be easily recognized as a cop on campus?"

James snorted. "Too late for you and for me. And Char's photo has been in the paper a couple of times, too. It sure as hell can't be Lorne Fisher."

Adam and Charlotte laughed, trying to picture enormous Lorne Fisher, the biggest cop on the force — maybe the biggest cop in the province, or even the country — going unnoticed undercover at the Light Source.

"Here's a thought," Charlotte finally said, wiping her eyes. "Those young women, who were trying to get it on with their professor. Maybe they'd talk to someone like them. Like Joan Karpinski. Young. Smart. Attractive."

"That's brilliant, Char. But has she ever been in the paper? Or on TV?" Adam asked.

"She's been quoted, but I don't remember a photo."

Adam swiveled his chair over to his computer. A quick internet search showed no sign of Sgt. Joan Karpinski's face in the media.

"Sold," he said, and dialled a number. When someone answered, he said, "Karpinski."

"Yes, Sarge."

"Want to be a mushroom for a few days?"

"The kind that stays in the dark and gets fed bullshit?"

"Exactly."

Chapter Eleven

Grace couldn't sit down. She shifted her weight from one foot to the other, practically hopping with excitement and tension.

The damned plane, with Hope and Lawan on it, was late and her patience had long since snapped. Grace stood, or rather vibrated, in front of the wide windows overlooking the tarmac, not really trying to hide her frustration.

"I'm going to check the arrivals board," she told Adam, turning to leave the area where, oddly, there were no information screens.

"For the tenth time."

"Well? What else am I going to do? Just stare out the window?"

"Come here."

Adam's arms encircled her, and his lips touched her forehead.

"Babe, it's frustrating, but it's going to be okay. They're a little bit late, and Thailand is very far away. Any number of things — minor things — could have delayed the plane. Besides, they had two connections, right?"

"Three. Bangkok to Paris to Toronto, then home."

"Yeck, that's a hell of a trip, especially with a little one. Hang in there, honey. It should be only another half hour. Want to get a drink or something?"

"Nope. I want to glare at the stupid empty tarmac."

It wasn't exactly empty. Domestic flights landed and took off in the gathering gloom, but Adam knew what she meant. He simply stood behind her, his cheek against her crazy, curly bright hair, and held her back against his chest, trying to soothe his agitated love.

"Going to be fine," he crooned.

Finally, half an hour later, in October darkness, a massive aircraft suddenly came into view, lights flashing as it taxied toward the airport.

"Eep! Is that it, Adam?"

"Must be. You wait here. I'll go check the board."

"No, I'm coming with you."

Hands clasped, they hurried around the corner and almost ran physically into Jay Griffin, who was standing below the arrivals board staring upward.

"Jay," Adam said. "Sorry, just about knocked you over. What are you doing here?"

"Adam," said the young man, clearly surprised. "No problem. I'm here to meet Emmy. She's on the plane from Toronto."

"Right, I remember now. We're meeting that plane too. Grace's sister is on it. Grace, meet Jay Griffin. Jay, this is my . . ." Adam nearly said fiancée, and barely bit it back. "Girlfriend," he finished, lamely.

"Nice to meet you," Grace said, holding out her hand.

Jay's eyes betrayed him; they widened with appreciation as he gazed down into her face. The look was not lost on Adam, whose chest puffed out with . . .

no, not jealousy. Pride. He took a breath. He had to get used to men looking at Grace that way. How could they help it?

"Nice to meet you, too," Jay said. "We'd better get over to the arrivals lounge. I don't want Emmy to think I'm not here to greet her."

"Yes! Let's go," Grace agreed, enthusiastically. "I can't wait to see Hope. My sister. She's been away for a long time and I've really missed her. And I'm going to have a new niece!" She stopped. "I'm sorry. I'm babbling."

Adam and Jay both smiled at her.

"I think it's great that you're so happy to see your sister," Jay said, earnestly. "It's hard to miss your people."

Man, thought Adam, this is an amazing kid. Although, he supposed, Jay was only what, seven years younger than himself?

"That's so sweet of you," Grace said. "I'm sorry you're meeting Emmy at such a hard time."

"Grace knows about Taras," Adam interjected. "And about Emmy. She's covering Taras's death for the StarPhoenix."

"Right. You're that Grace. Rampling, is it?"

"Yes . . . oh! Look, it's Hope! Hopey!" she squealed, pushing through the small crowd.

Grace stopped in front of her sister to briefly gaze at the tiny child in her arms, and a second later threw her arms around both of them.

"I'm so glad you're home," she said in Hope's ear.

"I am too," said Hope, returning the embrace with one arm. "Grace, meet Lawan. Lawan, this is your Auntie Grace."

The child stared at this new person, but she did not cry or scream. Lawan had met too many people in the

Thai orphanage to react much at all, and Grace looked a bit like Hope. Lawan seemed unphased by the hoopla in the airport. She'd been through three of them already; maybe it was becoming old hat.

Adam loomed over Grace's shoulder, waiting patiently to meet the little girl who would also be his niece. In his heart, she already was. Beautiful, tiny, too thin, her wide brown eyes took in the new world around her. He had to swallow hard around the tightening in his throat.

"And this," said Hope, pointing to him, "is your Uncle Adam."

That did it. Adam stepped forward and embraced all three members of his new family, blinking back emotion.

"Hello, Hope. Hey, little one. Welcome home."

"Aw, Adam," Hope said. "We're so glad to be here." She adjusted Lawan on her hip and pulled away to look into her sister's face, and then into Adam's. "So, what's new?"

"Oh, not a lot. Adam's working on a crazy case, and I'm covering it . . ." Grace said, only to be interrupted.

"That's not what I meant, Grace, and you know it." Hope grabbed her sister's hand and gave her a quirky grin. "Ah. So I was right, then. Something new on this finger."

"Damnnn," Grace said.

"Hope," Adam said. "We haven't told anyone yet. We were waiting for you."

"Squeee! When did it happen? Congratulations, you two! I'm so happy for you!" More clumsy hugging ensued around Lawan, who this time was slightly crushed by the group embrace and squeaked.

"Oh! Baby, I'm sorry," Hope said. "It's okay, it's okay. Happy. We're happy. Remember that word? Happy!"

"Appy?" Lawan repeated.

"Yes. Happy! Now, can we get the hell out of here? Let's go see if the luggage has landed. And you, sister. You will tell me everything later."

Adam blushed. Grace smiled.

"Can I carry her?" Adam asked. "Or will she cry?"

"Hey, wait, Adam. I haven't held her yet," Grace protested.

"Well then, get on it, Auntie Grace," he said, laughing.

Grace held out her arms to Lawan, who, after a moment's hesitation and a look at Hope, said "appy" and reached out with her own little arms. And Grace, tears streaming down her cheeks, finally held this little person who had brought so much joy to her sister.

They made their way to the carousel, where the luggage had not yet arrived. Adam spied Jay speaking to a diminutive brunette and led his little group over to stand next to them. He hoped Jay would introduce him to Emmy; he didn't want to lurch into her life at this moment, in a professional capacity, but he did want to meet her.

"Hey, Adam," Jay said, as soon as he noticed him. "Let me introduce you to Emmy. Emmy, this is Adam Davis. He's the sergeant on Taras's case."

Sad eyes looked up at Adam, and Emmanuelle Bisset Petrenko extended her hand.

"How are you, Sergeant?"

"I'm well. I am so sorry for your loss. How are you holding up?"

She shrugged. What could she say, after all, Adam thought. But there was something odd in her demeanour. She was clearly devastated, but somehow she seemed, what? Resigned, he thought.

"We will speak soon, I am sure," she said, a slight accent betraying her French birth. "This is my daughter, Clara."

"Hello, Clara." What should he say? "I'm sorry."

The girl, probably ten or eleven, nodded and looked down. "Thank you," she said, but it was barely audible.

Grace watched all of this, holding Lawan and fighting fresh tears; Adam could see her chocolate eyes were veiled in mist. He cleared his throat and turned to his right.

"Hope, this is Jay Griffin. He's, ah, helping us with that case Grace mentioned. Jay, this is Hope Rampling. And this," he added with a gesture toward Grace, "is her daughter, Lawan."

"Congratulations, Ms. Rampling," said Jay. "It's very nice to meet you."

"Thank you," Hope said, having to tilt her head back to look at this wide-shouldered, tall young man with the long hair, neatly tied back. "And you."

"The flights must have been hard on the little one."

"I think so, but she was very good. Slept most of the way from Toronto, so she's wide awake now."

"I gather it's her first time in Canada?"

"Yes, I just picked her up in Thailand."

"Amazing." Jay looked at Lawan, still peacefully curled in Grace's arms. "She's a beautiful little thing."

"She is, isn't she? And very sweet. I fell in love with her the minute I met her."

"Love at first sight. I guess that applies in more than one human situation." Jay held Hope's gaze.

"I — I guess it does." Hope looked down, then over to the carousel, cheeks flaming. "Oh, finally. Here comes the luggage," she said, and dove toward the emerging suitcases.

Adam's eyebrows shot upward as he gave Grace a meaningful, slightly confused look, and went to help Hope with the heavy bags.

"I get to hold her after we get to Hope's," he said over his shoulder. "So there."

*****

"What do you suppose that was about?" Grace asked Adam.

They were snuggled in bed, after dropping off Hope and Lawan at their home. Adam finally got to hold the little girl, who eventually fell asleep in his arms, while Grace arranged a family meal with her sister and promised to visit the next day. It was high time everyone learned about the engagement.

"Jay and Hope, you mean?"

"Of course."

"I don't think I've ever seen Hope blush before."

"Yeah, well, it doesn't happen very often. You know how composed she is, and how snarky she can be. Mother Lion, if ever there was one, including with me. As you've noticed."

"He got to her. And she to him."

"I thought so too. What was that comment about love at first sight? Who is this kid? He's so . . . intense, I suppose, and his manners are beautiful, if unique. He seems able to start a conversation with anyone."

"He doesn't hold back. He also told me he loved Taras Petrenko. As a mentor, a friend, a colleague and a genius. As we love Pasteur and Banting and Best. And I'm positive, at this point, that he's, uh, into women. Who says that kind of thing?"

"I know. Unique, like I said."

"You're unique."

"You are."

Adam turned Grace around, so that her back faced him, and tucked her into his body. He drew aside her auburn mane and kissed the back of her neck.

"It was love the moment I first saw you," he whispered, rising against her buttocks.

"Oh, Adam . . ."

"It always will be."

"I love you." Grace paused. "I want Hope to feel like this. To be happy, to not be able to get enough of her lover. Do you think it will ever happen?"

"If I saw what I think I saw, it could. Depends if someone can persuade her to let go and give it a shot."

"He'd have to accept Lawan."

"I'm pretty sure he already did that." Adam's hand had slipped around Grace's waist, and lower. "Let's talk about it some more tomorrow."

"Good idea," Grace gasped.

Chapter Twelve

Sgt. Joan Karpinski, aka Joan Carpenter, strode across campus looking exactly like a college student. It wasn't all that hard, considering she was in her early thirties and looked at least five years younger.

Her gear subtracted another couple of years. She had the obligatory backpack, water bottle, and Huskies paw-prints — the logo of the university's sports teams — on her jacket. Jeans, boots and long hair drawn into a swingy ponytail. Indeed, she hadn't been out of college long enough to have forgotten the drill.

Adam had rapidly wrangled her some new identification, a student card, and admission to two classes: one in plant sciences, and one in biology. He'd only been defeated when he attempted to get her a seat in a pharmacy class, but he was working on it. Dentistry was out. Karpinski could fake it through the sciences, but not through drilling teeth.

"Be careful," he warned.

"I won't give the game away, Sarge. I promise."

"That's not what I meant, Karpinski. We don't know much at this point, but I do know something ungood in the extreme is going on. Don't put yourself in danger. Don't ever go to the Light Source alone or any of the labs, especially at night, if indeed you can get in there. I mean it."

"Yes, Sarge. I'll be careful."

Joan slipped into an empty desk moments before the class's eight-thirty start time, in the College of Agriculture building. A substitute professor had taken over Taras Petrenko's agricultural biology class, and at the moment he had his back to the students as he madly wrote incomprehensible things on a white board.

Joan had looked up the ag biology degree description on the university website, to better understand what the hell was going on.

"Agricultural biology," she had read, "provides students with the ability to apply scientific principles to biotechnology, genetics, evolution and wildland ecology including but not limited to wildlife and conservation biology, toxicology and environmental conditions, as well as wildlife and domestic animals."

Nothing to it, then, she thought. Yikes. But it made sense to her, from the murder case perspective. Petrenko had combined his knowledge of plants, molecular genetics, toxicology and ecology in the study of this crazy mushroom. Got it.

Joan knew she was not an idiot, and she had taken several science classes while pursuing her degree; but most of those related to basic biology and human anatomy, in support of her ambition to become a police sergeant. Or chief, maybe, some day. She was definitely out of her comfort zone here, but hopefully would only have to fake it for a few days.

On the bright side, this prof likely wouldn't notice that one of his students was new to the class, which Joan took as a bonus.

She casually looked around at her fellow students, numbering about twenty-five. More than half were young women. Damn. Which of them had actively chased their professor? She had a couple of names, provided via Adam by Deanna Arlington, but who was who?

"Right!" said the professor, suddenly and very loudly, shocking Joan out of her musings. "For those of you who don't know me, I am Eric Bantle, and I will do my best to carry on with this class after the terrible events of last weekend. Let me say that I am personally devastated by the death of Dr. Petrenko, and I am very sorry for your loss, as well. Dr. Petrenko was a great scientist, a great teacher, and a great man."

He stopped bellowing to take a breath, and Joan peered surreptitiously at the students. Every single person in the room carried an expression of sorrow, even misery. But three of them were weeping, one openly. Joan made a mental note. *Start with the blonde in the blue sweater.*

The class was long — a weekly seminar — which was both good and bad. Bad, because Joan had to pretend to follow along for two and a half hours. Good, because it gave her time to evaluate the people around her.

Finally, it ended. Joan rapidly closed her computer, tucked it into her backpack, and rose to her feet, all the while closely watching Blue Sweater, who had fortunately stopped crying. Catching up to her at the door, Joan dropped her water bottle, lunged for it, and bumped into the blonde's leg.

"Oooh, sorry!" Joan exclaimed. "You okay? Gah, I'm so clumsy."

"Oh, no problem. I'm fine, thanks."

"I love your sweater, by the way," Joan said. "Where did you get it?"

"At Jenny's. It's my fave store."

"Where is it? I've just transferred here, so I need some tips on where to shop."

By now, Joan and Blue Sweater were walking together down the corridor.

"Downtown, on Second Avenue," Blue Sweater said, telling Joan something she knew very well.

"Thanks, I'll have to check it out. By the way, what was that about the professor? Um, Dr. Petrenko? What happened? Everyone looked very upset when Dr. Bantle talked about him."

Predictably, the young woman's eyes refilled with tears. Joan looked into her face with sympathy.

"My name is Joan," she said. "I'm sorry. You're obviously very upset. You don't have to talk about it."

"I'm Melanie," the blonde sobbed. "Thank you. I . . . um, really liked Dr. Petrenko. It was so awful, what happened to him."

Joan scrabbled for a tissue, purposely packed for this eventuality, and held it out. "Awww. Here."

Melanie dabbed at her bright blue eyes and blew her nose. "He was found dead at the Light Source. You know the Light Source?"

Joan nodded. "I think every university science student in Canada knows the CLS. That's terrible."

"No one knows what happened, just that he's dead. The police say there may have been 'foul play'" — Melanie added the quotation marks with her fingers — "but that's all they've said."

"No one on campus knows?"

"No one I've talked to. Livia has kept her mouth shut, and so have Jay and Deanna. It's very upsetting. They should tell us."

Livia, Jay, Deanna. Joan recognized the names; the student members of Petrenko's team.

"Who are they?" she asked anyway.

"They were working on a project with him. Grad students. Jay is a PhD candidate."

"Oh, I see." Joan paused. She had to keep this conversation going. "Do you have time for a bite or a cup of coffee? I'd sure appreciate some intel on the campus. Like where to go for a drink on Fridays."

Sniff. Dab.

"Sure. Let's go down to the cafeteria."

Conveniently, if sadly, the two women encountered an enormous photo of Taras Petrenko as they left the elevator on the main floor. Surrounded by flowers and a large sign reading "In Memoriam," his incredibly handsome face could not be missed from anywhere in the atrium.

"Ohhh," said Joan, trying to sound both impressed and sad at the same time. "That must be him. My God, he was so gorgeous." She paused, and looked at Melanie, whose face was screwing itself into a mask of misery again. "I'm sorry, that was a dumb thing to say. I guess I was surprised."

"He was beautiful, wasn't he," Melanie said. "He shouldn't be dead. He can't be. It's not fair!"

"No, he shouldn't be. Here, sit down," Joan said, slightly appalled at the depth of feeling emanating from Melanie's vibrating body. "Can I get you something? Some tea, maybe?"

"Would you?" Melanie looked up as Joan stood. "That's very sweet of you."

"I'll leave my gear here, if that's okay," Joan said, turning. She didn't want her witness to escape.

"Of course."

"Milk and sugar?"

"Please."

Two minutes later, Joan returned with the tea, and handed a cup to Melanie as she muttered soothing sounds.

"It looks like everyone admired him," Joan said, indicating the students gathered around the photo — several of them delivering yet more flowers.

"Yes, he was one of a kind. He was a super good teacher, and so nice."

"Aww. In what way was he nice?"

"Well, he never yelled. If you screwed up an exam, he'd call you into his office and carefully explain where you went wrong. He wanted us to succeed."

Joan Karpinski knew when to shut up. She nodded encouragingly and patted Melanie's hand.

"He was so smart. Almost scary smart. But he didn't act that way, you know? It wasn't like he was one of us; more like an older brother, almost. Well, not quite. But he treated us with respect. He'd even have us over, once in a while."

"Over?"

"He'd have end of semester parties for us higher-years. They were really fun, and it was nice to kind of get to know him outside school."

"Like, at his house?"

"Oh yes. A little house, for a professor. But it was such a nice thing for him to do." Melanie snorted. "I don't think his wife liked it, though. Cold bitch. She always stayed in the kitchen. I don't know what he was doing with her."

"Yeah, no accounting for taste," Joan supplied. "Must be nice to have a prof who throws parties."

"Right?" Melanie dropped her voice. "I sneaked into his bedroom once. Just to see."

"See? See what?"

"I don't know. Where he slept. What he smelled like at home. If he was messy."

Oh shit, Joan thought. This girl had it bad.

"He caught me, though," Melanie added, giggling. Then burst into tears again.

"What happened?" Joan asked, a touch breathlessly.

"He laughed, took my arm and we went back to the party. I knew, then, that he liked me. Really liked me, if you know what I mean." Another ocular flood. "And now he's dead. And I'll never, ever see him again."

*****

"She sneaked into his bedroom? At a party?"

"Yep. So what do you think, Adam?" Joan asked, after a lively recounting of her conversation with the smitten Melanie, whose last name had proved to be Martens. "She is upset, with capital letters. I don't think she was the only one, either."

"The obvious conclusion is that if she was going to kill anyone, it would not be Taras. It would be Emmanuelle Petrenko. Who, by the way, does not strike me as a cold bitch, although she's certainly reserved."

"I agree, about Melanie. But who knows? Maybe he spurned her at some point, and she lost her mind. Possible?"

"Possible. Is she bright enough, do you think, to orchestrate a murder? I suppose all she had to do was feed him something vicious, but in what context? Would he have shared a meal with her?"

"Good question. And she's not the brightest bulb in the room, I'd say, but certainly smart enough to have made it to third year ag biology, which I'm here to tell you is no small thing. I wouldn't take her off the suspect list yet."

"Okay. So you're off to biology tomorrow?"

"Yes. Hope I find myself another nice suspect."

"Were you able to keep tabs on Jay?"

"Yes, I checked on him several times. Texting worked well, but I also went over to his office and hung around his afternoon classroom. Still, Adam, we may want to add a body up there. Where are we with the tox screen?"

"Not very far. They expedited it, but we only have results on the easy stuff so far. No cocaine, no heroin, no fentanyl, no meth. We knew that, more or less. Although I suppose it could have been a massive dose of junk, considering the vomit; but it wasn't."

"Melanie could probably get her hands on some interesting dope."

"As could anyone in the higher years of plant science. Or biology. Or pharmacy."

"True."

"Which means we have something like four hundred suspects, if you include faculty."

"Theoretically."

"And that's just on campus."

"Yup."

"Terrific."

*****

Adam and James walked up the path to the colonial house on University Drive for the second time that week. Emmanuelle Petrenko had agreed to see them in the afternoon.

She came to the door, sleek black hair framing her pale face. Petite and very pretty, Emmy Petrenko also had a soaring IQ, Adam knew. One of the genetic lottery winners. As her husband had been.

"Mrs. Petrenko," Adam said, quietly. "Thank you for seeing us."

"Please. Call me Emmy. Come in."

She led the way to the living room, where cookies and tea were already waiting.

"Do you like tea?" she asked. "I can also make coffee."

"Tea is great, thank you," Adam said. "Very kind."

"I will pour, then."

Adam waited until she had done so, wondering if small talk before questions would ease the situation. He decided it would not.

"Again, Mrs. Petrenko . . ."

"Emmy."

"Emmy. I — we — are so sorry about the loss of Dr. Petrenko. How did you learn of his death?"

"Doug Brennan called me in Paris. He had my number because I am also a professor. It was, I think, about eight in the morning, in France."

"About midnight here. That must have been a terrible shock."

"I think you know it was not, really."

Now Adam was shocked.

"What do you mean?"

"Jay has told you, has he not, that Taras encountered a problem in Berlin. *Oui*?"

"Yes. I don't know the nature of the problem, though. He said you, perhaps, could tell me."

She gave a sharp nod.

"Taras was a post-doc at the time but had not yet decided on where he would take a position. He had discovered something while at the synchrotron in Berlin. How do I explain? An issue with a new drug. He was helping a big pharmaceutical company prove the efficacy of this drug. For Alzheimer's. The drug contained nicotine, but also something else. In Taras's opinion, it would have had some very negative effects on patients. Do you understand?"

"I think so, so far. I know that Thalidomide had two molecules, one that worked, but the other caused birth defects. Would this have been similar?"

"Yes, in a way, although the chiral properties of Thalidomide affected the offspring, not the mother. In this case, the product they were developing, which was somewhat similar to Buproprion — that is a black-box drug for anxiety — would have caused depression, nightmares, and almost certainly suicidal thoughts. I don't think patients with early Alzheimer's disease would have coped very well with those side effects. Do you?"

"No, I see your point. Was he using the Berlin synchrotron to investigate this drug?"

"Yes, in part. Similar to the way they finally investigated Thalidomide."

Holy shit, Adam thought.

"And what happened?"

"Well, you can imagine the company was unhappy with his findings."

"He revealed them, of course."

"Of course. At the time, Taras was a bit naïve, I would say. He thought everyone on Earth, including big pharma, would only want to do the right thing when it came to human health. He was wrong."

Adam heard James release an enormous breath, which he had clearly been holding while Emmy spoke. Then he heard a whispered "God Almighty" from his Catholic partner. Adam had to agree.

"And then?" Adam prompted.

"He was fired for insubordination. And later, threatened."

"In what form?"

"A letter came to our apartment. We were living together by then. It suggested Taras either consume the contents of a small bag tucked inside — to emphasize the threat was serious, you know — or leave the country and never again work in anything related to pharmaceuticals. And to keep his mouth shut. Or else."

"Obviously he did not take most of that advice. Did he keep his mouth shut?"

"No." Emmy vehemently shook her head. "Taras could not possibly have held back that information. He reported the company to the German authorities. A week later, he was followed, but we were lucky; there was a police officer nearby, and Taras struck up a conversation with him. We left Berlin the next day."

"How?"

"By car. We did not feel safe going by train or air. Too public, too easy to be captured on a surveillance system."

"Where did you go?"

"Paris. We hid with my parents for several weeks, as Taras worked to find a position somewhere far away. He had been offered several. He ultimately took an assistant professorship at the University of Toronto and confined himself to teaching plant biology. But then he learned that the Canadian Light Source was to be built in

Saskatoon. He had to come. The university welcomed him. And me."

"Did you test the contents of the bag?"

"We had no resources to do so at the time; we were on the run. Later, it proved to be a garden-variety rodent poison. At least, it contained such a poison. There may have been others, as well. We discarded it after that."

"Did he ever hear from the pharmaceutical company again? Why has this happened now?" Adam asked in a low voice.

"Taras Petrenko was born Marko Taras Petrovich, Sergeant. He changed his name before we came to Canada. As did I. My real name is Amélie. It took some time, but someone found him."

"Was he born in Ukraine?"

"No. In Germany, but to Ukrainian immigrants. And so, Sergeant Davis, no. I was not shocked to hear this news."

Chapter Thirteen

Two for the price of one, Joan Karpinski thought as she plunked her bag on the floor of the biology classroom.

This upper-year seminar was going to kick her ass — she prayed silently that no one would ask her a question — but Petrenko's master's student, Livia Balan, sat two desks ahead of her, and Dr. Evan Gorsalitz, dean of biology, stood at the front of the room.

Excellent people-watching opportunity. Joan pulled out her computer and settled in.

"And who might you be?"

The professor's voice shocked Joan as she straightened in her seat.

"Joan Carpenter, sir," she said quickly. "I've just transferred here."

"Welcome, Ms. Carpenter. What degree are you seeking?"

Ugh.

"Ag biology."

"Ah. Well, we'll give you a little space today. All right, people. Let's dive in."

Joan looked down and allowed herself a small exhale. She'd better get on this investigation if her cover was to remain intact. Obviously, she couldn't very well show up to this class more than a couple of times. She'd be busted.

The subject matter Gorsalitz delivered soared over Joan's head, as she expected. She watched him closely. His movements were tidy, precise. His clothing was clean, if not pristine. He was not specifically handsome, skin being rather pocked from acne, but he presented well. Smart, of course. Not too arrogant.

This morning, unlike yesterday, Joan focused on catching up to one person. Livia Balan. Even so, she took notes on all the young women in the room — only six of them, this time. Since the dean had not mentioned Petrenko, Joan couldn't go by the students' reactions to his name as she had in yesterday's class. Livia first; then she'd determine next steps.

Livia, if Joan read her correctly, was quite a different beast from Melanie. While Melanie was far from stupid, she was also an emotional wreck. Livia was cool, controlled, beautiful and, judging by her input during the class, brilliant. Was she another Einstein, like Jay Griffin?

Bumping into her was unlikely to work, as it had with Melanie. Besides, if they compared notes, they might wonder why Joan was always so clumsy. A different tactic, then.

At the end of the seminar, Joan watched Livia pack up her gear and approach the dean.

"Dr. Gorsalitz, may I book an office visit for Monday?" she asked, as Joan hurried to close her computer. "It's about lab time. I really need more of it."

"Why is that, Livia?"

"My project . . . it's . . . oh, hello."

"Hello. I'm sorry, I didn't mean to interrupt," Joan said. "Please, go on."

"No, that's fine. What did you need?" Gorsalitz asked.

"I was actually also wondering about lab time, not to mention how I find the lab. Where is it?"

"You'll have to pop by to schedule your time. My secretary can help you."

"Great, thanks. And where is it?"

"Livia, if you have time, could you show Ms. Carpenter?"

"Joan, please."

"Joan, then. Livia? Can you show her the lab?"

"Yes, all right." She sighed. "I have half an hour. Do you want to go now? And can I come by about ten on Monday, Dr. Gorsalitz?"

"That should be fine. Send my secretary an email to confirm."

"Thanks, I will." Livia jerked her head toward the door. "Let's go."

Well, that turned out better than I'd hoped, Joan thought.

"Thank you so much," she said, nodding to the dean and following her prey. Now to drag Taras Petrenko into the conversation.

Joan hurried after a clearly aggravated Livia, trying not to let her own annoyance burble to the surface.

"I'm sorry if this is inconvenient," she tried.

"No problem."

"What kind of a project are you working on, if you don't mind my asking?"

"Just the usual, but I'm not getting enough lab time."

"The usual?"

"I'm studying some soil samples. Oxygenation, nitrogen uptake and all that."

Okay, Joan thought. Good. I get that.

"Do you ever get to use the Light Source?"

"Why? Is that why you transferred here, to get in on a CLS project?"

"Well, partly, yeah. I mean, I don't have a project right now, but I'd love to use the synchrotron."

"It's pretty awesome."

Joan waited. Livia's pride won over annoyance.

"I'm doing a project there right now," she said. "Except I don't know where it's at, after the professor's death. Have you heard about that? Everyone on campus is talking about it."

"Yes. I was at the ag college yesterday and saw his picture. You couldn't miss it. That's terrible, by the way. I'm sorry. I didn't realize you knew him."

The young woman's jaw was clenched, Joan noted, but she did not cry.

"Yes. I did," Livia said, after a short pause.

"Was he as nice as Dr. Gorsalitz?" Lame, Joan. Lame.

But Livia snorted.

"Totally different."

"In what way?"

"In every way."

Joan had the feeling that she was pulling teeth. Open wide, Livia . . .

"He sure was handsome," Joan offered. Again, lame.

"Yes. He was."

Progress.

"Married?"

"Yes."

"Oh, too bad," Joan said, and waited to see how Livia would take that comment.

"Yes. It was."

A shadow, fleeting and inscrutable, fell over Livia's face. But Joan had her answer. It was too bad, then, that Taras Petrenko was married. Not too bad that his wife was now living in unbearable grief.

"Here it is," Livia said, opening the door to the lab. They'd come down two floors, wound down serpentine hallways. Good thing I don't really need to know where this is, Joan thought. I may not find it again.

"You know, I'd love to see the CLS. Any hope of getting a tour there?"

"Yes, of course. You can book one anytime with the tour guides. Now, I've got to get going. I have a lunch date."

And I'll make a date with you and my sergeant, thought Joan.

After thanking Livia and watching her stride away, Joan left the biology building and called Adam.

"Hey, Alias Carpenter," he greeted her. "How did it go?"

"Tough nut, Livia Balan," she said. "That was probably the most clipped conversation I've ever had. She was definitely in love with Petrenko. Do we know, at all, if he played around?"

"No. So far, there's no indication of it, and you know what I thought after interviewing his wife. They were tight, and not just as lovers and parents. As scientists and partners. But I guess it's still a possibility."

"We're going to have to get at her officially, Adam. There's something there. I'm pretty sure of it."

"Not as forthcoming as Melanie, I take it."

"Not even close."

"Okay. I'm coming up to campus this afternoon to interview Gorsalitz and Horvath. You'll have to stay undercover for the time being. I'll see if I can crack this nut."

*****

Adam sat across from Gorsalitz in his remarkably messy office. It didn't fit with the man's personal grooming, and Adam wondered what it meant.

"Thank you for seeing me, Dr. Gorsalitz. If I may, I'd like to start with the dinner on Sunday night at Dr. Stockton's home. Did you and your partner feel well afterward? Any stomach complaints?"

"No. Well, not really. I have Crohn's disease, so nothing really agrees with me. My partner was all right. The food was a little greasy."

"Did you notice what Taras Petrenko ate and drank? Was it the same as what you and everyone else had?"

"Yes, although neither of us touched the gravy. Taras, as I'm sure you know by now, treated his body as God intended. An aesthete, our Taras."

"And did he have wine?"

"Yes. He would occasionally have a glass, maybe two. He accepted a glass that night."

"So just the one."

"Well, I think Grant refilled it, over Taras's protestations. He may have had a little more of the second glass."

Stockton hadn't mentioned that piece of information to James, Adam recalled.

"Did Taras look normal?" he asked. "Anything unusual about his behaviour or appearance?"

"I thought he looked a little bit under the weather. He had complained of toothache earlier in the week. I wondered if it was bothering him. He didn't say anything about it, though."

"Would you say he looked pale? Sweaty? Did he touch his face where the tooth hurt, or anything like that?"

"A bit pale, yes. A bit quieter than usual. He certainly didn't seem deathly ill, though, Sergeant. I rather thought he couldn't wait to get away to do his experiment."

"Do you remember when he mentioned his sore tooth?"

Gorsalitz furrowed his brow in the effort to remember.

"I don't. It was Thursday or Friday, I think, but I couldn't swear to it."

"I'm sorry to ask you this, but were you and Taras Petrenko on good terms?"

"The best. Taras was a good friend, Sergeant Davis. A very good friend. I cared about him very much."

You and everyone else on campus, Adam thought.

"What did you know about Taras's Gryphon project?"

Adam waited patiently as the biology dean tapped his pen on his desk, likely wondering what to say. How far to go.

"I knew more than I should have, perhaps. Or wanted to. I'm the biology dean, Sergeant. Apart from Doug Brennan and Grant Stockton, I knew more than anyone else except his team."

"Dr. Stockton told my colleague that Dr. Petrenko was investigating the anti-inflammatory properties of a specific fungus."

"True."

"But there is more to the project than that. Isn't there?"

"Yes."

"Why don't you tell me about it."

Gorsalitz sighed. "That's all Stockton said?"

Adam nodded.

"Hell," Gorsalitz muttered. "Have you talked to Jay Griffin?"

"Yes, of course. I need to hear it from you."

"Oh, I see. I'm a suspect, then."

"Not exactly. I'm trying to rule people out, especially the deans and team members."

"Or rule them in."

"If that proves to be the case, yes."

"Look, Sergeant Davis," Gorsalitz said. "This mushroom is potentially very interesting, especially to human health, but also to the conversation around chirality and specificity of environment — where it grows, and why. Not to mention plant breeding, biotechnology, and a whole host of other research avenues. But nothing has been proven. We're talking early days."

"So you do know quite a bit about Gryphon."

"Yes. Taras came to me for help a few times. Maybe help is the wrong word. He wanted to throw some ideas around, and I think he felt I could be trusted."

"And could you? Be trusted?"

"Of course. Our conversations were held in strictest confidence."

"Who else did Taras trust?"

"I couldn't be sure. Doug Brennan; he had no choice there. I thought he trusted Stockton — his dean, after all — but if Grant only mentioned the one research angle, I wonder. Naturally, Taras trusted Jay. It was his discovery."

"Any of the other deans? Or professors?"

"Again, I don't know. Possibly Eric Bantle. Maybe Devon Horvath, although I doubt it. The project wasn't far enough along to engage with Pharmacy yet."

"Do you have any idea who might have wanted to kill Taras Petrenko?"

Gorsalitz snorted. "Taras? No. Who the hell would want to kill him? He was gorgeous. In every way. Physically, intellectually, personally. And a good man, Sergeant."

"All right, Dr. Gorsalitz. Thank you. I'll be in touch."

Interesting use of language, Adam thought as he left the dean's office. Had Gorsalitz wanted more from Taras Petrenko than friendship and the sharing of scientific thought?

*****

Adam walked from Biology through the university's main quad, known as "The Bowl," toward the Thorvaldson Building. Built to resemble a small castle, the old building's stone exterior loomed with sturdy elegance over the students rushing in and out of its heavy doors.

The interior told another story. The floors creaked and moaned; the ceilings rotted and sighed. But it was historic, dating back to 1924, and one of the best-loved buildings on campus.

Adam took the front steps two at a time and was swept through the doors by a swarm of students during class change. A quick look at the front board, listing classrooms and offices, directed him to Dean Devon Horvath.

As Adam approached the door, ajar by an inch or two, he heard conversation within. Low voices carrying heat. A second later, a lithe young woman stormed out of the office, turned in the opposite direction and stalked off, her long, dark hair swinging.

Upset student? Adam wondered. Bad mark on her recent exam? Only one way to find out. He knocked on the now wide-open door.

"Dr. Horvath?"

The man turned, face remarkably composed. "Yes. Sergeant Davis, I presume."

"Yes. May I come in?"

"Of course. Take a seat. Would you like coffee or anything?"

"No, I'm fine, thanks," Adam said, folding himself into the proffered armchair. "Thank you for seeing me. I'll get right to it; I'm sure you're very busy. I understand that you and your wife had dinner at Dr. Stockton's last Sunday, along with Taras Petrenko."

"Yes, we did. Terrible news about Taras. Just terrible. How can I help?"

Adam asked Horvath the same questions he had asked Gorsalitz. Did you or your partner have any stomach problems after the meal? Did you eat the same things Petrenko did? Did you notice how much wine he had?

The answers were identical to Gorsalitz's. Right down to the second, partial glass of wine.

"Did he look well that night?"

"Not his usual perfect self. A little pale. But he didn't appear to be deathly ill, either, Sergeant."

Same answer. Almost.

"What do you know about the Gryphon project?"

"Well, I gather Taras and his team were investigating the properties of a fungus. They thought it may have remarkable anti-inflammatory properties. Fascinating stuff, Sergeant."

"Anything else?"

"Should there be? Isn't that enough?"

Adam decided to poke Horvath a bit.

"I had been told there was a bit more to it than that."

"Oh? Well. Maybe they had made more progress than I knew. I understood that Taras was wondering about the relationship of this mushroom to other species and investigating whether chirality was in play. Other than that . . ." Horvath shrugged, palms up.

"I would think that the pharmacy department might be interested in this fungus, should it prove to have healing properties."

"Oh yes, absolutely. But early days, Sergeant. Much too early for thoughts of preparing and testing pharmaceuticals."

Early days, again. Did all professors use the same words? Or had they discussed this murder, and aligned their stories?

"Any thoughts on who might have killed Dr. Petrenko?" Adam asked.

"Heavens, no. Everyone respected and admired him. Some even adored him."

Adam managed not to roll his eyes as he rose and offered Horvath his hand.

"Oh, by the way," Adam said, with what he hoped was a conspiratorial grin, "I couldn't help but notice a young woman leave your office in a bit of a state. Did she do poorly on an exam?"

"Something like that," Horvath replied. "I'm sorry, Sergeant, but unless it's important to your investigation, I really can't discuss student matters."

"Right. Thank you, Dean. I appreciate the time. If you think of anything else, here's my card."

"My pleasure. I can't imagine what else I could add, but I will certainly call if something occurs to me."

Adam smiled and left the office, wondering what exactly "something like that" meant.

Chapter Fourteen

Before leaving the campus, Adam checked in with the agriculture college, seeking Livia Balan. She was not in class, he was informed, and was it important?

"Yes, it is," he told the secretary, placing his badge under her nose. "Do you have a number for her?"

"I do. I'm normally not allowed to provide student phone numbers to the public . . ."

"I'm afraid I will need that number." Adam smiled, but there was no doubting his authority. The secretary looked up into his eyes, deep navy blue with long black lashes, under his powerful brow and over his wide cheekbones.

"Yes, Sergeant," she murmured in acquiescence, a faint pink creeping into her cheeks, and scribbled some numbers on a scrap of paper. "Is there anything else you need?"

"No, thank you. You've been very kind, very helpful. Have a good day."

He tried the number the moment he left the building, but the young woman didn't answer. Probably at the pub by now, and can't hear the phone ring, Adam thought.

Or at the Light Source. Adam retrieved his unmarked police car and drove the short distance north to the synchrotron. Driving up to the massive facility, he felt awe and amazement rising again. He parked, jumped out of the vehicle and strode up the steep path to the front doors; it was still open. At the front desk, he asked for Livia Balan, but she was not in the facility.

"Is Jay Griffin in, by chance?" he asked the receptionist.

"I think I saw him come in. Let me check." A few keyboard strokes. "Yes, Jay is here. I'll page him for you."

A few minutes later, Adam, who had remained standing with eyes focused on the locked interior glass doors, spied Jay coming toward him.

"Hello, Adam," he said. "This is a surprise. What's up?"

"Came to check on you. How are things going?"

"Okay, so far. You? Any progress?"

"A little, yes. Actually, to be honest, I came looking for Livia. We haven't caught up to her yet. And she's not answering her phone."

Jay laughed. "Yeah, not likely. Livia likes her social scene. She's probably at Louis' by now. If I see her, I'll tell her to call you."

"Thanks, that would be great. I did want to talk to you, although I thought I'd leave you alone until Monday. It's not all that important, but I'd really like to see your twisted forest, especially where your fungus grows. Would you have time next week to show me?"

"Of course. Pick a day and I'll check the beamline schedule. I think I'm free Tuesday and Thursday."

"Either one works for me. I'd like to bring Grace, but only if that's okay with you."

"Why? She won't report on it, will she?"

"No. She understands what's going on, the need for secrecy. But she sees things I don't. Perceives things I haven't thought of. Asks questions differently from the way I do. It obviously needs to be off the record — we don't want to expose your project, nor have more people than necessary tramping all over the area — but it would still be helpful if she came. To me."

"So she knows about Gryphon."

"Yes. She more or less figured it out, considering Taras's death. She's been investigating the properties of mushrooms. She wonders, too, if he could have been poisoned by inhalation, osmosis, or some other method other than by food or injection."

"I've been wondering that too. Um, Adam, speaking of Grace . . ."

"Yes?"

"Can we go outside?"

"Sure, of course."

Jay led the way out the door. He had about an inch on Adam in height, and possibly two across the shoulders, causing Adam to wonder if his stature, thick long hair and bright eyes attracted women — or men — in swarms. Probably.

They found a bench tucked in alongside the building, and Jay gestured to it with an open hand. Adam sat and gave the younger man a questioning look. Jay came to the point immediately.

"Adam. How can I see Hope again?"

"Ah. Hope. Mother Lion, as Grace calls her. And she is that, I'm here to tell you. Neither you nor I, nor anyone, will get between her and Lawan, or her and Grace for that matter. Just so you know."

Adam noted Jay's chest expanding with an enormous inhale.

"Yeah, I already got that," he said, exhaling. A warm flush painted his cheeks.

Adam again sensed that Jay was no ordinary man. So this, what, twenty-five-year-old genius was turned on by a woman with heavy, unshakeable loyalties?

"I keep seeing her in my mind," Jay finally added, "at the airport. I noticed her when she came into the greeting area, holding that little girl, her face lit from within . . . and then, right after, Grace hugged her, and I knew it was her sister."

"Right, we told you we were there to meet her sister, didn't we?"

"Yeah, but I would have figured it out. They look alike. Hope's darker, shorter, smaller, but yeah. Grace's sister, for sure."

"That skin."

"Oh yeah," Jay breathed. "That skin." He paused. "I gathered she isn't married. But is she . . . with someone?"

"No. She did that adoption all by herself. With support from her family, of course, but that's not the same as having a partner."

"That's amazing."

"Yes, it is."

"Can I ask . . . not that I care, but . . . how old is she?"

"Twenty-eight."

"Ooh. Older woman."

Adam laughed. "By the calendar, maybe. I get the feeling you might easily cover that divide. Not that — what, three years? — is a May-December thing."

Am I really playing matchmaker here? Adam asked himself. He barely knew this young scientist. He could be a murderer. A crazed psychopath. A philanderer. Really, anything. *Hell.*

What should he do? Adam trusted his gut, and he was powerfully inclined to believe everything that came out of Jay's mouth. He had rarely been fooled, but this was not the time to be wrong. Hope was at stake — and not just her happiness.

"Listen, Jay," Adam began, thinking he must be crazy to even explore this request. "Here's the situation. I haven't solved Taras's murder yet. You could be in danger; we both know that. Worse, if only slightly, you could be the killer. What do you want me to do? This is my sister-in-law."

Jay's eyes widened. "Does that mean you're going to marry Grace?"

Oops. Adam sighed. "Yes, I am. As soon as possible," he said, and then wondered why Jay picked up on his last comment instead of freaking out over being called a possible murderer.

"I see your problem, Adam. Okay, look. What if — and I know I'm asking a lot, here — what if I met Hope under supervised circumstances? Don't tell me where she lives, don't give me her number . . . just, I don't know. If you go out for dinner, maybe let me know and I'll sort of inadvertently show up?"

Adam knew he should be laughing at this suggestion, but he was not.

"Let me think about it," he said. "Okay?"

"Okay. Thank you for even considering it." Jay looked into Adam's eyes, held his gaze. "I need to see her again."

"What happened, Jay? When you met her? Obviously, something hit you in the gut."

Jay gave a restless gesture.

"I suppose I realized, seeing you with Grace, Hope with Lawan, that I've been completely absorbed in my research, my academic career. I mean, I'm no saint. But I want more in my life. I want a real relationship, not all these temporary hook-ups. I'm sick of it. There's more, though. Hope is tough, brave, compassionate. I know this from you, but also from just looking into her face. And oh my God, so beautiful. I think I want Hope, Adam."

"I get it. Because of Grace, I get it, Jay. I just have to be very careful."

"I know."

*****

Hope threw open the front door to her little house and flung her arms out to greet Grace and Adam when they arrived for the dinner party that night.

"Hi, guys!" she said. "Here, let me take that," she added to Grace, who held a casserole dish brimming with her mashed-then-baked cheesy potatoes. A big favourite with her clan. "Come on in."

Hope and Grace's younger but much larger brother David stood at the kitchen sink when they walked in, washing raw vegetables for salad. You had to look for the resemblance to his sisters, but it was there: the smooth skin, although darker in tone; the enigmatic dark eyes, also dark but blue like Adam's; the heart-shaped facial bone structure, although with a more pronounced, masculine chin.

"Hey, Grace," David said, hugging his sister and bumping fists with Adam behind her back. "Hey, bro."

"How's it going, David? I see you've been recruited," Adam responded.

"Always. I hear you're on a strange new case."

"Yeah, it's pretty wild."

"Can you talk about it?" said David, the lawyer-to-be. He was always interested in Adam's work.

"A bit. Here, let me help you and I'll tell you what I can."

"Where's Lawan?" Grace asked as the men got to work.

"Playing in the living room."

"Let's go see."

Grace and Hope turned to the attached living area as the doorbell rang.

"I'll go check on Lawan," Grace said firmly. "You can get the door."

Hope made a face and went to greet their parents, Wallace and Sandra, bearing a dish of roasted vegetables and a platter holding chocolate cake. They had just handed the food to Hope when Adam's parents, Elizabeth and James, came up the walk, having made the trip into Saskatoon from the farm.

"Adam!" Hope called, seeing him in James Davis's face. "Come and make introductions. Looks like your folks are here."

Behind them by a minute came James Weatherall and his partner, Bruce Stephens; Charlotte Warkentin and her husband, John; and behind them, Suzanne Genereux, Grace's friend, with Constable Lorne Fisher. They'd been an item since the summer, when Suzanne's life had been threatened and Lorne decided he would be her protector. For life, if possible. Lacey McPhail arrived a few minutes later.

Grace and Adam had told their parents about the engagement once they realized Hope was throwing a big party. Not cool to inform your folks about your impending marriage at the same time as your friends; and besides, Adam already let his intentions slip to Wallace.

Grace embraced Suzanne with one arm as she held Lawan with the other.

"How are you, Suzé?" she asked. "Meet Lawan, Hope's daughter. Lawan, this is Suzanne."

"S'anne," said Lawan.

"Yes!" Suzanne crowed. "Aww, she is beautiful, Grace. You look very happy to have a new niece. Very," she added for emphasis.

"I am," she said. "Very. Should we get a glass of wine?"

They joined the throng in the kitchen, where Adam was pouring Shiraz and Pinot Grigio, and handing out bottles of Stella Artois. Grace's face softened as she regarded him: he fit in, pitched in, reached out.

"Your turn to bartend," he said, as Grace appeared with Lawan and he held out his arms. The little girl reached for Adam without hesitation.

"Fine," she grumbled, and took over the beverage service.

"Soup's on!" Hope hollered over the conversational din.

Somehow, roast chicken, roasted vegetables, potatoes and salad and stuffing and gravy had appeared, buffet-style, on the table. The hungry guests dove in and were soon settled in every corner of the kitchen and living area.

"So, Hope," James Weatherall said, between bites. "You decided to throw a welcome home party for Lawan? God, she is so adorable. Congratulations."

"Thank you. She is, isn't she?"

James raised his eyebrows. Hope hadn't exactly answered the question. Clearly, she didn't intend to. After another bite, she scrambled up off the floor where she had been sitting and went into the kitchen.

He gave a "whatever" shrug and returned to his plate. He didn't notice Adam squirming in the corner.

"Maybe this wasn't such a good idea," Adam whispered into Grace's ear. "I'm feeling conspicuous."

"We'll make it quick," Grace said. "And soon."

"How about now? People are almost finished eating."

"I'll see if that works for Hope."

Grace slipped into the kitchen and found her sister pouring champagne into flutes. At this point, it couldn't be helped, and Hope was trying so hard to be celebratory.

"Honey, this is too sweet of you. Thank you. I think Adam wants to get the announcement over with," Grace said. "Looks like you're almost ready?"

"Whenever you are."

"Okay. Here we go, then."

Grace returned to the living room, suddenly speechless. She took one look at Adam and blushed deeply, overwhelmed by the emotion of the moment, the realization that she was really going to marry this beautiful man, and that they were going to tell everyone. Right now.

Adam read her face, stood up and came over to put his arms around her, in front of their people. Hugging her closely, rubbing her back, murmuring in her ear. Everyone watched and wondered.

"Aw, Grace, my love. It's okay," he whispered, and pulled himself together. "Hey, everyone," he continued in a much louder voice, turning but leaving an arm around Grace.

All eyes were on Adam. His big, resonant baritone never failed to draw attention.

"Thank you for coming. We — Grace and I — are so grateful for your friendship and support. A week ago, I asked Grace to marry me. I am beyond honoured that she said yes. Most of you know that I'm crazy in love with her, but some of you may not know that she is not just beautiful, intelligent, loving and kind. In the few months we've spent together, she has pulled me out of darkness; she has helped me heal; she has saved my life."

No one said a word; everyone stared, eyes misting, at the couple. Adam bit his lip, tightened his hold on Grace, turned his face back to her and blinked back a tear.

"I will spend the rest of my life with you, Honor Grace Rampling. Nothing and no one will ever, can ever, keep me away from you. You are my heart and my life."

Grace, still unable to form a word, threw her arms around Adam and kissed him passionately. Right there, in front of parents and siblings and friends. Finally, she whispered, "I love you so much, Adam Davis. You are mine forever."

They finally parted, still gazing into each other's eyes, and the room erupted into cheers and congratulations. Hope and Sandra emerged with champagne, and the toasts began.

"To Grace and Adam," Wallace said. "Be happy always. I love you so much, my girl. I can't imagine a finer son-in-law. Welcome, Adam."

"To Adam and Grace," James Davis echoed, coming up to stand with Wallace. "From the moment we met Grace, we knew this was going to happen." Elizabeth smiled and nodded vigorously. "Welcome to the Davis clan, Grace."

Hope, Lacey and Suzanne descended on Grace, while James and Charlotte hugged Adam.

"I knew something was up," Charlotte said.

"Me too," James said.

"How the hell?" Adam asked.

"You're different together. A little. Like you've settled the big questions of life — which I suppose you have," Charlotte said.

"In other words, my life is an open book," Adam said. "Here I thought I was so enigmatic."

"Ha," said Charlotte and James together. "When it comes to Grace," Charlotte added, "not so much."

The party continued until late. Grace, Adam, Sandra, Wallace and David stayed behind to help clean up.

"I'm going to check on Lawan," Hope finally said. "Be right back."

Adam gave her a minute, put down his dish towel and mumbled an excuse to Grace and her family. He caught Hope quietly closing the door to Lawan's bedroom and gestured to her own room. Hope nodded, a quizzical look on her face, and led the way. Closing the door, she turned to Adam.

"What's up?"

"I have to tell you something," Adam began. "It's a little, well . . . "

"Well, what?"

"Unusual, for me. I've never done anything like this before. It's about the PhD student you met at the airport. Jay Griffin."

"Yes?"

"Yes. I saw him earlier today on campus. At the Light Source. He asked me to follow him outside for a private conversation. It was about you."

"Me." She sounded dumbfounded. "Me?"

"Hope, I don't know if you understand that he is part of this murder investigation? He worked closely with the man who was killed."

"No, I don't know much about it. Does that mean he's a suspect?"

"Not exactly. But until we find the killer, or entirely rule people out — which is proving more difficult than I'd hoped — well, you see what I'm getting at."

"Go on."

"He wants to see you again."

"Oh," she said, in a small voice.

"Do you want to see him? He suggested a "supervised" meeting. I would be there, and likely Grace, as well. It's a little odd, no doubt, but I can't in good conscience set you up on a date with someone I barely know. Someone involved in the case."

Hope had recovered, slightly, from her surprise. "So why are you mentioning this at all, if you're concerned about Jay being a killer?"

Right. Good point, Adam thought. Obviously, he did not think Jay was the killer, or he wouldn't have brought it up; but this idea did seem insane.

"I — I guess I really like him, Hope. He's a remarkable human. Every time he opens his mouth, he amazes me. But you're right. Maybe this was a stupid idea. I didn't think through all the implications. I would hardly want you to get involved, if in fact you liked him, with someone dangerous." He paused. "I guess I can't believe that he's at fault. I'm sorry. I want you to be happy, too, Hope. With someone who deserves you. I think he might."

"I do like him," Hope said, so softly that Adam wondered if he'd heard her correctly.

"I wondered if you did."

"It's a risk, though," she said, more loudly. "Oh, Adam. I don't know what to do."

"Think about it? It's entirely up to you, of course. I'll make sure you're safe."

Those big brown eyes, so like Grace's, looked up — way up — into his worried face. Hope had gone pale, but now flushed pink for the second time that week.

"I have. Thought about it. Yes, Adam. Damn it. I want to see Jay Griffin again."

Chapter Fifteen

Murder didn't take weekends off, and neither did Adam Davis.

He did roll out of bed late Saturday morning; he couldn't resist Grace's soft skin and warm body lying peacefully next to him. Adam curled his body around her and waited for his own warmth and movement to awaken her. Finally, she stirred.

"Good morning, Babe," he said. "Sleep okay?"

"Mmmm. Morning, Adam. Yes. That party was exhausting. But lovely. And now they all know. What a relief. Now I can wear my beautiful ring to work."

"Bonus." He cuddled her, snuffling at her neck. "I have an idea."

"Yes, I can feel it."

"Is it a good one? Idea, I mean?"

"Oh, yes."

Love in the morning was urgent for Adam. He tried to go slowly, to gently rouse Grace from her sleepy, sweet awakening, but inevitably he found himself holding on, holding back, stopping for deep breaths. This morning, though, Grace turned and laced herself around him, ready and vibrating.

"Your words," she breathed, kissing him. "Last night. It was all I could do not to tackle you right there in front of God and everyone."

"I always feel like that," he grunted, pulling her on top of him. "Let me look at you."

He stared up at her breasts, tantalizingly peeking out from under her tumbling curls, and thought for the hundredth time that this woman could star in any man's mermaid fantasy. He had to remind himself that she was no exotic sea creature but human, and so much more than beautiful. It was hard to remember, sometimes, when he wanted her this badly.

"No going back now, Babe. You're mine."

"Never, Adam," she said, and slipped him inside her. "You're mine."

Grace rocked him deeply and slowly, leaning down to kiss his lips, murmuring love noises. They caught fire together, holding eye contact until they couldn't any longer.

Once the passion subsided, Grace carefully dismounted and said, a little sadly, "I'll make you some breakfast, if you want to hit the shower. You're going to work for a while, right?"

"Just a while. I should be home by one, two at the latest. Not a lot I can do, but there are a few things I should catch up on."

Livia Balan, for one, he thought as he climbed into his unmarked car.

And where the hell is the next installment of the tox report? Damn it. How hard could they really be?

Pulling up in the police station parking lot, Adam felt the tug of irrational frustration at the technical delays in his investigation. Increasingly sure that this poison was no over-the-counter mouse killer from the hardware store, he wanted all the obvious, and semi-obvious, toxins ruled out. He was still waiting to hear if Petrenko had been tested for ricin, strychnine and arsenic.

Weekend day or no, the station was buzzing as always. Adam greeted constables and sergeants on his way upstairs to his office.

"Adam," came James's voice, as he walked past his constable's desk.

"James. What are you doing here? Take a day off once in a while."

"I knew you'd be here. Got a minute?"

"Of course. Come in."

James followed Adam the few paces to his office. Adam unlocked the door, and James fell into the chair across from his sergeant.

"What's up?" Adam asked.

"That ring you gave Grace. Where did you get it?"

"The goldsmith on Second Avenue. You got a look at it last night?"

"Yeah. It's amazing. Unique, am I right? You had it designed for her?"

"Yes. Grace is unique. Her ring should be too." James said nothing, so Adam pressed him. "Why are you asking about Grace's ring, James?"

"Um . . ."

"You don't have to tell me. But I could guess."

"You could."

"You want to get Bruce a ring. Something . . . unique?"

James nodded. Adam waited this time.

"I've asked him to marry me twice," James finally said. "This time, he has to say yes."

"I didn't know that, James. I'm sorry. You're not thinking of bribing him with a ring, though?"

"No, of course not. But maybe he'll see what he means to me. Isn't that why we give people stuff like that?"

"Yeah, I buy that. You didn't try a ring the last time?"

"Nope. I tried it the first time, though. And he wears it — on his right hand. He said he'd think about it. The marriage part." James exhaled. "I understood, the first time. It was before it became legal. Bruce's argument was that there was no point in an actual marriage if the state didn't sanction it, and we might as well just live together. But that was two years ago."

"Something else is worrying him, then. James, it's not that he doesn't love you. It surrounds him like an aura."

"I know. I know that. Just the same, I'm getting him another ring." James shook his head, as if to change the air in the room. "So, what are you doing here today?"

"Stewing about the tox report. And I'm going to try to find Livia Balan again. And I have another call to make, as well. Why don't you head over to see the goldsmith, then pop back?"

James looked slightly alarmed.

"Or not," Adam said quickly, wondering if his friend and constable might be afraid of being turned down again. "Want to wait while I log in?"

Adam turned on his computer, rapidly typed in his password, and watched until his emails loaded.

"I've got something from McDougall," he told James, opening the document and scanning it. "It came yesterday at six, while we were getting ready for the party, damn it." He leaned in. "It wasn't any of the usual poisons."

"We kind of figured, right? Does that limit our suspect list to professors and genius students?"

Adam's stomach clenched. When considering genius students, Jay Griffin topped the list. *Hell.*

"Well, it's not going to be your average citizen," he said, slowly. "But again, we knew that, too. And maybe it's not anyone on campus. Maybe Emmy Petrenko is right, and it's someone else? Someone from his days in Berlin?"

"Right. I'll start going through the list we have so far and see if anyone ever worked or studied at Max Planck," James said.

"Good idea. We should also cross-check Petrenko's appointments from the week before his death. The NSERC guy, for example. He was in Saskatoon on the Friday."

"There's a thought. Come to think of it, he hasn't returned our calls, has he?"

"No. I planned to try him again first thing on Monday."

"Okay. I'll get at it, and let you know if I find anything."

"Thanks, James." Adam decided not to mention the ring again. There was nothing he could really do to help James and Bruce come to an agreement on the big question looming between them.

He picked up the phone to try Livia Balan again, when a thought struck him. Hard. He almost gasped at its force, piercing his brain, and dialled Jay Griffin.

"Sergeant," he answered. "It is Saturday, you know."

"I do know. How are you, Jay?"

"Fine . . . I think. Am I?"

"So far, so good. I need a favour. Can you send me a photo of your mushroom? By email, and now?"

"Right now?"

"Yeah. Got one?"

"Sure. Just a sec."

Adam heard Jay fiddling with his phone. Seconds later, Adam's email pinged. He opened it to see a flaky, grey-white and faintly blue fungus.

"Got it," he said. "So this is basically a shaggy mane?"

"It is a shaggy mane. Its DNA is just different from the usual."

"How do you tell them apart?"

"You don't, visually. You have to test them. Which is why this is a tricky project. Well, one of the reasons."

"Are there other mushrooms that look the same, but have different properties?"

"Sort of. The inky cap is similar to the shaggy mane but doesn't have those flakes you can see on the head of the mushroom. If you're any good at mushrooms, you wouldn't get them confused."

Oh, for fuck's sake, Adam thought. Why didn't this occur to him before? He'd considered that Petrenko had eaten the Gryphon but had gone no further down fungus road.

"Inky caps. Are they poisonous?"

"Not really, except that they create a substance called coprine . . . holy shit, Adam," Jay said, his deep voice dropping another half an octave. "That could be it."

"Tell me. You said they're not really poisonous."

"So you know how with some antibiotics, you're not allowed to drink alcohol? Because it can give you the hangover from hell? Like metronidazole, for example. It's a very similar effect with coprine. It inhibits the enzyme in the human body that metabolizes alcohol. You're going to puke, almost for sure. Nausea, vomiting, flushing, the whole magilla."

"But it's not lethal?"

"Not usually. You can get very sick, but I've only heard of one person dying from the combination."

"Could it be lethal?"

"Maybe. I suppose it could be." Jay stopped, apparently to think. Adam held his breath. "It's possible, maybe, that it could be altered in some way. Think distillation, like a mega-dose. And then you give it to someone who doesn't drink much . . ."

"And when he has a glass or two of wine . . ."

"Yeah."

"So would the coprine have to be administered at the same time, or within a few hours of the alcohol?"

Jay gave a sharp laugh.

"Nope. You've got about seventy-two hours. Three days."

"That makes our window of opportunity Thursday night to Sunday night."

"Correct. The coprine would probably come first, but not necessarily."

"It did this time," Adam said, with certainty. "Jay. I hate to ask, but I have to. Where were you that Thursday night through Sunday afternoon?" Adam knew where Petrenko was Sunday night, and it wasn't with Jay.

"It's okay, Adam. Thursday night I was at the Light Source until ten. Went home to bed, slaughtered. Friday morning I left for Hafford; went to see the folks. Of course I came back as soon as I heard about Taras."

"Which was when?"

"Right after Doug Brennan called me. It must have been about eleven-thirty Sunday night. I couldn't believe it. I jumped in my truck and drove like hell back to Saskatoon."

Jay's own window of murderous opportunity was closing, at least. If Adam could verify that he was actually out of town from Friday on.

"Who saw you in Hafford, besides your folks?"

"No one until Friday night. I went into town to play pool with friends."

"Anyone see you leave Saskatoon?"

"The guy at the gas station?" Jay gave a small, mirthless laugh.

"That'll work," said Adam, deadly serious. "Which station?"

"The Esso on Clarence Avenue and Eighth Street."

"Okay. I'll check with them right away. Do you have a picture of yourself you can send me? A text will be fine. And then, Jay, I'll have to go to Hafford and catch up to your friends."

"You were going to go anyway, to check out the mushroom patch."

"How's Tuesday?"

"Works for me. Anything I can do to clear myself. You know I did not kill Taras Petrenko, right?"

"It's high time you actually said it."

"I need to see Hope again."

"That's more important than being stricken from the suspect list?"

Jay laughed again, with a bit more humour.

"I think it is."

"Hang in there. Give me a couple more days, okay?"

"Like I have a choice," Jay said bitterly. "But thank you, Adam. Very much."

"Thank you for the help on the coprine. Later."

Adam hung up, and immediately called Jack McDougall at home. No way he was waiting until Monday to throw his theory at the forensic pathologist. Besides, Taras Petrenko was Jack's friend. He'd welcome a call. Right?

"McDougall," he answered. "Oh, hell. It's you, Adam. Must you always call me on weekends? It was only, what, three weeks ago that you called me on a Sunday from the middle of nowhere."

"Hi, Jack," Adam said, mildly. "Good morning to you, too. Listen, I have a theory."

"Terrific," Jack said with an exaggerated groan. "Let's hear it."

"Coprine."

Dead silence, for a moment. Adam didn't have to say "I may know what killed Petrenko" or anything else. Jack got it, as Adam knew he would.

"Okay. Coprine doesn't usually kill, you know."
"Yes."

"So what are you thinking? Some mega-dose? Maybe mixed with something else?"

"You mean besides alcohol?"

"I do. I'm not sure coprine would do it."

"What if some scientific genius came up with a way to really slam someone with it? A really big mega-dose?"

Jack laughed. "The hyperbolic mega-mega-dose. Let me think about that. I suppose it's possible, but it is unheard of. Then again, most people get sick on coprine if they've inadvertently eaten the wrong mushroom with a bottle of wine, not if they've been injected with a lot of it. You'd have to be seriously piggy to eat enough fungus to kill yourself on coprine."

"So that's my other question. How else could he have received it?"

"You're sure he didn't eat it?"

"As sure as I'm alive. No way Petrenko would mistake an inky cap for a shaggy mane. Is inhalation or skin transfer possible?"

"I don't think so. Not inhalation. You'd have to hold him down and get him to snort it. A puff in the air wouldn't do the trick. And skin transfer . . . I doubt it, but it's possible."

"So we're left with injection and ingestion. And it wasn't the latter."

"Damn it, Adam, I told you there were no injection sites."

"Just test him for coprine. If that's the poison, so to speak, we'll figure out how it was administered. But I have to know what the hell killed him first."

"I'm on it, Adam. I'll haul the tox guy out of bed."

"Thank you, Jack. You know I appreciate this."

"Well, Adam, for once . . . I appreciate this, too. I want to catch the bastard who killed Taras as much as you do."

"I know, Jack." The air between them hung heavy with sympathy for a quiet moment. "Stay in touch."

Adam replaced the receiver and gave himself a few moments to gain control over his excitement. It had to be. The killer likely doubted that a tox screen would cover coprine, leaving the cause of death a complete mystery. Furthermore, a poison borne by a fungus was the only thing that made sense, the only substance that carried the weight and meter of poetic revenge. For a killer with something to gain.

Or lose.

Chapter Sixteen

Adam strode into the redolent coffee shop across from campus an hour later, wondering if he would recognize Livia Balan. Joan Karpinski had given him a good description, but no photograph. He sought her likeness online, but Livia used avatars. She was apparently dark-haired. That was all he could glean from his search.

However, she was taller than average height, had brown eyes, medium skin and carried herself with swagger, according to Joan. That should do it.

No one in the coffee shop remotely fit her description. Adam approached the counter and ordered an Americano, no room. As he was paying, a voice at his shoulder said, "Looks like you beat me here."

His head snapped around, and he was looking at arched eyebrows over liquid chestnut eyes and a faint smirk on full red lips. Adam's jaw almost fell open in shock, but he caught himself in time.

He had seen Livia Balan before. Storming out of the pharmacy dean's office.

"Hello, Miss Balan. What can I get you?"

"Well, thank you, Sergeant. A cappuccino would be remarkable."

"And a cappuccino, please," Adam said to the young woman ogling him from behind the counter.

"Yes, sir," she said, blushing and smiling. "I'll bring your coffees over as soon as they're ready."

"Thanks. Should we take that booth at the back?" he suggested to his witness.

"That would be lovely, Sergeant."

Once they were seated, Adam started with small talk.

"How did you know I was me?" he asked.

"I've seen you before."

"Oh? Where?"

"In the paper. After you called, I looked you up. So that, of course, I would recognize you. You get a lot of press, Sergeant Davis. Besides, we had agreed to meet here, no?"

True, sadly, he thought about the press exposure; and of course, they had arranged to meet at the café. Adam smiled.

"We had. Thank you for agreeing to the interview."

"Did I have a choice?"

"Not really, but still, thank you. I'm going to have to ask you some questions that might seem a little rude and may also be uncomfortable. I'm afraid I have to ask you where you were from last Thursday night through Sunday afternoon."

"My usual routine, Sergeant. At home Thursday night, writing a paper. On campus Friday. At the bar Friday night." She stopped, pursed her lips, and thought for a moment. "Saturday. Let's see. It was a busy day. Shopping with friends. Dinner with friends. Clubbing with friends. And Sunday . . . I was home in the morning and went to my parents' place for dinner. That's about it."

"Could you please email me the names of your friends? It would be very helpful in ruling you out as Dr. Petrenko's killer."

Livia Balan appeared unperturbed by the suggestion that she might be a murderer. She waited for the coffees to be delivered before responding.

"Of course. Your card?"

Adam handed it over. "If you could send them as soon as possible, I'd appreciate it. About Dr. Petrenko, then. What was your relationship?"

"His student, of course. His partner in mushroom science. We saw each other quite frequently."

"I gather that Dr. Petrenko . . ."

"Could we call him Taras for the purposes of this conversation? We were on a first-name basis."

"Taras, then. I understand that several of his female students were very fond of him, and not as a professor. Would you say that's true?"

Livia gave a large, husky laugh.

"Oh yes. All of it hopeless adoration. Taras was, of course, very handsome. Sexy, even. Perhaps not unlike yourself. Dedicated. Intelligent to the point of ridiculous. Women like those things. He was also extremely married."

"Did the young women care about that last part?" Adam asked, carefully ignoring the reference to himself.

"Probably not much, no. There are always a few who think their feminine and youthful attributes will overcome the professor's finer qualities, such as fidelity."

"And he was faithful?"

"As far as I know."

"What were your personal feelings for Taras, Ms. Balan?"

Livia cocked her head and gave Adam a frank appraisal, her eyes travelling from muscular chest to navy blue irises, and back to his left hand with its naked third finger.

"We were colleagues, Sergeant. Close colleagues. Very close, in fact."

"What does 'very close' mean?"

"I'd say we had a friendship."

Adam's hands formed into fists as he restrained himself from showing his frustration.

"Did you have any kind of a physical relationship with Taras Petrenko, Ms. Balan?"

"Not the way you mean, Sergeant. No."

"What do I mean?"

"You mean, were we having sex. We were not."

"Please, go on."

"Let's just say the sparks flew, but we managed to blow them out."

"Ms. Balan. This is a murder investigation, and no ordinary one. Be specific. Now."

She sighed, and contemplated Adam again, her gaze raking over him. It sent his spine curling against the back of the booth. This young woman was a predator, and no question. With her beauty, intelligence and fierce personality, it likely worked for her, very well.

"We were very attracted to each other," she said, in a soft voice intended to tug at a man's ear. "We did not ever do anything about it. You'll have to trust me on this, Sergeant. It would not have been appropriate."

"Was there touching, or conversation about these feelings?"

Livia Balan reached out with a forefinger and drew it slowly, delicately down the back of Adam's hand.

"Like this, you mean?"

Adam locked his gaze on his interview subject and did not move his hand. "Yes. I do mean like that."

"Perhaps once or twice."

"Were you in love with him?"

She shrugged. "Maybe a little. Everyone was. Jay, Deanna, the girls in his classes. Even most of the profs."

Was she purposely being difficult? Trying it on? Or was this a deflection? Adam couldn't be sure, yet. Livia Balan was arrogant and composed. He'd have to find the chink. He changed the subject.

"How was he killed, in your opinion?"

"Lord, I have no idea. I thought that was your department."

"It is. I was asking for your point of view."

"Again. No idea. I didn't see his body."

"Let me ask it this way, then. Did you kill Taras Petrenko, Ms. Balan?"

"Do call me Livia. Of course not. Why on Earth would I? This project is a long and beautiful feather in my hat, Sergeant. Think of how it will look on my resumé, when I seek my first professorial position. Why would I want him dead?"

"Perhaps because he turned you down. Or because you wanted a bigger piece of Gryphon."

"Ooo, ouch, Sergeant. That did hurt. I'd enjoy hurting you back, just a little." A highly polished nail, instead of the soft pad of her finger, retraced its earlier path down Adam's hand.

Hell, thought Adam, slamming his eyelids shut. She really was coming on to him.

"Ms. Balan . . ."

"Livia."

"No. Ms. Balan, you are a suspect and a witness in this investigation. You do understand that."

"Well, I didn't kill Taras, and now you have my testimony. So?"

"So, don't leave the city, please."

Finally, a real reaction. Livia's eyes widened in surprise for a second, and Adam saw her shoulders tense.

"Are you serious?"

"Deadly."

"Fine. Well, if you change your mind, you have my number. Goodbye, Sergeant."

Change his mind? About what? Adam feared he knew the answer to that.

"Wait a moment, Ms. Balan. I have one more question. What were you arguing about with Dean Horvath yesterday?" God, Adam thought. Was that just yesterday? Time was swimming in his mind, a watery kaleidoscope of strange colours and fractured visions.

"Whatever do you mean?" Livia's frown transformed her beautiful face. Suddenly, she looked like a child preparing to throw a tantrum.

"I heard you. I was waiting outside, to speak to the dean. And I saw you storm out and down the hallway. Are you taking a class in pharmacy?"

"Yes. One. Toxicology. It was Taras's idea. He, and I, thought it might help with the Gryphon project, not to mention other, similar investigations down the road. I have a couple of first year pharmacy classes, and a lot of biology, so it's not too hard."

"What," Adam repeated, "were you arguing about?"

"An exam. I was unhappy with my mark. Eighty. I thought it was worth at least eighty-five, possibly ninety."

"I see. Not a multiple-choice exam, then."

"No." She looked at her watch. "I really must run, Sergeant. Is there anything else?"

"Not for now. Thank you for meeting me, Ms. Balan. And remember, please do not leave the city."

She gave Adam a toss of the head as she rose and swung out of the café. He gave her a few seconds, then followed her and watched as she crossed the street, back to the university.

Adam turned to walk away, but out of the corner of his eye, he noticed that Livia Balan had stopped stomping and stood, hands on hips, head thrust forward, speaking angrily with a young, blonde woman. Even from across the street and over the relentless traffic, Adam easily perceived that this was a fight in progress.

He couldn't hear what they were saying, but he could certainly hear the occasional shout of anger. The blonde woman raised her hand and, in a flash, slapped Livia Balan across the face.

Whoa. What the hell?

Adam quickly looked both ways and dashed across the busy, multiple-lane street, dodging cars and trucks. Once he hit the campus sidewalk, he ran full speed toward the women. By this time, Livia Balan had slapped back.

"Ms. Balan. What is going on here?"

Her head snapped toward Adam so sharply he feared she might break her own neck.

"What the hell are you doing here?" she asked.

"Breaking up a fight, apparently. Who are you, miss?"

"Melanie," mumbled the blonde, looking down, face on fire.

"Melanie Martens?"

A nod. Then she looked at him in surprise.

"How did you know my name?"

"That's not important right now. I'm Detective Sergeant Adam Davis, Ms. Martens. Investigating Dr. Petrenko's death. Why did you slap Ms. Balan?"

"What does that have to do with anything?" Livia spat.

"I don't know. That's why I'm asking. Ms. Martens?"

"We were — we were just disagreeing. It's no big deal."

"It's usually a big deal when someone is assaulted. Not to mention in public, where everyone can see what's going on. You must have been very angry. Why?"

"It has nothing to do with your case, Sergeant Davis," Livia said imperiously.

"I'll have to be the one to decide that," he said. "Ms. Martens?"

Tears flowed down her cheeks; her mouth was screwed into a moue of misery.

"She . . . she's a witch!" Melanie declared. "A slut. I hate her."

"Okay, okay, let's take this down a few decibels," Adam said. "What are you talking about?"

"I saw her," Melanie whispered. "I saw her and Taras. Um, Dr. Petrenko."

Livia made a noise to demonstrate her annoyance and turned on her heel to leave. "I've had enough of this," she said, over her shoulder.

But Adam reached her in two long strides and took her, as gently as possible, by the arm.

"Just a minute, Ms. Balan. What did you see, Ms. Martens?"

"I saw them together in the lab. Kissing." Melanie recovered herself as she spoke and sneered at Livia. "I thought you were going to eat him alive."

Chapter Seventeen

Adam hauled both Melanie and Livia down to the station and planted them in neighbouring interview rooms.

Melanie knew more than she had revealed to Joan Karpinski, and Livia Balan had outright lied to him — assuming Melanie was telling the truth, of course; she certainly seemed outraged by what she believed she saw.

Adam let them stew for a while. He stopped in the washroom and splashed cold water on his face, mainly in an attempt to chill his own mood. Adam seriously hated it when people lied to him. He particularly hated it when he believed those lies, or at least didn't entirely disbelieve them.

He stretched his shoulders, arms and back, and tried to shake off the strange feeling Livia Balan inspired in him. What a piece of work.

"James," he said, after leaving the washroom and finding his constable. "I've dragged a couple of young women down here for interviews. Melanie Martens and Livia Balan. I'll need you with me, especially with the latter. Behind the mirror, though. I want to see what happens."

"Yeah, of course, Adam. What do you mean, though, see what happens?"

"Melanie claims she saw Livia kissing Taras Petrenko. Slapped her for it today, right out in public. Something's up, because Livia just told me she and Taras were attracted to each other but nothing sexual ever happened."

"Okay . . . and?"

"And she came on to me."

"Ah."

"I need you to observe. I wonder what might happen in the interview room."

"Got it. Melanie or Livia first?"

"Melanie. Ready?"

"Yeah. Let's go."

At the interview room door, Adam waited until James had walked by and slipped into the adjoining space with the one-way window before entering.

"Ms. Martens. Do you need anything?" he began. "Water? Coffee? Soda?"

"Water, please," she snuffled. Melanie had been weeping, off and on, ever since the altercation on campus.

Adam stuck his head out and requested water for both of them, before seating himself across from the overwrought young woman. He handed her a clean tissue.

"Now. Please tell me what you saw, and when. The truth, now, Ms. Martens. No embellishing."

She nodded, her face clearly displaying how disconcerted she was to find herself in a police station. After a big, shuddering breath, she started in.

"It was a few months ago. Three, four? I happened to be at the Light Source that day. I wasn't there very often, but I had a two-week practicum on a project. Some of us lucked into those. I was helping with a soil sample. It was Taras's project, too. So I was in a hutch down the way from the Gryphon project, and something went funny with the robotics. Okay, actually, I didn't really know what I was doing.

"Anyway, Taras was there that day, keeping an eye on me and on Gryphon, and so I hustled down to the other hutch. The door was open about halfway, so they hadn't started up the beamline yet — at least, I assumed so. I pulled it open, and there was Livia, all over Taras."

"Can you please describe exactly what you saw?" Adam asked.

"Taras was leaning against the wall, and Livia had her hands on his chest. And her mouth on his. Wide open. I could see that, because they were standing sideways to me."

"Was Dr. Petrenko engaged in this kiss, Ms. Martens?"

"Well, I thought so. I mean, she was kissing him."

"I'm asking if he was kissing back, if you know what I mean."

Melanie's face twisted in confusion, with the apparent effort to remember her professor's exact body language.

"Did he, for example, have his arms around Ms. Balan?" Adam prompted.

"Ummm . . . no. I don't think so. His arms were sort of plastered against the wall. I kind of thought he looked like he'd surrendered, or something."

Oh, surrender, Adam thought, remembering lifting Grace onto the kitchen table, covered in blueberry juice and his mouth. Don't think about that right now, he scolded himself. Stupid word. Surrender.

But surrender was usually demonstrated by arms up, not down. He asked the question.

"No. Arms down, against the wall," Melanie answered.

"Is it possible you misinterpreted the scene? Could Taras Petrenko have been taken by surprise?"

"I suppose . . . yes, I suppose it's possible."

"I assume they noticed you."

"Actually, not at first."

"Really? What happened next?"

"Taras ended the kiss and sort of slipped out from under Livia's hug, sideways. He saw me a second or two later."

"Did he say anything? To Ms. Balan, or to you?"

"Not to Livia. When he saw me, he simply asked, what do you need, Melanie? I was kind of speechless, but I sort of stammered that I needed some help in the other hutch. He nodded and followed me out."

"Did you confront either of them about what you saw?"

"I did confront Livia, once. She huffed and walked away. But I wouldn't dare confront Taras. No, no. I couldn't do that."

"Because he was your professor?"

"Yes, mostly."

"And now you've slapped Livia, because she was kissing Taras. Why?"

Predictably, this question brought on a fresh flood of tears.

"Do I have to say?" she sobbed.

"I'm afraid so."

"Oh! God. I . . ." she trailed off.

"You wanted Taras yourself. Isn't that right? Was it jealousy that made you slap her?"

"Yes! That bitch. She always gets what she wants. And now, Taras is dead. Dead! And I will never, ever get to kiss him. But she did."

*****

"I'm going to take a wild stab here, Adam, and say Melanie Martens is not our killer," James said, when Adam emerged from the interview room. "I think she would have kept him alive for just one kiss."

"I'm inclined to agree. On the other hand, maybe she was so angry at his presumed spurning of her affections, she couldn't help herself, and stabbed him with coprine."

"Coprine?" James asked, bemused. "What the hell is that?"

"Sorry. I forgot I learned about that this morning after you left my office. It's a substance in inky cap mushrooms, which look a bit like shaggy manes. It's poisonous if you combine it with alcohol."

"Wow. You think that's the murder weapon. Or, I guess, those are the murder weapons."

"Yeah, I do. McDougall has the tox people checking. Can you see Melanie creating a distillation of coprine, injecting it into Taras Petrenko, and figuring out how to feed him wine?"

"Nope."

"So you're probably right that it's not Melanie, but she's still on the list."

"Right. On to the next subject?"

"Yes."

Adam took several deep breaths before entering the interview room next door, as James headed for the adjoining room. Adam suspected this would not be fun.

Livia Balan reminded him of someone; someone who made his stomach tighten in disgust.

Jilly. It was Jilly, the woman who had chased him from teenage years through to adulthood, and finally attempted to run Grace down on a grid road. Both manipulative, both beautiful, both somehow abhorrent and vaguely frightening.

"Ms. Balan," Adam greeted her. "Are you comfortable? Do you need anything?"

"No, thank you Sergeant. I'm fine. Let's get this over with."

"Let's start with the obvious. You lied to me about having sexual contact with Taras Petrenko."

"Whatever. It was just a kiss."

"Did it ever go further?"

"What do you think, Sergeant?"

"I don't know, Ms. Balan. Please tell me."

"Livia."

"All right. Livia."

"No, it didn't go further. We were . . . working on it."

"So you expected a deepening of the relationship, then. Why didn't you tell me this earlier?"

"I was concerned that you might consider me a suspect."

"I already do. And did. In what way did Taras suggest that sex was in the cards?"

She shrugged. "I could just tell."

"I see." Adam stood up and paced for a moment as if deep in thought. Instead of returning to his chair, he stood against the wall, arms crossed, one foot planted on the floor, the other braced behind him.

"And how could you tell?"

"Just like I can tell with you."

"Really? How?"

"Signals. Body language. It's obvious. You can't bear to be near me, can you? Because you want to be."

Livia Balan stood then, and walked slowly with hips swinging over to Adam, still braced against the wall, now with his arms at his sides. Adam would remember her next action as a pounce, like a cat in heat leaping on its sexual prey. She lunged at him, pushing on his arms, tongue flicking toward his mouth.

It only took a second or two before her lips — almost — met his. Adam knew his suspect by now and lifted his chin just in time. A tiny thrill coursed through him.

He smiled down at Livia Balan and gestured to James with one arm. *Get in here.*

"I think I understand now. Thank you, Ms. Balan." James came through the door. "Could you please take Ms. Balan down for prints and processing, Constable Weatherall? We will have more questions for this suspect."

Livia turned, hissing, to James. "No. I won't go with you. I won't."

Not "I'm innocent." Not "I'm sorry." Just feral fury.

James reached for her arm and was rewarded by sharp red nails clawing his face.

"For fuck's sake. Okay, Livia Balan, you are under arrest for assault," Adam said, grabbing her other arm. "Let's go."

*****

"Well, you called that one," James said, as the police station's medic dabbed his damaged face with antiseptic. He winced and emitted a small scream. "Shit, that stings."

"She got you good," agreed the medic. "Hold still, Weatherall."

"Sorry, James," Adam said. "That was probably meant for me. I was impressed that you didn't let go of her."

"Show no fear. Or pain. That's my motto," James said through gritted teeth. "You knew she was going to come for you, didn't you? I loved that sexy pose against the wall."

"Gee, thanks," said Adam. "It was vaguely similar to what happened with Taras; I thought I'd give it a go. Miss Balan likes men to surrender to her, and based on this conversation, we can't assume he was into the kiss. Unfortunately, we'll have to ask Emmy about it. See if he told her about Livia's attack."

"Why in hell did she go for him in the hutch?"

"They're pretty private, and I suspect it was hard for Livia to get him alone. Or for him to get her alone."

"Do you believe her about not having sex with Taras?"

"Yeah. I do. I think she'd have been talking that up, in the state she was in. It'd be worth bragging about. Every woman on the planet seems to have wanted Taras Petrenko."

"Something you have in common with our victim," James said, only partly teasing.

"Shut up, James."

"We're done here," said the medic. "I'll send the samples to the lab. Do you want the scratcher's blood tested?"

"Yeah. And her nails."

"Right. Got it."

Adam and James left the station clinic and mused about whether to go at Livia Balan again, or let her sleep on her sins. Ultimately, they decided to leave her overnight.

"It might scare some sense into her," James said.

"It might. She's not as forthcoming as I'd like her to be."

James raised his eyebrows. "I won't tell Grace you said that."

"Hilarious."

Adam sank into silence as they continued toward his office. Finally, James asked him what he was thinking.

"I'm trying to decide whether she's a realistic suspect. Why would she kill Taras if she wanted him so badly? If she thought sex was a future possibility? Alternatively, though, if she's lying and he pushed her away, could she be angry enough to kill him? Also, is she smart enough to pull it off?"

"I hate to say it, Adam, but she might be. She's also pretty screwed up, right? I mean, she goes for any man she wants, and to hell with location, timing, or even interest. She's intense. Not in a good way."

"No." Adam paused. "So let's go over this. Many years ago, Taras was threatened because he revealed a pharma company's flawed drug. Nothing apparently happened for years, after he and Emmy came to Canada. Then three months ago, Livia kissed Taras and Melanie witnessed it. Again, nothing for a while.

"Then Emmy left town. Taras went for lunch with the deans and the man from NSERC on Friday, the same day Evan Gorsalitz, biology dean, said he complained of toothache. Then Taras had dinner with the same deans — but not the NSERC guy — on Sunday. Grant Stockton, the ag dean, poured him two glasses of wine.

"He went home, puked, put in a load of laundry including his soiled shirt, felt slightly better and headed for the Light Source. And died horribly. None of the video cameras picked up anyone else in the facility at the time, except Brennan and the janitors."

Adam finally took a breath. What happened between lunch on Friday and dinner on Sunday?

"I want to talk to Emmy, James. Today, if possible. Can you call her right away? I should really call Grace. I told her I'd be back early this afternoon. It's four o'clock."

"You bet, Adam."

James returned to his desk and Adam to his office. He called Grace, told her he'd be home by six and suggested they go out for dinner.

"No way, Sergeant Overtime. I have pot roast in the oven."

Adam gave a whoop. "Can't wait. See you soon. I'm so sorry, Grace. I'll tell you all about it over dinner."

"You'd better, Mister."

Three minutes later, having established that Emmy Petrenko was at home, Adam and James made their third trip to University Drive. This time, Emmy seemed less composed. Deep black rings under her eyes contrasted starkly with her pale complexion; her posture was limp and her gait slow as she led them to the living room. She was clearly exhausted.

"How can I help?" she said, dropping into a soft chair.

"I'm so sorry we're here again," Adam began. "I'm sure this is terrible for you."

"You have no idea."

"You're right, I don't. I wish this wasn't happening, Emmy. I am truly sorry."

"When will they release Taras's body?"

"Soon. Very soon. I think we've made progress, and it shouldn't be more than another couple of days."

Emmy dropped her head and stared at her lap for a moment, then raised her ravaged eyes.

"All right. Ask me whatever questions you need to."

"This is a little . . . delicate," Adam said. "Today, I spoke to a witness who apparently stumbled on Taras and Livia Balan." He thought Emmy would know the names of Taras's assistants and colleagues and didn't elaborate.

"And?"

"They were, ah, embracing."

"Kissing, you mean." Emmy sighed. "It wasn't the first time a student flung herself at Taras. I suppose it was the last. As far as I know. Taras told me about it. He was quite upset, even though he should have been used to it. But he said Livia's little advance was different. More intense. He thought he might have to take her off the project."

"Did he speak to her about it? Removing her, I mean?"

"He did. He said that sort of thing could never happen again, and she agreed. Or so she said."

In his peripheral vision, Adam could see James's eyes lift from his notebook. A significant revelation, if Taras could be trusted. Adam steeled himself for the next question.

"I'm sorry. Did you believe Taras when he told you that?"

"Of course. Yes. Absolutely. You've met Ms. Balan?"

"Yes."

"And you, Constable Weatherall? Your face . . ."

"Yes. I've met her, too."

That was all he said, but Emmy nodded knowingly.

"She might be lovely, but she is a very strange and somewhat terrifying young woman. As I assume you both know by now. And to be clear, I trusted my husband. Completely."

Adam thought Emmy Petrenko pretty much nailed the personality of Livia Balan. He decided to move on.

"Did you know your husband may have been suffering with a sore tooth while you were away?"

"I didn't," Emmy said, furrowing her face. "He didn't mention it."

"When did you last speak to him?"

"Saturday morning, I think it was. Here, I mean. It was late afternoon in Paris. But unless it was excruciating, he may not have said anything. Taras . . . well, he tried to protect me. My feelings. If I knew he was in pain, I would worry, and he knew that. What could I do from France?"

"Would it be possible for you to contact his dentist? We can, but we'd need to request a warrant, due to confidentiality around health matters. Even after death, it's required."

"Of course. I'll call the clinic when it opens on Monday. What would a sore tooth have to do with his death?"

"Almost certainly nothing. But the dentist may have seen him when he was already feeling unwell. That would help us determine . . . the timeline," Adam added lamely. He didn't yet want to reveal his theory about coprine, since it was still just that. A theory. He was positive, but the tox screen was not. Not yet.

"Could you ask the dentist how he was feeling, apart from the tooth? If he will speak to you?"

"I'm sure he'll talk to me. And of course I will."

"Thank you. I'll call you Monday morning, say around ten?"

"Make it nine. The dental clinic opens at eight-thirty. I'm anxious to have my husband's murder solved," she said. "And avenged."

Chapter Eighteen

Adam finally came home at six-thirty and Grace, scanning his tired face, also detected a brightness in his eyes. Something had happened.

She handed him a glass of red wine and told him to sit down while she took the roast out of the oven.

"You look pooped, my love."

"I am. But Grace, I think I've figured something out. The poison."

"What? What is it?"

"Coprine."

Adam launched into his poison theory while Grace brought plates of beef, roasted potatoes and carrots to the table, which already bore a crunchy green salad. Once he had finished, he finally took a monstrous bite.

"Adam, if you're right, this is a very clever killer. He or she wasn't even there when Petrenko died. Am I right?"

"Yes. It's much easier to cover your tracks if you haven't made any at the murder scene."

"There's a terrible symmetry to this, as well. Gryphon wouldn't kill him, but a similar mushroom could." Grace bent her head over her plate again, and in so doing noticed Adam's hand as he raised the fork to his mouth. "What happened to your hand? You've scratched it."

"I had a little help. That's the other thing. Taras's assistant."

It took fifteen minutes to relay the entire Livia Balan encounter, from the meeting in the café where she dragged a nail across his hand, to the strange interview at the station.

"Grace," he added slowly, "I have to admit I felt a thrill at being able to pull her into that ruse. I don't feel good about it."

"No, I can see why." Grace smiled sympathetically. "It's all right, Adam. It worked, after all."

"You should see James's face."

"Ow. Poor James. Although it might give him a handsomely rakish look. Do you think Livia could be the killer?"

"I don't know. She really wanted Taras sexually — and otherwise, I think."

"Well, she wanted you, too. The woman is messed up, obviously."

"Thanks a lot."

Grace laughed and gently touched Adam's cheek. "I didn't mean it that way. I meant that her predatory behaviour seems extreme. Something happened to her, along the way."

"If you had to guess?"

"Sexual abuse. Or a colossal rejection; maybe a parent's departure? Or loss?" Grace thought for a moment. "She may not be the killer, although I'd say it's remotely possible. But I'll bet she has a role to play here. Maybe more betrayal than actual murder."

"Go on."

"Well, Emmy told you Taras was going to fire her, basically. And if he rejected her twice — sexually and professionally — she may have wanted revenge. Maybe it backfired. Maybe she intended to mess with his reputation, but it went too far and resulted in his death. I'm spit-balling here, but if there was abuse or rejection in her background, it would make sense. She could be thinking, no one is ever going to screw with me again."

"Following your theory, why did she come on to me, then? I'm no help to her, career-wise or otherwise. In fact, quite the opposite."

"Let's see. Because you're ridiculously gorgeous and sexy?"

"No."

"Oh yes. But I think, in addition, she can't help herself. Yes," Grace said, warming to her profile of Livia Balan. "She's desperate to attract a man in authority, but I think that man also has to be very attractive, or the victory is hollow. She's lost Taras, immutably, so you were next. She's screwed up, for sure, but also frightened."

"Of what?"

"Hmmm. Possibly she has something to prove to someone, and fears that she'll never be good enough? She needs approval. And social standing. And sex. Sex demonstrates love and devotion."

Adam, by now finished his dinner, stood up and pulled Grace to her feet.

"You're incredible, Grace. That is all. Except, I'm going to marry you."

"I'm going to marry you, too. Amazing and so convenient, how that works out."

Adam laughed and kissed her. "I forgot goofy."

"All part of the package."

"Thank God." Adam held her tightly. "I have to tell you one more thing."

*****

Grace couldn't decide if she was pleased or horrified that Adam was playing matchmaker between Jay Griffin, an unlikely but potential murder suspect, and her sister.

That he had not told her about it for twenty-four hours suggested to Grace that he was struggling with his decision to arrange for the two to meet again under supervision. Was she angry? Worried? Thrilled?

As Adam left to check out Jay's gas station alibi, Grace climbed into her car and drove to Hope's. Grace knew she only had to look into her sister's face to sense what she wanted.

Grace called ahead, to say she was coming to play with Lawan. Hope had coffee and muffins on the table; Lawan sat in her highchair with a glass of milk and dry cereal strewn all over the little tray. And the floor.

After half an hour of chatter and interacting with Lawan, the little girl visibly began to droop. Hope swept her up and away to her crib, returning moments later.

"I assume you're really here to talk about Jay Griffin," Hope said, sitting down.

"Yes." Grace was unsurprised by the sudden launch into the topic. That was Hope, all over.

"Why is this such a big deal that you had to come over?"

"Because it is. When's the last time you heard of a murder suspect begging to meet the sergeant-in-charge's sister-in-law-to-be?"

Hope chewed her lip. "You have a point."

"Yes, I do. It's a bit unusual. And so is he."

"Yes. He is."

"What does that mean to you?"

Hope stood again and began to pace the kitchen. "Oh, God, I don't know. I've never met anyone like him, but it was only the once. I felt like he could see right through me. To the good parts. The ones I try not to show anybody."

"Well, it's not working. Everyone sees those parts, despite your best efforts."

"Ha."

"Hopey. What do you want to do?"

"I told Adam I want to see him again."

"And if he is a murderer?"

"He isn't. I know it in my bones."

"Adam is out there right now trying to prove it. For you, as much as for the resolution of the case. Can you wait until he's done that?"

"Depends."

"On?"

"How long it takes."

"Oh. It's like that, then."

"Yes."

"You've only met him once. Could you be wrong?"

"Anything is possible. But no. Remember when I found you on the bedroom floor weeping, after the first time you kissed Adam? And I told you I would have done the same thing — kissed a man regardless of the repercussions. And yours could have been significant. You were his witness, suspect and a victim of a crime. No way he should have come near you, legally or ethically, and no way you should have touched him, much less kissed him."

"And I said there's no way you would have done that. And you agreed. And then we laughed until our sides literally ached." Grace grinned at the memory.

"I've changed my mind about that. I didn't get it then — why you two would risk the case, Adam's career, the possibility of a future with him, someone you barely knew. But I do now." Hope's eyes, soft with sadness and longing, met Grace's. "I do now."

"Oh, honey." Grace put her arms around her sister and felt a warm tear on her neck. "This isn't quite the same thing, though. He's a suspect."

"So were you," Hope mumbled into Grace's hair.

"Fair." Grace sighed. "I was unlikely to murder Adam."

Hope broke away from the embrace and looked intently into Grace's face.

"Jay is unlikely to murder me. Because he is not a killer."

Grace's phone pinged. She glanced at it to see a text from Adam and relayed the information to Hope, who put down her coffee and hurled herself into Grace's arms.

*****

A mile away, Adam had identified himself and showed Jay's photograph to the gas station attendant. It would seriously have helped if Jay had kept his gas receipt, but so far, he hadn't been able to find it.

"Do you know this man?" he asked.

"Yep. He's a regular customer."

"Do you usually work the early shift?

"Yep."

"Can you recall if he was here a week ago Friday?"

The young man, really a kid, screwed up his face in the effort to remember. "Friday, Friday. What happened Friday? Shit. I can't remember for sure. How did he pay?"

"Credit card. Is that traceable?"

"Yep. Well, more or less. We'll have the last four digits. Got the number?"

"No. But I will in a minute."

Adam texted Jay, who was on full alert with his phone constantly charged. In a minute, he supplied the number. The kid punched it into the system with incredible speed, fingers flying over the keys, and a look of great satisfaction spread over his face.

"Boom," he said. "That credit card was used on Friday morning a little before ten. Like, I see him at least a couple times a month, right? Hard to remember when the last time was. So yeah, he was here." He beamed at Adam, clearly happy to exonerate a regular.

He couldn't possibly have been as happy as Adam. The window was closing. Jay's whereabouts from Thursday night, after he left the Light Source, until Friday at ten in the morning meant Adam only had to verify his location for about twelve hours. It would be tricky, if not impossible, since Jay had said he'd been alone all that time. Asleep, for much of it. But things were looking up.

"Thank you very much, ah, Jason," Adam said, taking a glance at the young man's nametag. "You've been very helpful. More than you know," he added, thinking of Hope.

"Cheers, Sergeant. Glad to do it. Come on by for gas sometime," Jason added, winking.

"I will," Adam said, and meant it. "Thanks."

Adam texted Grace immediately upon leaving.
Jay was at gas station, 10 on Fri. Phew.

Chapter Nineteen

Taras Petrenko had not visited the dentist before he died.

Neither had he made an appointment for a subsequent day.

Adam was surprised at this news from Emmy Petrenko at nine on Monday morning. Maybe Taras had decided to gut it out over the weekend in the hope the pain would subside. Maybe Evan Gorsalitz had been wrong about his toothache.

Damn. Adam hoped the dentist could have shed some light on Petrenko's condition immediately before his death, but no such luck.

And where the hell, he asked himself for the tenth time, is my tox report?

He picked up the phone and paused, finger poised, for a second. Who should he call first? James, he decided.

"Hey, James. Checking in on the NSERC guy. Have you tried him yet today?"

"I have, but damn it, Adam, he's travelling. In Europe on business. They've given me his cell number, but no answer yet."

"Were you able to leave a message?"

"Twice. The third time, his voicemail was full."

Adam had to chuckle. His constable was a bulldog.

"Keep me posted. And we'll have to re-interview Livia Balan sometime today, but I'm really hoping to get the tox report first. I'll call Jack next."

But he didn't have to. The phone rang within seconds of hanging up with James.

"Jack," Adam said. "What have you got?"

"I have a very tired tox screener who worked all day yesterday, which you will recall was Sunday, figuring out how to test for coprine. It's not on the usual list of substances, you know. Hello, Adam. Good morning."

"Sorry. Good morning, Jack." He held his breath.

"Well, he did it in good humour. Was quite excited about it, actually. Said it was 'cool' to test for something out of the ordinary."

"You're killing me here."

"There was coprine in Taras Petrenko's system."

Adam exhaled and pumped a fist in the air. "Say, 'you were right, Detective.' Out loud, please."

"No chance of that. Anyway, as we know, his blood alcohol was point-zero-five. Borderline for driving, but shouldn't have been a problem, realistically. But there was something else."

"What? What else?"

"Procaine."

"Like novocaine, only different?"

"Yes. Today they usually use lidocaine. The original procaine is an old anaesthetic, rarely if ever used these days. I think, although you'll want to check, it's only used if someone is allergic to the modern equivalents."

Baffled, Adam glared out the window and thought, what the hell?

"Jack, Emmy Petrenko told me that Taras did not see a dentist that weekend. She called their clinic and checked."

"Tox screens do not lie, Sergeant."

"But people do."

"You're not suggesting Emmy was withholding dental information, are you?"

"No. Why the hell would she? Even if she killed him, she did it from afar — like leaving a tainted frozen dinner or something — and so his sore tooth would have been moot. If he didn't get procaine from his dentist, where did he get it?"

"That's your department. Also, Adam, I have no idea whether procaine would have contributed to his death. I'll have to do some thinking, and probably researching. This is, and it shouldn't surprise you, my first victim with those three substances in his dead body."

"That was my next question, so thanks for anticipating. And I appreciate that you expedited this. Very much."

"Thank the tox guy. Two bottles of Glenlivet should be on your shopping list."

Adam laughed. The old Scotch joke. Came up every time.

"You're on. I'll let you know what I know, when I know it. Cheers."

"Goodbye, Adam."

Adam hung up and could barely restrain his glee. That lasted for five whole minutes, when James knocked and opened the door, his face like thunder.

"Shit, James. What's wrong?"

"Livia Balan has lawyered up."

"Well, I guess we shouldn't be surprised. She's not exactly an idiot. Damn it. Who is it?"

"Donna Hunter."

"Hell. She's good. Has she appeared yet?"

"No, but she's on her way down."

"Okay. Let me know when we can talk to her. And James, on the bright side, we have the tox report. There was coprine in Taras's system."

"Really? Well, at least you've made some progress. I'll get back to you when Hunter arrives." James retreated, leaving Adam to figure out what to do next.

Right. The Dean of Biology Evan Gorsalitz's partner. Silas. They hadn't had time to talk to him yet, nor Ellen Stockton, nor Andrea Horvath, the spouses of the other two deans at dinner. Adam had to cross off those witnesses.

Silas Cosgrove, apparently, was a stay-at-home father and writer. He and Gorsalitz were the adoptive parents of two boys, aged four and eight. Adam realized he had heard of Cosgrove; he wrote long articles for the paper, on occasion, as well as books — non-fiction, mostly, but also a novel or two. He called; Cosgrove answered and agreed to see Adam immediately.

Stopping only to inform James, Adam pulled on his coat and headed out into the bright, cold day. Gorsalitz and Cosgrove, as with most faculty, lived near the university on Elliott Street, in an old character home that had seen considerable renovation. Adam pulled up two blocks away; parking was always a challenge in this neighbourhood, due to the proximity to campus.

Cosgrove answered Adam's knock with a small boy clinging to his leg.

"Come in, come in, Sergeant. This is Adrian. Adrian, this is Sergeant Davis."

Adrian gazed up at the tall police officer, mouth wide open, for a few seconds before burying his face shyly into his father's thigh. Both adults smiled, and Cosgrove lifted the child into his arms, gesturing the way into the living room.

"How can I help, Sergeant?" he asked, sitting down with Adrian on his knee.

"I'm hoping you can tell me about the dinner at Grant Stockton's home, the night Taras died. Do you remember anything unusual?"

"Not really. It was the usual dinner. The usual yawn."

"Yawn?" Adam asked, a grin quirking up a corner of his mouth.

"Stockton is such a bloody stick. You've met him?"

"No, but my partner has. He gave me a good description. What about the others? Are they boring as well?"

"Ellen is, for sure. I don't mind Andrea and Devon quite so much. Taras was always lovely to be around, though, if only to stare at." Cosgrove winked, then seemed to remember the man was dead. His face fell. "Sorry. Taras was a wonderful human, Detective. I'm simply in the habit of commenting on his considerable beauty. It was a thing."

"Did he seem himself? Healthy, happy and so on?"

"He did," Cosgrove said, then paused. "At first. Now that you ask, he was behaving a little strangely when he left, but I put it down to his desire to get the hell out of there and over to the Light Source."

"When you say 'strangely?' How was his behaviour different?"

"Taras would normally leave a party with a hearty goodbye and many thanks for the hospitality. On that

Sunday, he was in quite a hurry. Kissed Ellen on the cheek, waved to us and said he had to go."

"How did he look? Was he pale, sweating, shaking, anything like that?"

"Maybe a shade paler than usual. A little drawn. I thought he was just tired, and he definitely was missing Emmy. I asked him when she was coming home, and he said next week; it couldn't be soon enough for him."

"Did you have any stomach troubles after the meal?"

"No. Evan did, but that always happens."

"How long had you known Taras?"

"Several years. Evan was already teaching on campus when Taras came to Saskatoon."

"Would you say you knew him well?"

"Yes, I'd say so. We were definitely friends, if not intimate ones. Unfortunately."

"Did he say anything about a tooth that was bothering him?"

"No, he didn't."

"Would anyone you know have any reason to kill him, Mr. Cosgrove?"

"No. Not that I know of. Why would anyone want to kill Taras? Although I can think of several young women, and possibly men, who would have liked to kill Emmy. Or at the very least, have her extradited to another country."

Adam was beginning to enjoy Cosgrove's slightly irreverent and snarky comments; besides, he was probably right.

"Any in particular?"

"Not really; they were legion. I did notice one young woman following him around like a puppy at one of his campus parties. Melanie, I think. The girl has no filters. I'm sure they all wanted to do the same."

A thought struck Adam. If every female, and possibly male, student had a thing for Taras, what about the other, more mature women in his life? Not to mention the men. Cosgrove had certainly admired him.

"Were any of the women in your social circle equally interested in Taras?" he asked.

"Oh yes. All of them, I would say. Did any of them try it on?" Cosgrove narrowed his eyes. "I think you should ask Ellen Stockton that question."

*****

"Come in, come in, Sergeant."

Ellen fluttered and fussed as annoyingly as the White Rabbit, apologizing for the state of the house — spotless to Adam's eyes — and offering him an entire menu of hot and cold drink options. His brain flew back to his school days, the image of a bunny wringing its hands and crying "Oh, dear" leaping into memory.

"I'm fine, Mrs. Stockton, please don't bother. I won't keep you for long. Just a few questions."

The agriculture dean's wife, vaguely pretty, short and buxom, seemed fuzzy around the edges: pink woolly sweater, flyaway hair, constantly in motion. Nerves, wondered Adam? Or a normal state of confusion and anxiety?

Adam began with his usual queries about the dinner — how Taras appeared, whether anything unusual had happened, had anyone else felt unwell.

The last sent Ellen into a tizzy.

"Oh, no, Sergeant, I don't think so. I would hate to think I had prepared anything other than a healthy meal.

No one said anything and I certainly hope they would tell me if they suspected unwholesome food."

"I'm not implying anything, Mrs. Stockton, but I have to check considering what happened later." He paused, wondering how she would react to his next avenue of inquiry. Maybe a little flattery would pave the way.

"I understand that you have your finger on the pulse of the social circle, Mrs. Stockton," he said, mentally rolling his eyes at the phrase. "Your knowledge and intuition may be of great assistance to our case."

She actually blushed. "Anything I can do, Sergeant. Anything."

"This is a little delicate . . ." he continued, trying to look uncomfortable.

"Oh, I see. It's all right, Sergeant. Don't worry; I can handle it."

He doubted that. He leaned in conspiratorially.

"Our investigation indicates that Taras was, well, universally admired, if I may put it that way. We've learned of at least two women who were, ahhh . . . interested in him. Personally. I was wondering if you, with your knowledge of human beings, were aware of any others."

She blinked rapidly several times before looking down at her hands, which she carefully folded in her lap. Adam instantly grasped Ellen Stockton's own feelings for Taras Petrenko. Good Lord, did every single woman on campus, or off, have a crush on this man?

Collecting herself, Ellen looked up and smiled. "I think perhaps many others."

"Of course. He was quite remarkably handsome. But were there any who were particularly enamoured? To the point of revealing their feelings?"

"You mean apart from his assistant?" It came out with a sharp edge, like a knife on the tongue. Ellen Stockton did not like, did not approve, or was jealous of Livia Balan.

"Yes. Apart from her."

"Must I really say?"

"I'm afraid so. It's a murder investigation, Mrs. Stockton."

"Are you sure Taras was killed, though? I've been thinking, perhaps he just caught a bug or something."

"No. It was not a bug."

"What was it, then?"

"I can't say at this point, I'm sorry."

"Oh."

"Please answer the question, Mrs. Stockton."

"I — I feel so . . . oh, dear. I hate telling tales on my friends. And I'm sure it was nothing."

Adam's frustration began to rise, and his patience frayed. He waited, keeping his eyes firmly on her face. Finally, he simply said, "Tell me."

A heavy sigh.

"We were at the Petrenkos one night for a party," she said, slowly. "I was in the . . . in the bathroom, and when I came out I heard raised voices. I admit, I was curious. I thought I recognized them. A man's and a woman's. I thought at first Emmy and Taras were fighting. But it wasn't Emmy. I heard the woman say something like, 'if you don't, I'll tell Emmy about us.' He laughed, rather nastily, and said, 'go ahead.'"

"Who was the woman?"

"Well, I didn't see her. But once I realized it wasn't Emmy speaking — she has that tiny touch of a French accent, as I'm sure you know — I, ah, I did continue to eavesdrop."

Adam deliberately pasted his most encouraging expression on his face and nodded in a way that he hoped absolved her of her sin.

"Very understandable. And?"

"It was . . . it was Andrea. I think."

"You mean Andrea Horvath? Dean Devon Horvath's spouse?"

A nod.

"What does that mean to you, Mrs. Stockton?"

"Oh, dear. I don't know. I assumed I either misinterpreted their conversation, or that . . . that something had happened between them."

"Did you tell anyone about this?"

Shame overcame her; blood rushed to her face. "Y-yes."

"Who?"

"My husband. And Evan and Silas."

"Not Emmy, though."

"No!" Ellen was clearly shocked. "I couldn't hurt Emmy."

"But you did gossip about what you overheard."

"I'm afraid so."

"Did you mention it to either of the Horvaths? Or to Taras?"

"No."

"So Andrea doesn't know that you were eavesdropping."

"No. Not as far as I know." Her eyes flew wide open in alarm. "Will you have to tell her? I don't think I could stand that."

"Yes, I'm afraid I will. I'll have to ask her about her relationship with Taras. Speaking of which, what was your own relationship with him?"

"We were very good friends with the Petrenkos. Still are, with Emmy."

"I wonder, Mrs. Stockton, if there's more to it than that."

"No. Certainly not."

"Perhaps you wanted there to be."

She didn't have to answer. It was written all over her.

"Did you . . . try? With Taras?"

"No. It was hopeless; I could see that," she said, capitulating. "Who would want a little mouse like me? Especially someone as beautiful as Taras?"

Chapter Twenty

Adam began to see the noose tightening around Taras Petrenko's neck. Erotic passion may not have literally killed him — no spurned lover, nor lover's husband, had plunged a knife in his back — but it was in play. Which one of these besotted women, or men, had braided the knot?

Dr. Andrea Horvath grudgingly agreed to fit Adam in between her two afternoon classes, pointing out that she had only an hour and at least half of that would be taken up with a student appointment.

Determining that Donna Hunter had not yet appeared at the station, Adam returned to campus and wandered the now-sere quad before heading to the professor's office. Her student emerged, and Adam knocked.

"Come in," said a husky voice.

She stood as Adam entered, smiled and shook his hand firmly.

"Thank you for seeing me today," Adam began, as he took a seat. "Greatly appreciated."

"My pleasure, Sergeant. I'm glad I had the time. What can I do for you?"

"Did you have a personal relationship with Taras Petrenko?"

She started, and then laughed. "So much for small talk. Of course I did. We were very good friends."

"That's not what I mean. You know it."

Andrea Horvath looked across her desk at Adam, eyes narrowing as she prepared to lie. And then she didn't.

"It was before Emmy, a long time ago. We were master's students at the time. We met at university."

"Which university?"

"Prague. In the summer. An international, highly coveted placement. As I'm sure you know, any courses you can pick up outside your own alma mater are prized by universities, and we were both very ambitious. We hoped to achieve our doctorates outside our own institutions."

"Would you describe your relationship as an affair?"

"I suppose so. He was gorgeous. So was I, if I may say so." She still was, Adam thought. Willowy, a bit exotic, elegant. But he felt no sexual pull. Grace exuded warmth and sexuality; Andrea Horvath did not.

"Do your spouses know?"

"Oh yes. At least, I told Devon."

"Had it come up with Taras in the recent past?"

"No. Why would you ask such a question?"

"Ellen Stockton heard you arguing. I wondered if there was a remnant of the old feelings you had for him."

"Ah. I see. Bloody busybody. Well, yes, we did have an argument one night. I told him to keep his damn distance from Livia Balan. That young woman is a terror, and she could have ended Taras's career, if he wasn't careful — not to mention his relationship with Emmy. But he dawdled over it. He was . . . too kind, sometimes."

Adam rapidly processed what Ellen Stockton had told him; did that fit with Andrea's explanation?

"Mrs. Stockton said she heard you say, 'if you don't, I'll tell Emmy about us.' Was that accurate?"

"Not quite. What I told him was, 'if you don't' — get rid of that girl, you know — 'I'll talk to Emmy about it.' That was all there was to it. It wasn't a threat, Sergeant. I thought Emmy should weigh in to save Taras and his reputation from Livia, if he wouldn't do it himself."

Adam wondered if that was the truth, but for now, he'd have to accept it. It did make a kind of sense.

"One more thing, Dr. Horvath. Were you aware that Taras had a sore tooth the week before he died?"

"No, I wasn't," she said. "He didn't mention it to me."

"So he didn't come to you for treatment, then. Or anyone else in the department?"

"No, and not that I know of. I don't do clinical work. And I don't recall seeing Taras that week, apart from at the dinner party. He seemed fine, apart from a little anxious to leave. As we all were." She smiled. "I don't really mean that. But dinner at the Stocktons can be a little stultifying."

"So I understand. Thank you, Doctor. I appreciate the time. Oh . . . one more thing. Do dentists use procaine anymore for freezing? It's usually lidocaine, right?"

"Yes, it is. Procaine is a very old drug and doesn't work as well as today's novocaine equivalents. I can't think of anyone who uses it, unless a patient has a very bad allergy to the newer drugs. Why do you ask?"

"I'm afraid I can't say. Thank you, again."

"My pleasure, Sergeant. Any time."

Adam raised an eyebrow at that, but simply shook Andrea Horvath's hand, nodded and left to return to the station. James waylaid him the moment he appeared.

"Donna Hunter is here, sitting outside your office," he said. "She showed a few minutes ago."

"Thanks. Want to join me?"

"Yes, I do."

The lawyer rose as they neared, visibly ready for battle. Adam smiled to deflect her weapons.

"Hello, Donna. Can I get you some coffee?"

"Your station dreck? No thanks, I'd rather die of thirst. And I don't have time."

"Good decision. Come on in."

Adam unlocked his office door and gestured for Donna to precede them in. Once they were settled, he got to the point.

"So, when can I talk to your client? Now would be good."

"Sorry, nope. I have some work to do before I can let that happen. I'll be asking for bail as soon as I get out of here, by the way."

"Good luck with that. You have seen James's face?"

"You two set her up."

"To attack James?" Adam said, incredulity dripping from the words.

"You, Sergeant Davis, used your manly wiles to provoke her. You can see she's a mess, right? I have to dive into a few issues before you get near her. Understood?"

"Look. All we want to know is what happened between her and Taras. The truth."

"That's what you think."

"What does that mean? Is there more to this than I can imagine?"

"Ah ah ah. Don't even try. I'll need at least twenty-four hours, maybe more. Don't worry, Adam. You'll get your interview. Now, I have to get on the bail request. See you in a day or two."

She grabbed her briefcase, stood, grinned at Adam and swept out the door, leaving Adam and James gaping after her.

"What the hell was that about?" James asked.

"No idea. Can't wait to find out. Call Sanj Kumar, would you? Give him the heads up on Livia's bail hearing. If we can keep her sweating it out in cells for a couple of days, I'd be much happier."

"You got it." James left to contact the Crown prosecutor but returned a second later. "Should I warn him about your little ploy?"

Adam had the grace to blush.

"Yeah. Thanks." He looked at his watch, amazed at how the day had flown by. "The hearing won't happen today; it's almost five. I doubt we'll be able to talk to her before Wednesday. If it does line up, you'll have to interview her. I'm off to Hafford tomorrow."

*****

In the morning, Adam and Grace packed up the big black truck with work gear, a thermos of coffee and snacks, and pulled up in front of Jay Griffin's apartment before nine. A second later, Adam's phone buzzed.

"It's Jay," Adam said to Grace. "Just a sec."

Adam. Do you see that blue van?

Adam scanned the street and immediately saw a filthy dark blue Caravan on the other side.

Hi Jay. Yes.

It was there last night before I went to bed. Still there. Someone was in it.

There still was, a shadow behind the dirty window.

I see it.

Am I paranoid?

No. Stay put.

"Grace. That van. Can you make out the licence plate?"

"Damn, Adam. What are you thinking?"

"Not sure, but Jay says it's been there all night, with someone in it. Why didn't he call me?" Adam grunted. "I can see an A and a seven."

"I think it's a one. And there's a C."

"Okay. Get down."

Adam opened the truck's door, hand on his holster, and stepped into the street. Probably nothing, he thought. Some drunk kid sleeping it off. *Still . . .*

Trying to simultaneously peer at the licence number and the person's face, Adam was in mid-stride when the vehicle roared, reversed and pulled out, speeding away.

"Shit!" Adam yelled, and grabbed his phone, dialling the station with one touch. "It's Davis," he said, wishing he had decided to drive his unmarked car, equipped with radio, instead of the truck. But it would take on the crazy rural roads far better. "Dark blue dirty Caravan, took off from Thirteenth Street near Clarence. Speeding. Possible suspect in the Petrenko killing."

"Got a plate, Sarge?"

"One sec."

Adam jerked open the truck door. "Grace, any more luck with the plate?"

"C1V, best guess, and then an A and an eight afterward. Sorry, I couldn't get the rest."

Adam grinned, and relayed the information. "Plate dirty too, but this is what we have."

"Okay, Adam. On it."

"Davis out," he said, and returned to grinning at Grace. "Well done, Babe."

"Do you think he was staking out Jay?" she asked. "Why would he do that? Wouldn't he just go up to his apartment and . . . do something terrible?" Grace shuddered.

"Good question. I'm going to take a look around before anything else happens. He might not have been alone. Lock the doors and stay down, love."

Adam loped down the block, one side and then the other, but saw no other occupied vehicles.

OK, Jay. R u ready? Come on down.

K. I see he took off.

Yes. Come straight to the black truck.

Even as he texted, Adam thought twice about that.

Stop. I'm coming up to get you.

That's stupid.

No. Wait.

"Let's go get him, Grace. I don't want to leave you here, and I don't know what's going on in there."

"Right."

She scrambled down from the truck as Adam came to her side, and they buzzed Jay's apartment number.

"Come on up, if you really think it's necessary," he said over the intercom.

Not deigning to respond, Adam yanked open the door, pulled out his sidearm and warned Grace to stay behind him. They crept up the flight of stairs to Jay's little home on the second floor. Once they reached the landing, Adam exhaled and began to reach for the door handle; but in that second, the heavy fire door flew open, crashing into Adam's shoulder, which in turn slammed into Grace and knocked her into the wall.

A huge man, head completely covered in a balaclava, burst through the opening, leaped down the half-flight of stairs, landed on all fours and charged down the second flight.

"Go to Jay's suite!" Adam yelled to Grace and turned to make chase, ignoring his sore shoulder.

He thundered down the stairs, but the would-be assailant had several seconds on him; by the time he reached the exterior door, the man was gone from sight. Adam picked a direction, tore after him, but there was no sign of him.

Adam swore at the top of his voice and yet again called the station.

"Davis. Just got slammed into by some brute. Wearing a balaclava, black, leather jacket, black, jeans, six-four or so, fit as hell. Big. Really big. He ran out of Jay's building, 1028 Thirteenth Street."

"Are you hurt, Sarge?" the staff sergeant asked.

"No," Adam lied. "Come find this fucker."

He raced back to the building and buzzed, hoping like hell he'd made the right decision to chase the assailant and not stay to protect Grace. Jay buzzed back. Thank God.

When Adam reached the suite, he found Jay and Grace both standing in the tiny kitchen, wild-eyed. Grace lunged at him.

"Is your shoulder okay?" she asked.

"Imperfect, but okay. How are you? Did you hit your head?"

"A little; mostly the back and shoulders. A little sore, but I'm all right."

"I guess it was necessary to come up here," Jay interjected, sounding somewhat sheepish. "Shit, Adam. Who the fuck are these guys?"

"Hitmen," Adam said, sourly. "Clearly not ready to hit yet, although who knows what this guy was up to? He was inside. Maybe we got here in the nick of time; maybe he was still casing. You're not staying here, Jay. Pack up some stuff. Now."

"Where am I going?"

"Hafford, first. Then anywhere but here. We'll figure it out."

Jay obediently strode off to his bedroom. Grace and Adam took the moment of privacy to hold each other, breathing in the sweet air of relief. Then Grace removed her face from Adam's chest and looked up at him.

"No way Jay's getting near my sister."

"He's obviously not the killer."

"No. But equally obviously, someone wants to kill him."

Chapter Twenty-One

The truck's occupants refrained from conversation for the first seventy kilometres of the journey to Hafford. Adam and Grace allowed Jay to simmer in a morose silence until they reached the town of Radisson, when Grace suggested they stop for coffee.

Inside the Red Bull Restaurant, they took a booth, ordered coffee and toast, and spent a moment or two staring at the table. Adam cleared his throat.

"Jay. Are you okay?"

"I've been better, frankly. That was crazy shit."

"Yeah, it was. Why didn't you call me last night when you saw the van?"

"I didn't think anything of it until this morning, when I realized it was still there."

Fair, Adam thought. Even he had wondered if it was a kid with a hangover.

"Well, there won't be a next time, not at your apartment. But if you notice anything strange, and I mean anything — being followed, for example — call me right away. I mean immediately. Don't even breathe, just dial."

Adam paused, and Grace put a hand over Jay's shaking fingers.

"He will solve Taras's murder, Jay," she said, as soothingly as she could. "This will end."

"There is a bright side," Adam added.

"What would that be?" Jay asked.

"Looks like you're not a suspect anymore. I'm still going to check up on you, but as smart as you are, I can't see you hiring two guys to pose as hitmen just to throw me off the trail."

Jay brightened considerably, a small smile playing at the corner of his mouth.

"I told you so," he said, but the gratitude in his eyes spoke different words. Then he coughed them up. "Thanks, Adam, for believing in me."

"Don't thank me yet. There's also a downside to this."

"I know. Hope. Oh . . ." he said, glancing at Grace.

"She knows, Jay."

"Okay, good. Grace, I — I want to get to know her. I, um, I kind of . . . "

"Fell for her a bit, at the airport," Grace finished, as Jay trailed off again. "She is amazing, Jay. But for God's sake, I can't — we can't — put her in the proverbial line of fire. Sorry," she added. "I didn't mean to remind you of what just happened. But let's be open and honest here. I mean, we're sharing the same truck cab, on the way to your parents' place."

Jay managed to laugh at that, and everyone's shoulders came down an inch or two.

Adam's phone tingled in his pocket, and a text from James popped up.

No luck so far, sorry, Adam. Still looking.
OK. Keep me posted.

They drained their coffee cups and climbed back into the truck after filling it with gas. The Twisted Forest, alias Crooked Bush, was still more than half an hour out, down groomed grid roads that passed through fertile Saskatchewan cropland.

Neither Grace nor Adam had ever seen the strange little clump of gnarled aspen. As they neared it, Grace asked, "Does anyone know why the aspen grew that way? I've looked it up but haven't found any answers."

"No. They've taken cuttings of the trees to see if they'll grow anywhere else, and apparently they do — similarly twisted, somewhere in Manitoba. It's really a strange phenomenon. When I was a kid, I used to dream that odd little people lived in the forest and had put a spell on the trees. To what end, I can't say," he said, laughing.

"What about your fungus? I'm not clear about what's so special about this mushroom, but do you think its properties are related to the crooked trees?"

"I do think so. I have little reason to, but it is a fact that tree root beds have strong associations with their fungi. So, whatever is happening to the trees . . . did that have an effect on Gryphon? It's one of the questions we're asking. That's why there's a related investigation into the soil here."

"You mean someone is bombarding the soil with light, too?"

"Yes. Livia has been involved with that project. Me, less so."

Adam stayed silent. Jay didn't know that Livia was sitting in a police station cell, nor what had preceded her arrest. He wanted to keep it that way for now.

As they approached the town of Hafford, Adam decided to make a short stop. He pulled up at the bar, turned and asked Jay if this was his local hangout.

"Yep. No one will be there now, though. It's only eleven."

"The bartender might be. Wait here."

Adam jumped out and walked quickly to the aging building. Grace, to keep Jay from stewing, asked him questions about his family.

"What kind of a name is Griffin?" she asked, although she already knew.

"Welsh. Dad's Welsh, but Mom's Ukrainian. This is Ukrainian farm country, for the most part. Mom's parents were immigrants. Dad's from down the road some distance, but he agreed to come and help farm this land after they were married. Having a son-in-law involved allowed my grandfather to grow his land holdings. Dad still runs the smaller Griffin farm. He has a manager out there."

"What was your mother's maiden name?

"Nykiforuk. Sofia Elena Nykiforuk," he elaborated, softly. "Dad's name is Ioan. He calls Mom Sofie. And I have a sister, Christina."

"Do you feel a pull to the Welsh or the Ukrainian side?"

"Both, except that Mom's roots have led her to the forest and the meadow. My Baba brought her love of foraging to this country. She always took Mom with her when she went picking — berries, flowers, and mushrooms. When I was young, Mom took me along, too — me and Christina."

Jay took a small breath and went on.

"I think that's why Taras took me seriously when I brought him the Gryphon," he said quietly. "When I showed it to him, he said, 'that's a shaggy mane.' I said yes, but that I thought it was a unique shaggy mane, and why. The scientist in him gave me a sharp, questioning look, but the Ukrainian in him . . . well, that guy bought it."

"How long did it take before you were able to start the research project?"

"Not long. By anyone else's standards, it was immediate. Taras fooled around with the samples I could bring him while he was trying to figure out how to fund the project without giving too much away. So I wrote the abstract, put my name on it — he insisted — and we got a few bucks from some ag organizations, as well as NSERC. He added some of his own money. We were rolling within a few months."

Adam opened the door to the truck. Grace had been so absorbed in Jay's story she hadn't noticed Adam running across the street.

He got in and said to Jay, "That guy does not love you."

"Nope."

"Why not?"

"Had an issue with him over a pretty girl. A long time ago. Never forgave me."

"Why am I not surprised? You were here, though, that Friday night before we found Taras. Pretty good witness, the bartender, since I think he'd much rather see you in jail."

"I'll try to remember to buy him a drink," Jay said, dryly.

Ten minutes later, they turned into the Griffin farmyard. Jay's parents were not in the house, so they carried on a few more miles to the edge of the strange, small forest.

Leafless by now, the trees stood twisted together in a copse, black knots standing in stark contrast to the white bark. They got out of the truck and headed for the boardwalk erected alongside the eerie cluster.

"I've seen pictures, but this is bizarre and amazing," Grace said. "I can see why you imagined elves and gnomes when you were a child. It looks like an arthritic hand reaching out from Mother Earth."

"Yeah, I had these fantastical ideas about the place when I was a kid," Jay said. "Mom encouraged that sort of thing; she loves fairy tales and Tolkien. I was always on the lookout for a Hobbit."

Adam laughed. He had to agree that a little hovel inhabited by short creatures with large hairy feet would suit the place.

Jay led them to the right, nearly to the edge of the bush, and pointed down. "Shaggy manes. And Gryphons. They grow right here."

There were none, of course; it was too late in the season, and even if it wasn't, his mother would likely have picked every last one.

"When will they come back?" Grace asked.

"In the summer. They come up fairly early here, at least when we've had some good early rains."

"Does their short season delay the research?" Adam asked.

"We harvest and freeze as much as we can. If we get in here before Mom does, anyway."

"How much do you get?"

"Not a lot. A few pounds. See, that's part of the problem. Will they grow elsewhere? Can we cultivate them? We don't know yet. We're trying a test plot right now."

"You have to promise you will not go there. Not until I find Taras's killer. Agreed?"

"No one knows where it is, except me," Jay argued. "Except, of course, Taras did."

"They could follow you."

"I'd know if I was being followed."

Adam turned to Jay and grabbed him by the shoulders, forcing the young scientist to look at him.

"That's the first stupid thing you've said to me," Adam growled. "I have a very bad feeling that these are professionals. You will not see them coming. No civilian would. I'm not sure a cop would. I don't care how brilliant you are, how big you are, how good a fighter you are. You will not see them. Am I clear?"

"So you're kicking me out of my apartment and curtailing my ability to do research, Adam? Is that what you're saying? My life is not my own?"

"Got it in three," Adam replied with a small smirk. "When we get back to Saskatoon, we'll find you somewhere to stay. And from now on, you go nowhere where you will be alone. Ever."

Jay visibly sagged. "Is this necessary? Like really?"

"Do you think those men this morning were just arbitrarily hanging out at your apartment block?"

"No. No, I guess not. This is surreal."

"Not unlike your Gryphon. Welcome to surreality, Jay. And what about Hope? And your parents? Quite apart from your life?"

Grace laid a hand on Adam's arm. "Gently, love. I think Jay's getting it."

Adam's arms dropped to his sides, and he nodded.

"Sorry, Jay. I have to make you understand. This is very serious."

The two men stared at each other for several seconds. Finally, whatever Jay saw in Adam's eyes, whatever he had understood from his words, made him capitulate. He nodded.

"Say it," Adam demanded.

"Yes. Okay. I promise."

Still they stared. Grace made a small noise, a little "oh" of reaction to the intense scene. It spurred Adam to grab Jay's hand, not in a shake but as if his own hand were a lifeline, the space between thumb and forefinger inserted into Jay's. He responded by tightening his own grip.

"I won't let you die, man," Adam said, his voice low.

"I — don't know what to say, Adam," Jay said, clearly as moved as the police sergeant who was so focused on his plight. "Thank you doesn't seem to cover it. I can't find the words."

"Yeah, I can't either. Stay the hell alive. Who else is going to save the world?"

*****

Jay expressed a hope to see his parents, but they had not returned by the time Adam reached the farmyard on the way back to Saskatoon. He asked Adam to hold up a minute so he could text them.

Mom. You around? All ok?

A minute later . . .

Fine, dear. We're in town. Sorry to have missed you.

OK, see u soon.

And so, they drove on for a few kilometres, until Adam's phone began to ring.

He pulled over, and saw the caller was James.

"What's up?" he asked.

"We found the van."

"Okay. Hold on." Adam lowered the phone and asked, "Grace, could you drive? I'd better talk to James, and I'd rather not waste time getting home."

"Of course."

They quickly switched sides, and Adam was back on his cell with James.

"Right. Tell me."

"It was abandoned, of course. We had Fisher out with us — Lorne can find acorns in a pine forest, don't know how he does it — and he saw it parked in an alley in old Nutana."

"Not far from Jay's."

"About ten blocks away. He must have dumped it pronto."

"Wise move, damn it."

"Yeah. We found nothing unusual inside — fast food wrappers, plastic cups and CDs — except one thing." James paused.

"Do you want me to guess?" Adam asked, a bit testily.

"Do you want to?"

"Nope."

"A gallon jug of piss."

Adam's first, fleeting reaction was to feel vaguely satisfied that he — and Jay — had read the situation correctly. On the heels of that was a kind of horror: how long had the man been staking out Jay's apartment? Enough to need bladder relief over an extended period of time.

Fuck, Adam thought. *That was close. But why had he left the jug behind? Not that urine is a good source of DNA. Right. Scratch that.*

"Not good," James said, breaking Adam's train of thought.

"No. What else? Vehicle registration? Plates?"

"Tell Grace she has a good eye. C1V F8A. Belongs to a guy called, if you're ready, Jon Smyth." James spelled it out. "But here's your big news of the day." James paused again for effect. "This van used to belong to . . . Douglas Brennan."

Shocked, Adam couldn't stop himself. "What!?" he almost yelled. "You're kidding me."

"Would I do that to you? I haven't talked to him yet; I called you first."

"Okay, good move. I think we'd better tag team Brennan. Can you think of any explanation, other than the obvious?"

"Not really. It's an old van, though, Adam. I'd assume he drove it when his kids were young, assuming he has offspring. The question is, who did he sell it to? I'm thinking Jon Smyth might be a pseudonym." James laughed. Adam didn't.

"See if you can get Brennan on the phone and get us in to see him as soon as possible. I'll be back in about an hour. Did Livia make bail?"

"No. Sanj was awesome. I appeared at the hearing with my cheek as Exhibit A, and your behaviour was played down with an expert air of 'no big deal.' Still, the judge told us to get on with the lawyered interview. Hunter says tomorrow. And one more thing."

"You're a fountain today. What?"

"The NSERC guy called me back. Eaton Walter is his name. He's still in Budapest. I grilled him first on Gryphon, and he told me it was a . . . just a sec," James said, and pulled out his notes. "And I quote, 'A very interesting project investigating the future benefits of cultivating mushrooms for pharmaceuticals, mainly antibiotics and antioxidants.' I asked him if there was anything else, and he said, 'should there be?' We've heard that before. And then . . ."

"What? James . . ." Adam knew his constable was enjoying this. "What?!"

"I asked if anything unusual happened while he was in Saskatoon. Anything at all. Remember that luncheon the deans had the Friday before Taras died? At the faculty club?"

"Yep."

"Walter said he was sitting next to Taras. About three, four bites into the meal, he heard a small crunching noise. A moment later, Taras excused himself, his hand to his face. When he returned, Walter asked if he was all right. Taras said it was nothing; just that he had bitten down oddly on a molar."

"The toothache."

"Right. The toothache."

Chapter Twenty-Two

Adam dropped Grace off at The StarPhoenix and Jay at the police station, where he was exhorted to stay until Adam returned.

Turning him over to the watchful care of Charlotte Warkentin, Adam found James and they headed for the Canadian Light Source. Brennan had agreed to see them at four.

"Did you give him a hint?" Adam asked, as they turned onto the campus.

"No. I said we had a new piece of evidence that we had to run by him."

"Perfect."

At the front desk, the receptionist recorded their names, gave them visitors' badges and asked them to wait for someone to take them inside. No one was allowed to roam the synchrotron without a guide. Too much could go wrong.

After a short wait, one of the communications people arrived and led them to Brennan's office. He greeted them and asked if they wanted coffee.

"I'm fine, thanks," Adam said, and James indicated that he was, as well. "Something has come to light, Dr. Brennan. We have found a dark blue van that appears to be connected to the case. The van once belonged to you."

Brennan's big, shaggy head reared back. "To me?"

"Yes. You owned this van for four years, I believe. May I ask if you have children?"

"Two. It seemed the best thing while we were driving my teenage son to hockey and my daughter to soccer. How is my former vehicle connected here?"

"I can't tell you that, I'm afraid. It's now licensed to a Jon Smyth. Does that name ring a bell?"

"No, I can't say that it does. Look, when I decided to sell it, I traded it in on a sedan. I didn't sell it privately. Could this simply be a coincidence?"

"It could be." But Adam didn't believe in coincidences, and that was evident in his voice.

"You don't believe it, do you?" Brennan asked.

"No. Is there anyone who would like to see you in trouble?"

"Not this kind of trouble. Do you think someone is trying to frame me?"

That, or you're involved in this, Adam thought, but didn't say it out loud.

"It's occurred to me. You sold it about two years ago?"

"That sounds about right, yes."

How long did the killer have his eye on Taras, Adam wondered, if he had been planning far enough ahead to buy Brennan's van? Had it been parked outside the Petrenko home on dark nights for months?

"How long have you been CEO here?"

"Five years."

"Where did you trade in the vehicle?" James asked.

"Well, I kind of upgraded. I took it to the Lexus dealership. They don't argue about the vehicles you bring in for trade when you buy a new Lexus."

"Okay. We'll contact the dealership and let you know if it checks out. Thank you, Dr. Brennan."

As they drove back, Adam asked James to check on the van, then nail down a time to speak with Livia Balan the next morning.

"Two other things," Adam added. "We need to learn more about this pharmaceutical company Petrenko did internship work for. I'm going to start with Jay, see what he knows, and then we'll talk to Emmy again. What was the name of it? EPI or something?"

"I think that's right." James flipped the pages in his notebook. "Yes. Well, close. Euro-Pure Pharma International. EPPI. What's the other thing?"

"Have you seen the goldsmith yet?"

"Um, no."

"None of my business. Sorry, James."

"You have something to say, Adam. Out with it."

"I had a . . . moment this morning, with Jay out at the Twisted Forest. He's taking the danger of the situation seriously, but not seriously enough. I kind of let him have it. But afterward, I realized a couple of things. This is going to sound like it walked off a bad motivational poster, but James, life is short. For Jay, it could have ended this morning."

"I'm with you so far."

"That would have been . . . I don't know, somehow the worst thing that could possibly happen. He's like a mini-Taras, you know? Despite his size. He could do some very important work. Is doing, I should say. Where could that lead?"

"Right. Go on."

"Remember when we met him, and the first thing he said was, 'I loved Taras Petrenko.' I wondered what that meant. Was he actually in love with Taras? No, as it turned out. But he loved him, as a mentor, friend, colleague and genius. Imagine that loss. I realized that I couldn't imagine the loss of Jay Griffin. I didn't exactly say that to him, but I came as close as I could."

"Holy shit, Adam."

"The kid got to me. I don't really know him, but I'll be damned if I'll see him die at the hands of some jealous or greedy asshole."

"Okay . . ."

"What I'm trying to say is that it sometimes takes a shock or a strange encounter — like running into these guys at Jay's place — to make you realize what's important. I'm always aware of how much I love Grace, every minute of every day. God, when she was attacked, I'd just met her, and I'd have done anything to protect her. I still would, of course; even more so, but I don't think about it every minute because she's safer, living with me, and she hasn't been at risk lately. But now, I feel sort of the same way about Jay. It's bizarre, but there it is."

"You're asking if I feel that way about Bruce. Would I move heaven and earth and all the stars to protect him, be with him. Forever."

"Yes. I'm not trying to pry. I'm only saying."

James said nothing, and Adam shot him a look: His jaw was tight, and the cords of his throat were taut and working hard.

"James. For fuck's sake. Do what you've got to do, to be happy."

*****

"What do you know about EPPI, Jay?" Adam asked.

"Quite a lot, actually," Jay said, sitting across from Adam in his office. "What do you want to know?"

"Well, not the share price. Tell me the stuff I can't look up. Like word-on-the-street reputation."

"I'm not in pharmaceuticals, Adam. I'm a primary researcher in agricultural biology. That being said, I have friends in pharmacy and medicine, and we talk. So EPPI generally has a pretty good rep. Solid drug portfolio, global reach, good labs. But there was one thing that sullied their image. It was some time ago. They've bounced back, speaking of share price."

"And that was when?"

"This is a long story, Adam. You probably could Google it, although it might take some keyword know-how."

"Give it to me."

"Okay. Get comfortable."

Jay explained that, many years ago, a group of international medical researchers had worked to find a cure for a debilitating and often fatal genetic disorder that mostly seemed to affect remote northern populations. It involved introducing adapted genes through an utterly novel device, and it worked. Not for a while, not for a few months. It seemed to completely reverse the condition.

The science and method were turned over to EPPI, which in turn would theoretically generate and deliver the therapy.

"But they didn't," Jay said. "They simply removed it from their list. When challenged on it by the medical press, they argued that the therapy was too expensive to provide — in the range of a million dollars per 'dose.' No one would, or could, pay that, they said. They may have been right."

"I hear a 'but' coming."

"Yeah. Three of them. First of all, withholding life-saving therapies is, in my view, abhorrent and unethical. Second, I don't believe that price tag, although it would certainly have been enormously expensive. And third, EPPI sells a drug that, in theory, mitigates the worst symptoms of this disorder."

"Does it work?"

"Not worth a shit."

Adam considered how much he could or should tell Jay. But he needed his insight.

"Jay, you told me soon after Taras's death that 'something happened in Europe' but you didn't know all the details. Did you know Taras worked for EPPI very briefly in Berlin?"

"No. It was EPPI, then. Why do you think he wouldn't tell me?"

"To protect you. No question."

"Why are you telling me now?"

"It's too late to protect you from that knowledge. We're at the point where you need physical protection. Whatever you know is enough for these people. It doesn't matter anymore."

"So what happened?"

Adam explained that Taras had learned a drug the company had been working on was flawed and brought it to the attention of authorities. After being threatened, he came to Canada, and changed his name.

"I believe they eventually found him, after he came to the Light Source."

"And now they're pissed about Gryphon."

"Yes."

Jay's eyes suddenly blazed with understanding.

"Oh my God," he breathed. "They want to kill the Gryphon project, don't they? Because it has the potential to replace some of their drugs."

"Based on what you told me about the genetic disorder treatment, I think I just came to that. Yes."

"Or, alternatively, they want Gryphon, the mushroom itself, for themselves." Jay shook his head, correcting himself. "Although I don't think that's the motivation. EPPI, based on what we know about its past, won't want to put the funds into developing an antibiotic. It would cost billions, and they don't want to spend that kind of money."

"Right, good point. But I also wonder if they want to find it so they can destroy the actual mushroom — not just the project. Wipe it from the planet. Is that possible?"

"Sure. Why not? It would come back, but it could take a long time. There are definitely ways to poison and kill the mushroom. And the land. God, what a disaster that would be. Mom would kill me."

Adam had to laugh. "She'd blame you for all this, would she?"

"Well, I did steal her mushrooms and bring them to Taras."

"You're right. It's all down to you."

"Very funny. Adam, now what? What the hell are you going to do? Fly to Prague and Los Angeles to arrest the board and CEO of EPPI?"

"I'd like to, but I might need evidence to pull that off. And there are very bad guys on the ground right here. We have to find them first."

*****

Adam finally decided to take Jay home with him. The kid needed people, a hot meal, a safe bed, comfort. They'd look for a safe house or hotel room tomorrow, although Adam couldn't stand the thought of isolating Jay in a lonely room at the Circle 8 or whatever the hell.

Not under the circumstances.

Adam knew he had become far too fond of Jay Griffin. He hoped it wasn't affecting his judgement. Jay reminded him of the younger brother he had often imagined, but never had.

"Adam, that's very kind of you, but way beyond the call of duty."

"Shut up, Jay, and get in the truck."

Jay planted his legs shoulder-width and crossed his arms. "Are you sure about this?"

"It's the best plan I have right now. I have to think about it some more tomorrow. It's not like the Saskatoon police force has dozens of safe houses all over the city."

Jay sighed, relented. "It's very kind, Adam. Very. Too kind."

"I reiterate. Shut up, and get in."

They drove the short distance from the station to Grace and Adam's little bungalow, originally Grace's. Adam felt gnawing — and growing — guilt over not discussing it with Grace, but there simply had not been time. He had tried to call her, but she had gone to cover court after their return from Hafford.

Adam couldn't decide if it would be easier to explain if Grace was home when they arrived, or if she came home to find them there. Court cases often kept her at work late.

He parked in the garage and took a suitcase out of the back as Jay removed two more. Everything he needed — clothes, papers, computer, shaving kit — had been quickly tumbled into the three bags he'd packed that morning.

Lights were on, so Adam assumed Grace was home and tried the back garden-door knob instead of inserting the key.

"Grace," he called. "Where are you?"

"In the kitchen, love."

They dropped the luggage and Adam led the way in, Jay behind him looking a little like a fish out of water, bearing the posture of an imposing guest.

"Hey, love. Oh . . ." Adam said.

As Jay came up even with Adam, a smile of gratitude on his face, both men realized Grace also had a visitor.

"Hello, Hope," said Jay.

Chapter Twenty-Three

Grace's heart thumped in her breast as she watched Hope's face, a study in amazement, awe and something else — something so tender, so open, Grace caught her breath with a little gasp.

Hope, being seated, gave the impression of a small child grasping the enormity of a large gift as she slowly looked up into Jay's face, eyes wide, lips formed into a small 'O'. Jay took a short step toward her, then stopped. Grace thought, for a moment, he was actually going to grasp her sister, pull her to her feet, lift her into his arms and carry her off.

Since Hope was momentarily speechless, Grace found her voice and came to the rescue.

"Hello, Jay," she said, trying to sound as if this tableau was the most normal of scenes. "Welcome. Can I get you a drink? Beer? Wine? Something stronger?"

"A beer would be extremely great," Jay said, his gaze never leaving Hope. "Where is Lawan?" he asked, apparently trying to pull it together.

"Having a nap," Grace answered, seeing that Hope had not yet closed her mouth. "Hopey? Do you think she'll be up for dinner?"

Hope managed to nod, as Grace handed Jay an open beer.

"I'll take these to the living room, get them out of the way," Adam said, picking up a suitcase. "I don't want to wake Lawan. Have a seat, Jay. It's been a long day."

"I'll help you, Adam," Grace said, grabbing another bag and following him into the other room. Once there, she grabbed his arm. "What's happening?" she whispered. "Did you bring a stray home with you for keeps?"

"I did," Adam said at an equally low volume. "I'm so sorry, Grace. You were in court and I couldn't arrange anything quickly enough. Nothing safe, anyway."

"You mean safe enough by your standards. A little notice might have been nice, though."

"I know. I've been feeling very guilty for the last hour."

"Well, you can stop now. I understand. As long as you're sure no one saw you bring him in."

"Lorne followed us over. He sees all."

"True. But we can't let them get together. It's too dangerous. What are you going to do about that?"

"I don't know yet. I'll have to speak to him. And you to Hope."

"It's all we can do, I suppose. How long should we leave them alone in there?"

"Long enough to say hello. Hello, Grace. How was the rest of your day?"

She laughed, threw her arms around his neck and pressed her body against him, lips reaching for his.

"You are the most amazing man," she said against his mouth. "I love you to pieces."

"I love you. But what brought that on? I just brought you a house guest without permission. A slap might be more in order."

"It's the way you handled Jay out at the forest. You were pretty aggressive, but you got the point across, along with your concern. And the way you live up to your motto, to serve and protect — me, for starters, but also Jay, Hope, and Suzanne, among many others." She removed her arms from his neck and wrapped them around his waist. "Hold me for a moment."

"Babe. My love." Adam smoothed her wild, curly hair, to no effect.

Finally, reluctantly, they parted and crept back to the kitchen. Jay and Hope sat facing one another; Jay was saying something simultaneously quiet and urgent, his head thrust forward. Hope continued to stare at him, face flushed, silent. Grace had never once seen her this way. It was rather frightening and beautiful at the same time.

"We're going to have to break this up at some point. Or we could go out for dinner," Grace said to Adam.

"The former. I'm not leaving anyone alone, Lorne Fisher notwithstanding."

"Okay."

Grace cleared her throat as loudly as possible, and made vague "right, then" noises, ostensibly to Adam. She stomped into the kitchen, and both heads turned to her.

"So, anyone hungry? I was planning spaghetti, since the sauce is already made. Is that okay?"

"More than okay. Grace, I'm very grateful, and sorry to barge in," Jay said.

"Jay, you are very welcome here." Grace glanced at her sister, and saw her give a vigorous, single nod behind his back.

Conversation over dinner saw a relative return to normalcy; four people enjoying one another's company, chatting and laughing. Lawan awakened and joined in the laughter with her gurgly giggle. At eleven, however, Hope had to leave for home.

"It's late, and Lawan should have been in bed two hours ago," she said. "I must go."

"I'll help you take things out to the car," Jay offered.

That caused a look of consternation to cross Adam's face. He rose, went to the living room window, and peered into the dark street. Seeing no strange vehicles parked outside, nor humans, he simply returned to the kitchen and sat back down.

Hope bundled up her child, and packed up the little case of toys, blankets and other necessary kid paraphernalia. Jay reached out to take Lawan while Hope pulled on her coat and shoes and refused to hand her back.

"May I? I'd like to carry her."

"Yes. Sure. Thank you," Hope said.

They looked like any couple leaving the house, bearing a babe and her gear. Jay tucked Lawan into her car seat as Hope threw the bag in beside her, then locked her into the device.

Adam and Grace turned off the living room lights and surreptitiously watched through the window.

"I hate spying on them," Grace said.

"I know. Must be done."

Hope straightened after bending down over Lawan and turned to face Jay. He said something — Grace couldn't read his lips in the dark — and Hope looked at her feet. Then, very gently, he touched her face. Cupped her chin. Said something else. She raised her eyes. And Hope tentatively, slowly, reached out a hand and placed it on his chest.

They stood that way for a minute. Then Hope spoke, wiped a tear, and ducked into the car.

"Oh my God," Grace breathed. "What just happened?"

"They've got it bad," said Adam, putting his arms around Grace. "But they're trying to be good."

*****

Grace called her sister first thing the next morning.

"Are you all right, Hope?" she asked without preamble. "I barely slept, wondering."

"*You* barely slept," said Hope, sounding a bit more like herself. She sighed. "I'm wonderful. Frightened. Horrified. Overwhelmed. Messed up. Blown away. Don't know what the hell to do with myself. So, am I all right? Not exactly."

"Eek, Hopey. Do you want me to come over?"

"No, Grace, but thanks. I have to get to work. Mom's taking Lawan today. What about you? Don't you have to get to work?"

"Yes, but you come first. I do have to say one thing, though."

"No, you don't. I know where you're going. You're going to warn me not to see Jay unless Adam is nearby, not to get too involved, and not to get a room. Right?"

"That more or less covers it. Besides, you've only met him twice, for God's sake."

"In this life."

"Oh. You've found an old, familiar soul, then."

"I can't even explain. I'll try later. Go to work, Grace. Don't worry about me."

"I love you, Hope. Breathe deeply."

"Ha. Love you too."

Hope hung up, and Grace kept worrying.

Adam had taken Jay with him on the way to work and dropped him off on campus. Grace wondered how their conversation had gone, as she grabbed her purse and went out to the car. She also wondered how safe Jay was on campus, but twenty thousand people were there to keep an eye on him.

She'd been finding work frustrating in the extreme. Nothing about the case could be reported; indeed, there were few hard facts, and everything else landed under Adam's cone of silence. Slowly, her file on Taras's death and the fascinating mushroom became fatter but remained useless until the police caught a solid break.

It was why she had agreed to run over to court late the previous afternoon. The appearance by a drug trafficker had been short and resulted in only a six-inch story, reporting his name and the charges against him. She had gone home in time to welcome Hope, who had called to say she wanted to pop over.

Hope had arrived fifteen minutes before Jay and Adam, and Grace still wasn't sure why she needed a chat; they had played with Lawan and gossiped about family before putting the little girl down for a nap. Then the men appeared.

She had probably wanted to talk about Jay, and that conversation was likely moot now.

Grace turned on her computer and rolled her chair over to speak to Claire Davidson, hoping something exciting had happened overnight.

"Nope," Claire said. "I suppose we're nowhere yet, with this Petrenko case."

"Afraid so," Grace said. "I have the impression that Adam is starting to sort it out, but as to hard evidence or anything that can be reported, I have nothing for you."

Grace didn't tell her that she and Adam had been slammed behind a door by a hitman on the fly the day before. That episode was off limits, for now.

"Well, maybe head over to court and check the docket. We might get lucky. I could use a page one story, or at least page three. Things have been pretty quiet."

"Okay. I'll check my email and go to Queen's Bench."

"Perfect, thanks. Hey, wait . . . what's that bruise on the side of your face?"

Hell. So much for makeup, Grace thought.

"It's nothing. I bumped into a door. Really, Claire. I did."

"It had nothing to do with your escapade yesterday, then."

Grace, who fully knew she was a terrible liar, sighed.

"It did, yes. But I'm fine, and . . . well . . ."

"You can't tell me about it."

"No."

"Someday soon, maybe?"

"I hope so." Grace gave her editor a crooked grin as she heard her phone ring. "Gotta go," she said, and wheeled back to her desk.

She caught the call on the fourth ring. Saskatoon Police. If it had been Adam, it would have said so on the call display, so she simply answered, "StarPhoenix newsroom, Grace Rampling speaking."

"Grace, it's James."

"Hi, James. Should I get my hopes up, since you're calling and not Adam?"

"Yes. We found a dead guy early this morning. We think it might be the van man."

"What? I assume you'll issue a press release."

"I will. Not until later this morning, though. I thought I'd give you the head's up. You can ask me questions if you'll keep it under embargo until noon, or whenever the release hits your mailbox."

"Done. Where did you find him?"

"Under the Traffic Bridge."

"How was he killed?"

"Stabbed."

"Where? On the body, I mean."

"Sorry, can't tell you that."

"Are you identifying him? Did he have ID on him?"

"No, and yes. Except it was probably fake. But you can't report that. We have to find the family first, of course, which is going to be tricky if it is fake."

"Right. But James, how are you positioning this? Are you going to link him to the van, the Petrenko case, or anything useful?"

"We may link him to the van. We haven't figured that out yet. But we won't connect him to Petrenko, no."

Grace understood but squirmed at the inability to write a real story about the case.

"Anything else?" she asked.

"I don't think he's from around here," James said. "We found a photograph folded into quarters and tucked inside his hat. Obviously, he wasn't expecting to be caught, or killed for that matter. And the killer likely didn't know it was there, or he would have removed it. It looked like it was taken several years ago, in a city with much older buildings than ours."

"Do you mean like a European city?"

"It looks European, yes. Maybe Eastern European? It's hard to tell. It's not in great shape from being folded up like that. And it's not like the Eiffel Tower or the Cologne Cathedral is in the background; nothing obvious. Just old stone buildings."

"Who else is in the picture?"

"I think his girlfriend. Maybe a sister. A young woman."

"Ah. It's always a lover, sister or mother in those keepsake photos. Can I see it?"

"I'll ask Adam. He'll probably let you. And you can't report on the photo, but you can say there is evidence that the man wasn't from Saskatoon. I think we can go that far."

"Why didn't the killer take his ID, do you think?"

"That's one of the reasons we think it's fake. We're having it checked. The other is the name. Much like John Doe, only slightly more believable."

Grace paused, wondering what else she could ask James, when a horrific thought struck her.

"James. Why was he so easy to find? Under the bridge, for God's sake, when people are walking or running along that path every minute of the day?"

"You know the answer to that."

"Because the killer is sending a message. And he thinks he's untouchable, or unfindable, or he doesn't care if he's caught."

"I'm afraid so."

Chapter Twenty-Four

Donna Hunter appeared at the police station half an hour after James spoke to Grace. Livia Balan was brought to an interview room, and Adam and James entered shortly thereafter.

Without makeup, the suspect looked considerably younger and less assertive; even a little vulnerable. Hunter wore a grin that suggested her client's appearance would work in her favour.

"Present are Detective Sergeant Adam Davis, Detective Constable James Weatherall," Adam said. "This is an interview with Livia Balan and her counsel Donna Hunter at ten-oh-eight. All right, Ms. Balan. Can we start with you telling us, truthfully this time, what your relationship was with Taras Petrenko?"

"Most of what I told you was true," Livia said, in a much smaller voice than during the last interview. "Except that I was really angry with him."

"Why were you angry? Because he turned you away? Because he threatened to fire you?"

"Both, but mainly the first. We were so good together, on the job and otherwise. Getting fired would have looked bad on my resumé. And I thought he could see we should be lovers."

"Were you angry enough to kill him?"

"No! Of course not."

Adam thought her voice wobbled a bit and wondered if that was a tear in her eye.

"She didn't kill Petrenko, Sergeant," Hunter interjected. "Why the hell would she do that, if she wanted to be with him? Okay, Livia. Tell him."

"I wanted to make him jealous," Livia said plaintively. "It was the only thing I could think of, to make him want me."

"How did you do that?" Adam asked.

"I slept with someone else. I made sure he knew about it."

"How?"

"I told someone in his hearing. Kind of like a stage whisper. He knew."

"How long ago was this?"

"In the summertime."

"Were you taking intersession?"

"No. But research projects never sleep, Detective. Many of us are on campus year-round." She was bouncing back. Adam had to hurry this interview.

"Who was your dangerous liaison, Ms. Balan?"

A wild look suddenly in her eyes, she turned to her lawyer. "Do I really have to do this?"

Hunter nodded. "We talked about this, Livia. Do you want to be a murder suspect? Really? Tell him."

"We'll find out anyway, Ms. Balan," Adam said. "You've already told someone."

"Fuck." Livia paused to suck in a big breath, and on the exhale said, "It was Dean Horvath."

When it finally came out, Adam was not surprised. From the beginning, he had wondered what the contretemps in Horvath's office had really been about.

"When was this?" he asked, voice even.

"In June, I think."

"Did it happen more than once?"

"Yes. Three times. Within a couple of weeks."

"Why didn't you continue with the affair?"

"Affair! It wasn't an affair. It was disgusting. I didn't want Devon. He's not my type. At all." Her lips curled downward, punctuating her revulsion.

"So this was before you kissed Taras in the hutch at the Light Source. You were testing the water, after you'd had sex with Dean Horvath. To see if Taras had indeed become jealous."

"Yes."

"Where did the sex take place?"

"Hotel room."

"Did you talk as well?"

"Not much, no. We were only there for one thing, Detective."

"There was no discussion about work, for example, then."

"Very little. Just the usual. How's your project going, things like that."

"What did you say about your project?"

"I really can't recall. That I was excited about it, it was going well, that sort of thing. Again, we weren't there to chat."

"Okay. Thank you for being forthcoming, finally, Ms. Balan. We'll let you go, but as I said before, do not leave town. If you do, I'll have no choice but to arrest you again. Is that clear, Ms. Balan? Ms. Hunter?"

"Yes, it's clear, Sergeant," said Donna Hunter. "You have my word that Livia will remain in Saskatoon."

Adam officially ended the interview and allowed the lawyer to escort her client out. After the door closed, James said, "That isn't exactly conclusive."

"No, but she's not prevaricating anymore. We can't hold her; there's not enough evidence, and as angry as she was at Taras, she wanted to lure him into her clutches. That was the end game. Killing him would be counterintuitive. Now tell me where we're at with Jon Smyth. Have you called Grace?"

"Yes. She wants to see the photo."

"I can show it to her, off the record. She knows that, right?"

"Yes, I told her. Smyth's body is with McDougall; no other updates. Why do you think he was killed?"

"He fucked up. His buddy in the apartment may have heard him squeal out when I approached him; that building is made of paper. He almost got caught, so he was suddenly a liability. Buddy — we need a code name for him — doesn't know whether or not I got a look at Smyth's face. I assume he was also pissed because Smyth didn't warn him soon enough, that we were coming inside."

"Did you see Smyth's face, at all?"

"Not really. Caucasian, male, maybe thirty, thirty-five. I couldn't see his hair under that hat — and he was wearing dark glasses. I couldn't have identified him. But again, the dude in the building wouldn't know that."

"What should we call him?"

"Mercury. He's in flight. What do you think?"

"That's good. I'll get it out there. He'll be a son of a bitch to find now that he knows we're looking."

"Yeah. Now let's make a date with the undesirable Devon Horvath."

*****

Horvath proved to be teaching a class, so James booked an appointment for noon with his secretary. It gave Adam time to look up Horvath's own projects and research papers.

The pharmacy dean had published several of the latter; the most recent dealt with the surge in transdermal drug delivery. Apparently, Horvath's knowledge of 'patches' was extensive. Some hormones and substances such as nicotine were routinely delivered through the skin, but the dean sought new ways of allowing larger molecules to be absorbed by that route.

Would coprine molecules be small enough to absorb through a patch? Did the "ine" ending signify a similar molecule to nicotine, at least in size?

Adam felt certain that McDougall would have picked up on whether Taras had recently worn a patch during the autopsy. Still, worth checking.

Jack picked up the phone himself. "Adam. Now what?"

"Hello, Jack. I have another question about Taras's autopsy. Did you notice any evidence that he had been wearing a patch?"

"For transdermal drug delivery? No, there was no indication of it. Had there been, I would have said so."

"Is it easy to tell? Does a patch leave behind any markings?"

"It certainly could, more so with long usage."

"Is it possible that he had worn one for, say, a few hours and it left no mark?"

"Anything is possible. If it was a few days before his death, and he only wore it for a while, it may not have shown up. Also, Adam, it's worth checking whether he was allergic to procaine. That can make you vomit."

"And there was nothing unusual about his teeth?"

"Not really. A couple of fillings needed replacing or patching, but generally he had rather good teeth. Not perfect, but quite healthy."

Adam thought about that for a moment, and said, "Jack, let's not release the body yet. I'll let Emmy know. She won't be happy, but I think she'll understand."

"Okay, Adam. Anything else?"

"No. Not now." Adam heard a knock. "Thanks. I'll be in touch. I have to run. James is at the door; we have an interview. Later."

"Goodbye, Adam."

*****

James and Adam purposely arrived at the Thorvaldson Building early and stood waiting for Horvath in the hallway. If nothing else, Horvath had lied to them about his little fight with Livia Balan, and while Adam understood why — adultery was one thing, but sleeping with one's students could be grounds for dismissal — he was also cranky. Hence, the show of power.

Five minutes later, they saw the dean striding down the hallway. His eyebrows drew together in annoyance when he clapped eyes on the two officers.

"Sergeant, Constable. I'm very busy. What can I do for you?"

"Dean," Adam said, nodding. "It would be best if we went into your office. Shall we?"

"Could we make this quick, right here?"

"That depends. Do you want the entire student population to know you lied to us about Ms. Balan?" Adam kept his voice down, but it had the desired effect.

"I don't know what you're talking about," Horvath said. "But I suppose you'd better come in."

He unlocked the door and went inside first, dropping his stack of files heavily on the desk with a loud sigh, presumably to demonstrate irritation. Then he turned, arms folded.

"Well?"

"You might be more comfortable if you sat down, Horvath."

"No. This won't take long. Right? I have a lot to do. Get on with it."

"Your choice. You lied to us about the argument you had with Livia Balan, that it was a student exam matter, or 'something like that.' We understand now that you have had sexual intercourse with her."

"Little bitch," Horvath spat.

"Is it true?"

Horvath's face worked, and turned very red as he tried, Adam knew, to decide whether to deny or address the allegation. It might be hard to prove; it would certainly be her word against his.

"She was very convincing," Adam said, as Horvath's pause lingered on. "We could check with the hotel, you know. Unless, perhaps, you used an alias? But then again, I'm sure someone saw you. The housekeeping staff. The front desk clerk. We could take a photo down and ask around."

"You wouldn't."

"I would. Depend on it."

The man squeezed his eyes shut and swore.

"She seduced me," he finally said. "It was a one-off fling. I feel very badly about it."

"I gather it happened three times. And that she called it off."

Horvath did not respond but gave a small shrug.

"Does your wife know?"

"What does this have to do with anything? Why would the police care about a one-night or even a two-night stand?"

"Three nights. Please answer the question."

"No. She doesn't." Horvath's eyes flicked to the side. Adam wondered if it was nerves, or if he was lying. But why would he?

"Did you discuss Livia's work on the Gryphon project?"

"No."

"Ms. Balan said you did. She told you it was progressing well and that she was excited about it."

"Did she. I don't recall."

"Is that so. I have some more questions, if you'd care to sit down now."

"What else?" Horvath didn't move.

"Your research into transdermal patches. Who is funding it?"

"NSERC is the primary funder. It supports research into the biochemistry of drug delivery."

"Is that why Eaton Walter was here?"

"In part. NSERC provides funding to many of the university's projects. He was here for a series of meetings, including one with me."

"Any other funders?"

"A couple of minor ones. Secret partners, I'm afraid. I couldn't reveal their identities if I wanted to, under strict confidentiality guidelines."

"I assume they are not large pharmaceutical companies. That would have to be public record, would it not?"

"Yes, it would." Horvath cocked his head at Adam. "Anything else?"

"Not at present. I don't have to tell you that if Ms. Balan decides to come forward with your affair, your career and your marriage are in jeopardy. Stick around Saskatoon, Horvath. I'll need to speak to you again."

"We were planning a trip . . ."

"Cancel it. We'll be in touch."

Adam held Horvath's gaze for a moment, gave a curt nod and walked out the door, James right behind him. They said nothing until they were out of earshot, and even then, Adam remained quiet.

"What are you thinking, Adam?" James finally asked.

"We need to take a look at Horvath's curriculum vitae again. Let's make sure he has no connection to EPPI. Now, let's see if Emmy Petrenko is on campus, before we leave."

They walked across the quad toward the Biology Building as Adam dialled Emmy's office number; she answered and agreed to see them right away.

"Hello, detectives," she said, opening the door to their knock. She still looked exhausted, Adam noted. "Come in."

"We won't stay long. Thanks for seeing us on no notice, Emmy. I wanted to tell you in person that we won't be able to release Taras's body yet for a few days. I'm very sorry. I have the feeling that something was missed."

"Oh," she said in a small voice, and bit her lip. "Can you tell me what?"

"Not exactly, since I'm not sure what was missed. Emmy, I also have to ask you; did you know that Taras had a relationship with Andrea Horvath, many years ago?"

"Yes. They had a fling while he was studying for a summer in Prague. It was before we met."

"When did he tell you?"

"When the Horvaths arrived in Saskatoon. It didn't occur to him before then, he said. It was a brief affair, and it happened long ago. But when Andrea showed up, he thought he'd better tell me."

"What else did he tell you, if anything?"

"Not a lot. I gathered he didn't want to talk about it; it did not end well."

"Meaning?"

"Well, he'd had enough, he said. When he told Andrea, she swore and stomped and then flew at him."

"And yet you socialized with the Horvaths, yes?"

Emmy drew a sad sigh. "Not much choice. The deans of the science colleges stick together. She's Devon's wife."

"Was it tense, being around her?"

"A little. It was worse for Taras. I always tried to make sure we didn't spend time with them alone."

"What do you know about her?"

"She's quite brilliant, you know. But I find her a little, maybe, too passionate? Volatile, I suppose. I don't know her well; I keep my distance. Of course, she's not crazy about me, either."

"Do you know anything about her past? Where she's from?"

"She's American by birth. Wealthy family. I don't know how she landed here, but academics tend to go wherever the opportunity fits their credentials. And it could be because Devon is here, largely due to the CLS."

James scribbled madly as Emmy spoke. When she paused, he looked up and asked, "You don't happen to know her maiden name, do you?"

Emmy pursed her lips and lowered her eyebrows, clearly searching her memory banks. "Damn. I did know it, once. I think Taras mentioned it. Obviously, it's not something I'd ask her. We aren't exactly close."

"Not to worry, Emmy. It shouldn't be hard to search for; and we can always ask her," Adam said. "One more thing. Was Taras allergic to anything?"

"Cats. I can't think of anything else."

"What about dental treatment? Did he have any trouble with novocaine, for example?"

"No. Why are you asking me this?"

"There was procaine in his system."

"How much?"

"I'd have to check the autopsy report."

"Well, Sergeant, procaine can be life-threatening in large doses. It sensitizes the nervous system and can cause convulsions. He wouldn't need to be allergic for it to hurt him. Oh no," she suddenly said, in a different tone, as she realized the implications. "My poor Taras. He would have been so sick. He was, wasn't he?"

"I'm afraid so, Emmy. I'm so sorry."

"Find these bastards, Adam."

"I will, Emmy. I will. But when you say bastards? Plural?"

"It has to be more than one person. This is more complex than either of us know."

Adam's eyes narrowed. Of course there were more than three people involved: the two hitmen, and whoever had hired them. Possibly someone who worked for EPPI, or another pharmaceutical company. But what was Emmy saying?

"Are you suggesting a conspiracy?" Adam said.

"I think I am."

At her words, Adam experienced one of those moments of epiphany that rarely came to him, both thrilling and horrifying in their impact.

"Emmy," he said. "You must leave Saskatoon. Immediately."

Chapter Twenty-Five

Jay tried manfully to concentrate on the paper he'd been working on for a year. He was well into it now; it contained thirty thousand words and he profoundly hoped to have it published by spring. Yet he couldn't harness his thoughts; they jumped and spun and occasionally stabbed him in the brain.

I'm a fucking fugitive, he thought, *from my own life. Not to mention some enormous, scary prick who wants to kill me. Just when I've found Hope, I can't see her, touch her, maybe even kiss her; I'd be putting her into the same kind of danger if we were discovered together.*

Still, he had Hope's cellphone number. She had told him not to call, though; she didn't think she could bear it, to talk without the possibility of face-to-face interaction. Last night, when she had gently touched his chest, the message was both tender and forestalling. It had almost sent him to his knees.

He saw her face in his mind's eye — the pink flush that had risen to her cheeks when he came into the kitchen, bringing bright colour to her perfect white skin. Those enormous brown eyes, so like her sister's, widening with surprise and . . . and something else. A shiver ran through Jay's body at the memory. Please, Adam, he found himself thinking; please find Taras's killer. Yesterday would be good.

He knew he shouldn't. He had to. He couldn't. But then he did. He pulled out his cellphone and texted Hope.

I'm sorry. But I'm thinking about you. I keep seeing your face instead of the computer screen. I guess I had to let you know.

He waited, feeling the sweat form on his neck and brow. Would she respond?

Finally, he turned back to his paper and tried again to focus. Twenty minutes later . . .

I would come to you now, but I can't. And you cannot come to me. I must think of Lawan. Please take care of yourself.

Powerful surges of erotic longing mingled with fear that she might be pushing him away. He wasn't sure.

Wait for me, Hope.

Another long pause. Then . . .

I can do nothing else.

What could he say? His heart gave a monstrous thump and he simply sent back an emoji. A heart.

His body lurched when the phone rang in the same moment, but it wasn't Hope. *Damn.* It was Livia.

"Yo, Balan," Jay answered, trying to swallow the emotion in his voice. "What's up?"

"Hey, Griffin," she said. "I'm at the greenhouse. You should see your mushrooms. And there's something weird going on with the dirt. Can you come over?"

Jay realized with a small flicker of guilt he hadn't told Adam that Livia also had access to the secret greenhouse, tucked among fruit trees being bred for the Saskatchewan climate on the edge of the campus. Regularly testing the soil was an important part of the research project, and Livia was the soil expert. Did

Gryphon, for example, require high nitrogen to thrive? What levels of potassium did the mushroom need? Were certain insects or worms part of the equation?

Livia slipped into the greenhouse almost daily to check the nutrient levels. And the mushrooms were growing? Excitement balled in his stomach.

"Everything okay over there? No sign of a break-in?" Jay asked.

"No, all is well. You're getting paranoid. Just come and see. It'll blow your mind."

He hadn't been to the growth chamber in over a week, having been busy at the Light Source and with all the other madness surrounding Taras's death.

"Okay, but I'll have to walk over. My car . . . I left it at the apartment." Adam had insisted he leave it there, presumably to suggest he had not decamped. Having the villains watch his apartment might keep them from searching elsewhere.

"Well, hurry up then," she said, and hung up.

He wasn't getting anywhere with the blasted paper anyway, and maybe a walk would clear his head. He'd make sure to take the well-travelled route, he thought; and besides, Livia was at the other end. If he didn't show up, she'd wonder why and call the troops. She sounded strange, breathlessly excited. He had to go and check it out.

Jay turned off the computer, picked up his keys and wallet, grabbed his coat and slipped his phone into the big outside pocket. He left the agriculture building by the back door, nearest the Bowl, and quickly walked down the main sidewalks, avoiding his usual shortcuts.

His considerable height was supported by long, powerful legs and it took only a few minutes to reach the main drag. Looking around, he could see only streams of cars flying past; a few students straggled along behind him, likely heading home. He pretended to check his phone as he waited for them to pass, then ducked to the right under the sour-cherry trees and plunged into the thick grove of apples and saskatoons.

He saw no one, heard nothing, and began to breathe more normally. Before entering the little building, most of its glass obscured to refract rather than absorb sunlight, he did a rapid tour around the exterior.

Finally, Jay entered through the single door and blinked in the relative darkness, waiting for his eyes to adjust. Long tables held container after container of soil, liberally scattered with Gryphon spores. Overhead, a vast system of grow lights and water pipes hung from the ceiling. He stared into the half-light, trying to see his mushrooms.

"Balan, where are you hiding?" he called.

She didn't answer. That was weird, he thought. She had called only fifteen minutes ago, and she wasn't outside tinkering with the taps. Playing a prank, maybe; Livia loved practical jokes.

"She's here," said a low voice. A male voice.

Oh, fuck. Jay's gut dropped and clenched painfully.

His first instinct was to turn and run for help; but then he'd be leaving Livia in mortal danger, all alone. What could he do? He reached for his phone and tapped it wildly, hoping to reach someone — anyone — on his contact list. Adam, preferably.

"Don't even think of moving," said the voice.

Livia emerged first from the farthest corner of the building, a cloth crammed into her mouth, her hands tied behind her back and a massive arm curled tightly around her waist. The man towered over her, and Jay could see the shadow of his body on either side of her; God, he was a brute.

Shock was giving way to heightened perception, and Jay finally noticed the firearm trained on his own chest, a sliver of sunlight sparking off its barrel. He was more angry than anything — even more than he was frightened.

"Who the fuck are you, and what do you want?" Jay spat at Livia's captor.

"Oh please, Griffin. You know what I want. It doesn't matter who I am. And if you move," he added as Jay took a step toward Livia, "I will kill her. She is quite expendable."

Jay stopped and raised his arms. "Okay, okay, relax. Let her go, and I'll give you whatever you want."

"You won't give it willingly, Griffin. So we're going to have to do it my way."

"Which is?"

"You're going to show me where these babies come from."

Jay had no intention of doing that; he had to figure out a way to deflect this monster. He wondered if he could take him in a fight, assuming he could get the gun away. He doubted it, but he was ready to try.

"If I agree to go with you, will you put down the gun?"

A laugh emerged from the barrel chest of the man, harsh and mocking.

"Very funny, Griffin. Not happening. Let's move."

"Not until you let Livia go."

Jay could see her wild eyes rolling in their sockets; she was rapidly running out of oxygen, trying to breathe through her nose, stuffed and running from crying.

"Good idea."

The man released his grip and gave Livia a small push toward the wall, then turned and shot her in the forehead. The impact spun her body in a sickening, twisting half-circle.

"No!" Jay bellowed, lunging for his colleague as her body slumped, then slid down the wall. But the man caught Jay in both arms, in a vice-like hold, and whispered in his ear.

"Don't bother," he said. "She's dead. And now you know I mean business. Have you heard from your parents lately?"

Jay's brain swirled in a fog, thought backward to the day before when his parents had not been home. When he had texted his mother, and she had said all was well.

"My God," he said, unable to help himself. "Where are they? What have you done? Tell me!"

"They're very near the farmhouse. Not actually inside, but nearby. They're not going anywhere."

"What do you mean?"

"They're a little tied up right now. Too bad they wouldn't share the information I needed. Claimed they didn't know what I was talking about, but that's not true, is it?"

Jay pressed his lips together. This was moving too fast; he wasn't sure what to say or not say. He glanced at Livia's lifeless body and thought he might vomit.

"How do I know my parents are alive?" he asked, swallowing the acids rising in his throat.

"Come on, Griffin. Use that big brain of yours. I've got to make sure you're going to give me what I need, right? And if you don't, who will? Why, your folks. I suspect they'll cough it up fast enough if they see this gun pointed at your head. Besides, I think you're going to tell me fast enough to save the sire and dam."

He wasn't just a goon, then, Jay realized by his words. Damn.

"You do see this greenhouse full of spores, don't you? Isn't that good enough?" he asked.

"I don't see any fucking mushrooms. And even if there were, I have to find the source. So let's move."

Livia had lied — been forced to lie. The mushrooms had not come up. Whoever was behind this did want the originals, or to destroy them, Jay thought. And his phone rang.

The man unerringly reached into the right pocket, removed the phone, glanced at who was calling and turned it off. Then he put it in his own pocket.

"Sorry, Griffin, it wasn't the cops," he said.

Turning Jay toward the door, he poked the gun into his back and pushed with the other hand. Once outside, Jay felt his body being inexorably moved deeper into the grove, where after a moment a large vehicle came into view. And Jay understood how completely unprepared he was for this kind of murderous chaos. Of course the bastard hadn't parked nearby.

The man trained his weapon on Jay as he forced him into the truck, where he secured Jay's feet tightly.

"I assume," the man said, "we're going back to Hafford."

Jay nodded dumbly. He didn't know what to do, but he had to find out what had happened to Sofia and Ioan. He silently prayed his sister was somewhere safe in Saskatoon.

*****

Grace picked up her ringing phone to see that Hope was calling.

"Hey, Hopey."

Before she could finish the second syllable of her sister's nickname, Hope was already yelling.

"Something is wrong with Jay. I got a text from him that was this crazy jumble of letters and numbers. Like crazy. Z*slth10byrwjl . . . it goes on . . . Grace, I tried to call him, and he didn't answer but he had just texted me and . . ."

"Hope, stop. Take a breath. Shhh, now." Grace heard Hope suck in some air. "Okay. He had texted you? What did he say?"

"That he was thinking of me. Nothing more. We texted back and forth a couple of times. Then about half an hour later, I got the weird message. Then he didn't answer my call. He hung up on me without saying anything. There's something wrong."

Grace had to agree but decided that saying so was a bad idea. Hope was upset enough.

"Okay, Hopey, okay. I'll call Adam right now. You have to try to stay calm. Where are you?"

"At work."

"In your office, or out with a client?"

"Office."

"Stay there. Don't leave, okay? Cancel any appointments. I'll call you back as soon as I can. Got it?"

"Yes, okay. I'll stay here." Hope sounded robotic, but at least she was compliant.

"Hang in there. Love you."

Grace hung up and immediately attempted to call Adam, her hands shaking so hard she dialled incorrectly — twice. Finally, she got it right, and it rang four times.

"Grace," he answered, a question in his voice. "Love? What's up?"

"Hope just received a text from Jay. It was a bunch of garble. Then she tried to call him, almost immediately afterward, and he didn't answer; in fact, he hung up on her. She thinks there's something wrong."

"Fuck," Adam swore, the word exploding from his mouth. "Did Hope know where he was?"

"She didn't say, no. I didn't get many details. I told her to stay put at her office, and that I'd call you right away."

"Damn it. What did he do? Maybe he was just talking to a prof, or something, and couldn't take the call. Okay, I'm on it, Grace. Tell Hope. Tell her to breathe."

"I did. I don't think she can, though."

"No. I'll call you back when I can. Later, love."

Grace returned to her computer screen, vibrating. What could she do? She couldn't very well search for Jay; neither could she focus on the story she was writing.

Sighing, she opened the photograph Adam had remembered to send her that morning, in strictest confidence. The dead man who had been watching Jay's apartment appeared with a young woman, her face turned to him, partly in shadow. Grace recognized neither of them, but she hadn't expected to.

She leaned in and peered at the architecture behind them. Pretty, old buildings, built of stone and perhaps marble, many painted in soft pastels, rose in the background. Then it hit her. *Sorry, Adam,* she thought, as she fired the email off, then jumped to her feet and raced across the newsroom.

"Richard," she said to the photographer loading files into the system on his massive computer. "Can I bug you for a sec?"

He growled a little, but said, "What's up?"

"I sent you an email with a photo attachment. Could you open it? I can't see it very well on my own screen. It's too small."

He closed a file, opened his email and brought the photo up on his screen, then blew it up as large as possible without it pixellating.

"It's pretty beaten up," he said, pointing to the fold lines. "What are you looking for? The guy's face is pretty clear but not the woman's. Not much I can do; there's a dark shadow there."

"I'm trying to see the buildings. Can you do anything to clarify the background? Zoom in or something?"

Richard did so. The faces slipped away off the bottom of the screen, the buildings grew larger, and Grace stared at the sign on a coral-pink building with a bright green logo.

Hotel B, then L, then I. An X. Blixen. Like the reindeer. She turned and dashed back to her own computer, calling thanks to Richard over her shoulder. An Internet search of the name brought up countless listings for hotels, cafés and tourist attractions related to Karen Blixen, the famous Danish author. Most of them were in Africa.

Finally, on the fourth page, she found it, and clicked on the website. Hotel Blixen was in Prague, Czech Republic.

Chapter Twenty-Six

Lorne Fisher, the police force's missing persons co-ordinator, picked up the call from a distraught young woman who could barely speak through her panic.

"Missing Persons," he had answered. "Saskatoon Police."

"I — I need help," said a tight, breathless female voice. "I don't know what to do. Please, sir, help me . . ."

"Miss, please try to calm down. I'm here to assist you. I'm Sergeant Fisher. First, tell me your name."

"Christina. Griffin."

"What's the problem, Ms. Griffin?" Lorne asked, immediately picking up his cellphone as he spoke on the landline.

"My parents. I haven't been able to reach them in two days. And then I called my brother, to see if he'd heard from them, and he didn't answer either. I'm so scared."

"Why are you scared? Is this unusual?"

"Yes! It's never happened before. My parents are always around, they always answer or call back quickly, unless they're travelling, and I know they're not right now. And I went to my brother's apartment; he wasn't there. We're in touch every day, by text or call."

As she spoke, Lorne texted Adam, his enormous fingers struggling to punch the right letters.

Griffin's sistr on the phone. She gteakid. He tried again. Stupid autocorrect didn't work, the one time it would have helped. **Freaked**.

Adam, in the marshalling room madly gathering a team to search for Jay, glanced at his phone just the same, saw the name, texted back.

Thx. Put her thru.

"Detective Sergeant Adam Davis," he said, answering the phone as he left the room. "Ms. Griffin? You're Jay's sister?"

"Yes. I can't reach him, Sergeant; I've called and gone by his apartment. But I also can't reach my parents."

Adam stopped walking down the hallway — stopped dead as if he'd hit a brick wall.

"When did you last speak to them?" he asked.

"On the weekend. I've called them at least five, six times in the last two days. I need a signature on my student loan application, but that doesn't matter now. I'm scared. They always answer, or call back right away, as I told the other sergeant."

Adam was reasonably sure Christina didn't know much about the Taras Petrenko case, nor Jay's involvement in it; the level of danger had only become apparent very recently, and if Adam knew Jay, he wouldn't have wanted to frighten his sister.

But she must know something. The entire campus, if not the city, knew about Taras's death. In fact, Adam had intended to call her as soon as a search was organized.

"Ms. Griffin, I don't know if this will scare you more or comfort you, but I am organizing a search for Jay as we speak. An hour ago, I received a call from one of Jay's . . . friends, saying she had received a strange text from him. I'm sorry there hasn't been time to contact you. But I didn't know this about your parents. We'll call the RCMP and also get out to their place immediately. Where are you right now?"

"In Place Riel," she said, referring to the student concourse that stretched from the Arts building to the library.

"Okay. I want you to go somewhere safe, somewhere with friends. Can you do that?"

"Yes, I think so. I'll see if one of my girlfriends is at home."

"Good. Do not go back to Jay's apartment, okay? I have your number now, and I promise I will call you with updates."

"Okay. Thank you, Sergeant. Please find my family."

"I have every intention of it. Goodbye, Ms. Griffin."

Adam had to restrain himself from violently flinging his phone across the hall. Goddamn it, what the hell was going on? But he was forced to admit that it made sense. Mercury, or his boss, had figured out where Jay hailed from; it wouldn't have been all that difficult. How had he picked up Jay, though? Where were they now?

Instead of breaking his phone in a rage, he dialled Jay's number, hoping against hope that he'd pick up and the alarms ringing in his head were false. But there was no answer.

He strode back into the marshalling room, making rapid decisions and praying they were the right ones. The officers, who had been chatting in his absence, fell silent as entered.

"I just had a call from Jay Griffin's sister. She has not been able to reach her parents, nor Jay, by phone.

We'll have to head to their farm, out by Hafford. James, Lorne, Joan, you're with me. Charlotte, please organize a team to scour the campus.

"We're looking for codename Mercury, and we have no vehicle description. The man himself is six-foot-four, and probably 230, 240 pounds. Big, solid, fit. He has at least an hour on us, maybe an hour and a half. Okay, let's get dressed. Everyone in vests, full gear. Go."

The officers leaped to their feet and rushed out. James, Lorne and Joan awaited Adam's next instructions.

"We're going to have to fly down that highway. Sirens and lights. I'll call the Mounties in Radisson on the way. We'll take the SUVs. Let's roll."

They grabbed their Kevlar vests, checked their weapons, threw on coats and churned down the stairs to the parking lot. Once in the vehicle, Adam contacted the RCMP detachment office in Radisson and rapidly explained the situation, to be greeted with the unwelcome news that officers were at least an hour out from the farm.

"Get there as fast as you can," Adam told the sergeant on duty. "It could be life and death. And silence the sirens as you get close. If he's there, we don't want to give him warning."

"We're on it. We don't have a car in the area," the sergeant said. "Priority one, though. The Griffins are good people. This sucks."

"Yeah. It does. Thanks. I'll see your people there."

James drove as fast as he dared through the city, up Idylwyld Drive, over the curving left exit to the west, and then nailed the accelerator. By the time they passed the city's arena, he was pushing one-sixty. Lorne and Joan were close behind.

"We'll make good time to Radisson," he said, "but shit, Adam, those grid roads. At least harvest is long over, so there shouldn't be farm equipment."

"There better not be," Adam growled.

He had not expected utter chaos to erupt this afternoon. He'd planned to make progress on the evidence, to piece it together, to have a solid case for an arrest. Hell.

His cellphone buzzed. Grace was texting. It was hard to read the words in the vibrating, flying police vehicle; he held up the phone as steadily as he could, and peered at the screen.

The van man's photo was taken in Prague. Sending details.

How did you figure that out?

Blew up the photo, duh. See email.

Adam had to laugh, despite the dire situation.

LOL.TY, Babe.

He didn't need to open her message, although he would later.

Of course. Prague.

*****

"You could end all of this right now, Griffin. Just tell me where the damn mushrooms grow."

"And what? You're going to let me go?"

"I sure as hell won't unless you cough up," Mercury snarled. "I know they have to be near the farm."

Jay kept silent.

"It's too late in the season, right. So you'll have to show me. Or tell me."

"Go to hell."

Mercury's hand balled into a fist, shot out and slammed into Jay's cheek. Jay saw it coming and turned his head away, so at least he didn't get it in the mouth; but it hurt like hell. He wondered if the bone was broken, or only bruised.

His captor hadn't spoken much for the first half hour on the highway. As soon as he'd wrestled Jay into the truck, he'd planted a hat on his head and sunglasses over his eyes. Right around the tiny town of Borden, he started to prod Jay for information.

And now here they were, Jay's cheek swelling and blood flowing from a cut sliced open by Mercury's ring.

There was no way, Jay thought, no way on Earth, no way in hell he would say anything. He had to hold out until he found his parents. The exact location of Gryphon was the only thing keeping them, and him, alive. If they were brave enough to keep their mouths shut, even as this asshole threatened them and — if he was telling the truth — kidnapped and bound them, he had to find the same courage.

Hang in there, Mom, Dad. Hang in there, he thought desperately. How he would rescue them when they arrived at the farm, though, he had no idea.

Mercury didn't need directions when they reached Radisson. Without hesitation, he turned on the correct highway and headed north. Once at Hafford, he navigated the grid road without any forced assistance from Jay, nor even from global positioning. Jay's heart sank, and his stomach flipped. This guy knew where he was going. He had obviously been there before.

Jay's last hope that this was all a ruse evaporated. Horrific thoughts tumbled crazily through his brain.

"Where are they?" he asked Mercury.

"You'll find out soon enough."

"Are they alone? Have you been giving them food? Are they cold? Tell me!"

And what about bathroom breaks, Jay wondered, his heart breaking; what about his parents' dignity?

Mercury snorted. "Of course they're not alone. I have a guy watching them."

So there were at least two of them. That wasn't going to help him free his parents. He'd never felt so helpless in his life; in fact, he'd never really felt helpless before, and the sensation was starting to overwhelm him.

Stay calm, he told himself. You can't think if you're freaking out.

Finally, they arrived at the farm, but Mercury drove past the house and right into the fields; the truck bumped and rocked but took the undulating land easily. So his parents had not been in the house when he'd dropped by yesterday. The realization gave him the tiniest flicker of relief; at least he hadn't missed them, couldn't have saved them, couldn't have known they'd been taken. The guilt over that had been tearing him to pieces.

He knew, now, where the man was taking him, where his parents were being held. Most of the machinery and other equipment was kept in Quonsets and barns on the home quarter; but the Griffin-Nykiforuk farm was monstrous. Ioan had long ago erected two distant buildings, one on the back forty, thinking it would be useful for storing tools, an extra tractor and even food in a small refrigerator during seeding and harvest. It forestalled the need to come back in if a combine needed servicing, or if the men got hungry.

After the main work of farming was completed in the fall, no one went out to the secondary shed. Jay never gave the place a second thought.

The captor's reconnaissance had been comprehensive. He'd found the damn shed, which would not have been easy. If someone dropped by the house, there was no danger of finding Sofia and Ioan. Farmhouses in rural Saskatchewan were notoriously unlocked, and people often popped in. Unfortunately, it had also made it ridiculously easy for the man to grab his folks.

The shed came into view. Jay tried to breathe. He couldn't even imagine seeing his parents bound and possibly gagged; he equally couldn't imagine what the hell he could say or do to get all of them out of this serious shit.

And he knew this man would kill them all, the minute he'd figured out where Gryphons grew. Clearly his parents had understood that and remained silent. Jay also had to hold back that information. But the man might murder one of them, to show, as he'd said, he meant business. Jay steeled himself to confront a hideous choice.

Finally, the bastard pulled up, got out, and dragged Jay down from the truck with his ankles still bound. Grabbing Jay by the arm, he forced him to shuffle and hop to the door and drew it open.

And Jay yelled, before he could see anything in the dim light, "Mom! Dad! I'm here!"

Two sets of wide, terrified eyes gleamed in the dark, and Jay lurched toward his parents, wondering how a mushroom had brought them to this.

Amazingly, the man allowed him to fling himself, arms wide in embrace, at the Griffins. Jay was surprised, but quickly realized that the higher the emotion — the touch, the tears — the more he would be likely to talk.

Suddenly, Jay realized these men had not asked his parents about Gryphon. Either they assumed Sofia and Ioan were out of the loop, or it didn't matter: they wanted him as much as the mushroom.

Jay whispered in their ears. "Hang on. Don't say anything after they remove the gags. Okay? Don't tell them anything."

Mercury pulled him away, then, showed his gun and gestured to the other man to do the same.

"Okay," he said. "Let's get this done. Where is that fucking mushroom?"

Chapter Twenty-Seven

In full flight down the highway, Adam changed his mind about sending Charlotte to campus with the other officers. Just as Lorne could see things on the street that others missed, Charlotte was genius at tracking down information based on the slimmest of leads.

"Char. Can you go back to the station? See if Jonesy is available to help with the search instead. I need you to dive into EPPI, the pharma company. Where was it founded? Where is it located now? Who's the CEO? Who's on the board?"

"You bet, Adam. I'll radio Jones. By the way, Deanna Arlington saw Jay earlier in the day at his desk, but when she went to ask him a question later on, he was gone. That's all we've got so far."

"That reminds me. Can we alibi her up? I'd like to rule her out, if possible."

"I'm on it."

"Thanks, Char. I probably won't be able to answer the phone for a while but try me anyway if you find something on Jay's whereabouts. And also, call the chief. Tell him what's going on. I didn't have time. And ask him if we can get the surveillance plane out here. You know where."

"Got it. Good luck, Adam. Be careful."
"I'll try."

The cruisers screamed into Radisson and turned north. James was forced to lower his speed, but risked one hundred and thirty kilometres per hour, even on the narrower road. Joan, driving the second vehicle, followed his lead.

As they neared the farm, they turned off the sirens and flashing lights and finally parked on the road near the yard. Jumping out, they drew their weapons and made the last several hundred metres to the house on foot, creeping along the bushes and trees that lined the driveway.

Adam approached in a low crouch, silently signalling to James and Joan to slip around the back. Flattened alongside the door, he peered in the living room window; no one was there, but he saw a large plant, once placed on a small stand, lying on the floor. Signs of a struggle.

He nodded at Lorne, still crouched at the bottom of the front steps, and placed a hand on the knob, turning it slowly so it wouldn't make a sound. The door squeaked slightly as he opened it and Adam caught his breath; but nothing happened.

Lorne followed him inside, and they quickly separated to check every room, Adam first going through the kitchen to meet James and Joan at the back door. James shook his head to indicate he hadn't seen the Griffins, nor anything strange, out the back way.

James turned to the basement stairs, and Joan made her way upstairs, as Lorne checked the main floor bedroom and bathroom. Five minutes later, they convened in the living room.

"Nothing, Adam," Lorne reported.

"Nope," Joan added.

"Nothing in the basement, either," James said, "except a few bags and containers of food on the floor. If I had to guess, someone's ransacked the freezer."

"Makes sense, if they're looking for a stash of mushrooms," Adam said. "Damn. Okay. Let's check the outbuildings. And where the hell are the RCMP?"

They crunched over gravel and frost to a huge barn, to find hungry cattle lowing and snorting, their breath coming out in billows of frustration. Being a farm boy, Adam, undaunted, weaved in and out of the pens, patting the occasional rumps to comfort the beasts. Joan climbed into the loft; James and Lorne peered down the hallways and hutches.

"No one here. Obviously, I suppose," Adam said. "The cattle would be much more agitated. Let's hit the Quonset."

Crammed with machinery, the massive Quonset held no surprises, no clues, and no Griffins. Neither did the sheds.

"Where the hell are they?" Adam asked. "Let's go back to the house, and hopefully meet the RCMP there. And think."

Two Mounties had indeed arrived, quietly as promised, and were headed for the farmhouse as the Saskatoon police officers returned.

"Don't bother," Adam told them. "No one inside."

They introduced themselves to the Mounties, Powell and Yakubowski by name ("call me Yak," said the latter, "it's easier") and Adam asked them what they knew about the farm.

"We've checked all the buildings we can see," Adam said. "There's no sign of them. A plant was knocked over in the living room, and the freezer appears to have been ransacked. Where else could they be?"

"It's a damn big farm," Powell said. "Ioan has two sheds out on the land, that I know of. They'd see us coming, though; not a lot of cover out there."

"Right. But we have no choice. Can you lead us there? Do you know where they are?"

"I know where one is. We can start there."

"Okay. Should we take the vehicles?"

"Oh yeah. It'd be a long walk, and a hard one through the stubble and over the hills."

"Okay, let's go."

All six officers ran back to the vehicles. Adam, Joan, Lorne and James piled into the SUVs and waited for Powell and Yak to drive ahead. Powell, behind the wheel, drove a kilometre down the grid road, then turned left at a narrow, rutted track that led into a field recently harvested of its wheat. After a very bumpy few minutes that had Adam worried about the SUV's undercarriage, they saw a small building a few hundred metres out.

"Is it worth stopping and walking in, at this point?" Powell asked Adam via radio. "Or should we just blaze in?"

"We're running out of time," Adam said. "Let's get within fifty metres or so."

A minute later, they jumped out of the vehicles, leaving the doors wide open, and raced toward the building. Adam's heart sank as they neared it: ramshackle and unpainted, the door appeared to be padlocked from the outside, and there was no sign of life through the window.

"Shit," he said, under his breath. They checked it anyway, but the Griffins were not there.

"You said there were two buildings out here?" he asked Powell.

"Yeah. I've heard Ioan mention them. You can see this one from the other road, to the west, so I knew where it was, but no clue on the other one. We're going to have to drive the perimeter, Adam. But I would think it would be some distance away; no point in having the two close together, right?"

"Good thinking."

Back in the SUV, Adam fought to control his impatience. Would they be too late? Were the Griffins even on the farm? If not, where in hell could they be?

*****

Between his hobbled feet and aching cheekbone, the sight of his parents struggling and bound in two ancient wooden chairs, the horror of watching the murder of Livia Balan and the gun trained on his temple, Jay felt his brain skitter helplessly away from finding a solution to this mess.

Mercury asked him again.

"One more time, and it's the last time. Where are these mushrooms, Griffin?"

"Far, far away," Jay said, buying time.

"How far?"

"Well, we'd need a truck."

"I have a truck. As you know."

"And then we'd have to walk in. It's a very . . . bushy sort of place." And Jay felt a synapse fire. He made a decision. He had to get this asshole out of here and get his legs back. "I'd have to show you. As you said, it's too late in the season for mushrooms. You wouldn't be able to find it yourself."

"Okay, let's go." Mercury grabbed Jay by the arm.

"No. Not until you guarantee my parents' safety. I will show you the place, but my parents stay alive. That means he comes, too," Jay said, jerking his head toward the second man. "Don't even think about hurting them, because I swear to you, I will not disclose anything if you do. You can hit me, shoot me, I don't care. I won't tell you."

"This mushroom means that much to you."

"My parents mean that much to me."

"Fuck. Fine."

"Okay. I'm ready. Let's go."

Not that Jay trusted his captors; they'd certainly kill him once they made it to the Twisted Forest. How would they know he'd taken them to the right spot, though? Which he had no intention of doing. Would they actually trust him?

Jay felt more than saw his mother wriggle violently in her chair. He turned to her with pleading eyes, hoping she could see that he was silently begging her to trust him. She stopped moving but stared at him with fear in her gaze.

The two men each took an arm and half-dragged Jay to the truck, pausing only to lock the shed behind them. Jay prayed that Sofia and Ioan would be okay, and that he would somehow be able to kill his captors or persuade them to let his parents go. If he was dead, so were they. They'd seen the men's faces.

They pushed him into the back seat, where the second man joined him. Mercury drove.

"Got names?" Jay asked.

Mercury laughed. "Cochrane. This is Morris."

"Right."

Jay directed Cochrane over the land and back to the grid road, south toward the farm. Before they reached it, he told Cochrane to turn west. When they were a short distance from the gnarled, strange trees, he told him to stop.

"You're going to have to cut this strap," Jay said. "We have to go into that bush, and I can't walk like this."

Cochrane thought this over, then nodded at Morris to set Jay's ankles free.

"Don't do anything stupid," Cochrane growled. "I'll shoot you. I guarantee it."

Jay's knees nearly buckled, but he managed to stay upright. Again with one man holding each arm, he pointed with his chin and the three headed for the boardwalk. Jay stumbled, and they yanked him back to his feet.

"Sorry. I'm tired. Okay, now we have to go into the bush, to your right."

Stepping off the boardwalk and into the bush, captors in tow, Jay tried to remember the specific lay of the land. Where were the hollows and broken trunks? It was prairie, not boreal forest, so hiding spots were almost non-existent.

If he could get away at all.

They plunged into the densest part of the little forest, and Jay realized that one of the men would have to give up his death grip on his arm. It was impossible to walk three abreast. Cochrane let go and stepped behind Jay, following closely.

"We're almost there," Jay told them, as his eyes scanned the landscape.

There. His only hope.

Jay sucked in air and steeled himself. Now, or never.

Being relatively enormous had never before been a life-or-death advantage, although he'd once been forced to punch the bartender in Hafford when he tried to literally grab Jay's former girlfriend. Jay's size wouldn't get him far with Cochrane, who was a big man, but Morris came up to his chin. The weaker link.

Jay whirled to his right so violently that he was suddenly facing Morris and jammed his free left elbow into the bridge of the smaller man's nose. Morris, instantly spurting blood and howling in pain, released Jay's other arm as Cochrane tried to react; but Morris stood between him and Jay for several seconds, blocking the possibility of a shot or punch.

Jay lurched, bending as low as he possibly could, into the bush and behind a tree. He heard a shot ring out, a bullet slam into a trunk, and leaped across a puff of brush into a hollow. Heart pounding, he rolled down a small incline and found a rotting log at the bottom. He hoped Cochrane had not been quick enough to see him tuck his body into the tiny shelter.

More bullets rang out, pinging off the bark of the trees surrounding him. Is he firing for effect, Jay wondered, or does he know where I am?

A sudden, burning pain seared Jay's body; he clutched his biceps and bit through his lip in the effort not to scream. Even if Cochrane hadn't found him, one of his bullets had.

Chapter Twenty-Eight

The lowering sky threatened rain as the police officers drove around the Griffin farm, Adam feeling a sense of doom and desperation as time ticked inexorably on. Would the cop plane make it out? And if so, would it be in time?

"Powell, are you sure there's another building out here?" Adam said by radio.

"Yes, unless he's taken it down for some reason. I can't see why he'd do that."

Minutes felt like hours. Adam perpetually scanned the horizon and watched the dark clouds gather; a pouring rain would obscure the fields and make it nearly impossible to find a small building on the prairie. But hurrying wasn't going to help.

The radio crackled.

"I see it, Sergeant," Powell said. "Follow me. To your left."

They turned and drove at an unnerving speed over the terrain, fat drops splattering suddenly against the windshields. The shed was actually very large, Adam noted as they neared — certainly big enough to house a tractor or two — with two sides protected by shelterbelts of caraganas. The roof was shaded with trees. Adam wasn't sure if the plane would find it.

The six police officers, weapons drawn, jumped out of the SUVs and ran toward the shed, bodies hunched. Adam saw the lock on the door and thought, hell, not again; then dashed to the side window.

Two people sat bound and struggling in the middle of the room. He could see no one else, but that didn't mean Mercury wasn't there, hidden in the gloom.

He didn't pause this time. Adam raced back to the door and shot the lock off, flung it open and braced his back against the outside wall, bellowing "Police! Freeze!" at the top of his lungs.

Not a sound greeted his warning. He peered inside, head dodging in and out of the opening, eyes flicking around the space.

"Coming in. Do not move," he yelled, and the officers burst through the door.

There was nowhere to hide. Only the Griffins were inside. They stared at the police officers for a moment, then began to squirm.

Adam dove at them and removed their gags, as Joan and Lorne began to cut their ropes.

"Where is Jay?" he asked. "Was he here? Where is he?"

"He was," Ioan croaked. "Can't talk. Water. In the fridge."

James grabbed two bottles of water and brought them to Ioan and Sofia; they gulped, took deep breaths and Sofia, through tears of fear and relief, said, "They've taken him to the forest. Please, hurry."

"How many are there? And how are they armed?" Adam asked.

"Two. They have guns. Handguns. Please, officer. Please. Hurry."

"How long ago did they leave?"

"Maybe twenty minutes? Thirty? I can't keep track of time in here."

"Okay. Powell, can you drop the Griffins off at a neighbour's or something on the way? There's always a chance Mercury will return. Then meet us at the Twisted Forest. As fast as you can."

"The Graingers are on the other side of the road. I'll take them there. It'll only be an extra couple of minutes."

"Good. Let's go, people."

This time, Adam knew exactly where he was going, and got in on the driver's side. He sped toward the forest, and before long reached the edge of the boardwalk. Lorne radioed from the other vehicle.

"Sarge, there's a black truck parked to the south, partly behind some bushes."

Of course, Lorne would notice the truck. "Head over there and see if anyone is inside," Adam said, then parked and got out of his vehicle.

Seconds later, Lorne's voice crackled: "No one here."

He and Joan joined Adam and James, and Adam said, "We'll go out in twos, try to cover as much of the area as quickly as possible. Not enough people to stay with the truck."

But before they could move, a shot rang out.

"Hell," Adam muttered. "Never mind. Follow the noise."

*****

"You do know, Griffin, that there's little point in keeping you alive now. We know where the mushrooms grow, or at least, we will in the summer. Your plan backfired. You're fucked."

Jay could hear Cochrane clearly, which meant he was very nearby. It was all he could do not to breathe heavily, as the pain from his arm emanated through his chest and side. He's probably right, Jay thought. I am fucked. It was also amazingly difficult not to respond to Cochrane's tirade. With every fibre, Jay wanted to scream, "Go to hell."

Jay knew he was bleeding copiously and wondered how long it would be before he passed out. Or until Cochrane found him. Or until both things happened at once.

He heard crunching. Feet falling heavily on dry leaves, breaking twigs, coming nearer. Lying prone half in, half behind the rotting log, Jay could see only a horizontal sliver of fading light and autumnal detritus. And then, boots. Cochrane stood inches away, and emitted a loud, evil-sounding laugh, almost a cackle.

"Come out, come out, mushroom man," he sang.

Jay held his position, didn't speak, didn't breathe. He wasn't sure he could move; he felt incredibly weak, thirsty, cold, numb. He heard another shot, closed his eyes and waited for a second bolt of agony.

It didn't come. Then another shot, and the loudest voice he'd ever heard was bellowing something. It sounded like, "put the gun down now" but how could that be? He didn't have a gun. So he couldn't put it down. Cochrane knew that. He'd been thoroughly frisked.

More yelling. More shots. Where was Morris? Jay could make no sense of the noise. Confusion closed in. Then darkness.

*****

Adam heard the laugh, reverberating through the rain and the chilly late October air. He plunged into the trees, James sprinting behind him.

They saw him. Mercury. Standing like a mountain over a little hill, gun pointed downward. Adam thought he wouldn't recognize him, but he did, as someone might recognize the devil after a dream.

In the same second, Adam raised his sidearm and let his booming baritone rip.

"Drop the gun! Now! Police, you fucking bastard!"

Cochrane did not drop it. He lunged behind a tree, aimed and fired at Adam. But Adam, knowing what Mercury was capable of, had already flung himself to the ground. *No fucking way I'm getting shot today. Not again. No.*

Adam and James, sprawled on the forest floor, braced their weapons and returned fire. Cochrane shot back and ran toward a bigger tree for cover. He was getting out of range, so Adam scrambled to his feet and followed him, dodging behind trees as he went.

Lorne raced up behind Adam and threw him the rifle he'd removed from the SUV; Adam was by far the best shot, particularly at a moving target. He braced himself again, shot again. Heard a wild animal's cry, the sound of a body crashing to the Earth. Did he miss, hit a deer? He couldn't see Mercury.

"James, do you see him? Lorne?"

"No. I think you hit him, Adam."

All six officers, the RCMP having arrived minutes after the Saskatoon police, formed a line and stalked over the land.

"Police! Do not move!" Adam shouted as they walked.

They found Mercury lying prone and bleeding in a nest of leaves. Adam had indeed hit him squarely in the chest. He ran to the man, fell to his knees, checked the pulse. Thready.

"Who the fuck are you?" Adam asked Mercury.

"You will never know," he said, so quietly Adam was forced to lower his ear to the man's mouth.

"Call an ambulance," Adam told Lorne, but he knew it was too late. Lorne's eyebrows went up, but he stepped away and radioed as requested.

Adam's heart sank. He hadn't wanted to kill the bastard; he needed him as a witness. Yet trained as he was to aim for centre body mass, his rifle shot was true. Too true.

"Fuck you, cop," Mercury croaked. And died.

No time for self-recrimination now. Where the hell was Jay? Adam stood, left the body where it lay, turned and began to shout.

"Jay! Jay! Where are you? Answer me! Jay!"

There was no response. Frantic, Adam began to run in the direction they had come, but James flew after him yelling, "Adam! Stop. We have to do this more systematically. Okay? Slow down."

"Right. You're right. Sorry, James. Where the hell is he?"

"If he's here, we'll find him."

The officers once again formed a line and this time walked carefully, slowly, across the bush. Then it hit Adam. In the frenzy of chasing Mercury, he'd forgotten.

"Where's the second guy?"

"Hell," James said. "Right."

"Stay low, everyone."

They crept, now, looking everywhere for two men. There were few places to hide.

They almost stumbled over the log. If there had not been blood staining the scattered leaves, Adam might have walked right past it.

"Oh my God. Jay. Jay. Are you there?"

He was. Adam ducked down and saw him, pale, unmoving, silent. Unconscious. Dead? Adam reached for him, immediately placing two fingers on his throat, and dragged him from his hole.

"Jay. Wake up. It's Adam. Wake up."

A small groan gurgled in Jay's throat; one eye opened, as if to test Adam's proclamation that it was really him.

"Adam," Jay said.

"You've been shot?"

"Yes. Arm."

"Hold on, Jay. I've got you, brother. I've got you now. You're going to be okay."

"Parents?"

"Safe."

"Thank God."

Jay passed out again. Adam gathered him in his arms for a moment, found the wound, then tore off his shirttail to bind Jay's arm, and silently begged him to stop bleeding. James and Lorne helped Adam lift Jay and bore him back to the SUV, Joan going ahead, watching for the second man. They could hear sirens. An ambulance was coming.

The black truck had disappeared.

*****

The ambulance screamed back to Saskatoon, headed for Royal University Hospital; there were no medical facilities nearer to Hafford. Adam and James followed at full speed, leaving Lorne and Joan behind to interview the Griffins, and Powell and Yak to deal with Mercury's body. The ambulance had originally been called for him, but now Jay was its denizen.

The police plane had appeared, and Adam contacted the officers on board to search for the black truck, while also issuing an all-points bulletin for the second man driving said truck. Lorne had identified it as a Ford 150, which was supremely unhelpful; every second truck in Saskatchewan was a Ford, and eighty per cent of those were black. But he also had memorized the plate number and wrote it down for Adam while the paramedics loaded Jay onto a gurney and into the ambulance.

Adam knew he had to call Grace. He hadn't told her about the mad dash out to Hafford; there hadn't been time. He likely wouldn't have told her anyway. She would have been terrified for him, worried for his life, and failing death, his PTSD.

But Adam had made considerable strides in managing his trauma disorder since earlier in the fall, when he had been the hunted man in a paintball arena south of Saskatoon. He'd fallen apart. Six years after he had first been shot on the job, and had nearly died, the recent event had been the worst since, bringing on a severe flashback.

Grace persuaded him to seek help from her friend, Anne Blake, a psychologist with a track record in helping PTSD sufferers. Adam owed her a great deal. His sessions with her had calmed his horrific nightmares, and his reaction in the field today surprised him. He'd felt a flicker of the old fear, but his mad desire to find and save Jay had overwhelmed thoughts of past horrors.

She answered on the first ring.

"Grace. I have something to tell you," he said, without preamble or greeting.

"Adam. What's wrong?"

"It's Jay. I'm afraid he's been shot."

"What? How? Oh my God, Adam. Will he be all right?"

"I think so. I hope so. Hell, Grace, I don't know but I hope so. He was shot in the arm, but he's lost a lot of blood. We're on our way back to Saskatoon, following the ambulance. It's going to RUH."

"What happened? Where are you? Don't answer that. I think I know. I'll meet you at the hospital, and you can tell me then. But Adam, are you all right?"

"I am, Grace. I am all right. Not perfect, and I'm a bloody dirty mess, but I'm all right."

"Bloody? Were you shot, too?"

"No. Jay's blood. We should be there in thirty minutes, maybe less. Are you going to tell Hope?"

"Of course I am. It's not something we can hide from her, is it?"

"No. Shit. She's going to kill me."

Adam heard Grace laugh, just a little burst. It was an incongruous thing to say, he realized. Maybe he was a little more unhinged than he thought.

"Yeah," Grace said. "I'll see you at the hospital."

Half an hour later, James pulled up behind the ambulance at the wide glass doors of the emergency department. Adam was out the door of the SUV as the paramedics opened the back of the ambulance, racing toward them.

"How is he?" Adam asked. "Is he . . . "

"He's alive, Sergeant. But we have to get him into surgery as fast as possible."

Adam approached Jay and grabbed his hand around the tubes snaking in and out of it.

"Don't you fucking die on me now, you promise-breaker," he hissed in Jay's ear. "What the hell would I tell your parents? And Hope?"

Chapter Twenty-Nine

Adam paced the hallway between emergency triage and the patient rooms, feeling less like a tiger in a cage and more like a worm wriggling through the earth. How did this go so incredibly wrong? Somehow, Mercury had enticed Jay to a place where he could easily kidnap him. Adam couldn't fathom it. How did the bastard pull it off?

James called Charlotte with an update and asked her to relay the information to the chief. He had offered to report in, seeing Adam's distress mingled with a desire to think through the events of the last few hours. Hanging up, he watched Adam's back-and-forth for a moment, then decided to interrupt.

"Adam," James said, stepping into his sergeant's path. "What are you thinking? More importantly, do you know how awful you look? You're going to scare hell out of Grace."

"Do I?" Adam looked down at his chest, plastered with dried blood, and at his hands, equally bloody and covered in dirt.

"Maybe take a look in the mirror," James suggested.

Adam turned to look in the glass of a nearby window; his face was badly scratched, caked in blood and dirt, almost unrecognizable.

"Yours is only slightly better," he told James.

"Very true, but my fiancée and soon-to-be sister-in-law, who is in love with the victim, are not on their way. Yours are."

Then Adam felt the sting of the abrasions, mostly caused by sharp twigs and branches. His worry over Jay had held all self-concern, and apparently self-awareness, at bay.

At the edge of his peripheral vision, he saw a blur of auburn hair and creamy skin.

"Shit. Too late," James said.

One look at Adam and Grace threw herself into his arms, patting him all over to reassure herself that he was not hurt. Hope, right behind her, stood shaking and pale; James went to her and tentatively placed an arm around her shoulders. He knew her fairly well, but as an acquaintance, not an intimate friend. Hope, however, turned her body into James's and buried her face in his chest.

"Are you really all right, Adam?" Grace asked. "You don't look it."

"I am, Babe. A little scratched and bloody, but I'm okay."

"How's Jay doing?"

"He's in surgery. They got him in right away. The bullet hit the main artery, so he was bleeding a . . . um, a lot." He lowered his voice and spoke into Grace's ear, to avoid Hope overhearing. "They're hoping to save his arm, if . . . if he makes it."

"Ohhh. We'd better go help James with Hope. If you're sure you're all right."

"I'm sure."

They took the few steps to where James was holding onto Hope and put their own arms around her. All four stood there for a few moments, comforting Hope and each other.

Finally, she spoke.

"Tell me, Adam."

"He's alive. He's in surgery. He was badly wounded in the arm."

"Will he . . . will he . . ." she clearly couldn't say it.

"We have to wait for the surgeon, Hope. I'm sorry."

"How long will this surgery take?"

"Judging by mine," James said, "a few hours." James had been shot in the leg earlier in the year; it had been a similar wound, causing him to lose a great deal of blood, and came with the threat of the loss of his limb.

"I'm not going to make a few hours," Hope whimpered.

"You will," Grace said. "We'll be here with you."

They found a corner in the hallway, dragged chairs out of the waiting room, and tried to create a small oasis of peace and privacy. Adam took a moment to wash his face and dabbed at his shirt before deciding it was hopeless.

James wandered off to the cafeteria, and returned with juice, coffee and muffins. Grace called her parents, who were taking care of Lawan, to tell them there was no news, and they would be a while. Hope stared at the wall, fingers laced together as if keeping a death grip on herself.

Adam returned from his ablutions, and before he returned to the Rampling corner, he called Powell.

"How are the Griffins?" he asked.

"They're okay. They've just been seen by paramedics at their neighbours' home. They were given a small amount of food and water during their ordeal, and while they were quite cold overnight, they avoided injury and exposure. How's their kid?"

"Don't know yet. Can you bring them in, or could they drive themselves?"

"I'll bring them or get someone to. It's that bad?"

"It might be. They should be here, if possible."

"Okay, Adam."

"Were they able to give you any useful information? Any identifying details?"

"Not much. No names; just descriptions."

"They must be traumatized."

"Yeah, they are a bit, but you know, they're really strong people. They're dealing. They're worried about their son, and anxious to get into Saskatoon."

"With good reason, unfortunately. And there's been no sign of the second man on our end; I assume you haven't found him either?"

"No. We'll keep looking, though."

They signed off, and Adam returned to the waiting area.

And waited.

*****

Adam remembered to call Christina, who seemed to appear within seconds. Powell arrived with the Griffins ninety minutes later. Adam made introductions but refrained from trying to explain Hope's nascent relationship with Jay. Hell, he couldn't really explain it to himself.

But Sofia, after hugging her daughter, unerringly approached Hope and took her hands.

"You are Hope," she said, wonderingly. "Hope. I need that right now. Jay has spoken of you. How are you doing?"

Hope's worried face suddenly registered amazement. "He has? Ohhh . . ." she said, then gave herself a little shake. "I'm okay. But how are you, Mrs. Griffin? You must be exhausted."

"Call me Sofia. We are tired, but all that matters now is my son."

"Yes. All that matters is Jay."

Tears began to flow from both women's eyes, and they, strangers until a moment ago, put their arms around each other and held on tightly. Ioan, Christina and Grace joined them, until Grace persuaded them to sit and have something to eat and drink.

Dr. Brian Ashern finally appeared, looking exhausted. He nodded to Adam — they knew each other well — and Adam indicated Jay's parents.

"Mr. and Mrs. Griffin?" the doctor asked.

"Yes," they said in unison, heads turning toward him. "How is my son?" Ioan asked, fear shaking his voice.

"He made it through surgery," Ashern said. "Please, sit down. I could use a minute off my feet, too."

He sank heavily into a chair and took a breath.

"So the bullets, thankfully, did not hit any organs," he began.

"Bullets? Plural?" Adam asked. "I only knew of one."

"Yes. The one in his arm, and another in his side."

"How did I miss that? How did Jay miss that?"

"Probably because there was so much blood. The one in his side, near his hip, chipped the bone and went through. Nasty wound, but the arm was more serious. It shredded an artery. We were able to repair it. However, there may be some nerve damage. We can only wait and see."

Sofia released a moan and collapsed. Whether from relief that Jay had survived, or worry over his prognosis, Adam couldn't be sure. Ioan managed to catch her before she hit the hard, tiled floor.

"And the hip, Doctor?" Ioan asked.

"I'm hoping it will be all right, that it will heal properly and not force him to limp. He's young and appears to be very strong."

"When can we see him?"

"It'll be a while yet. He's in recovery, of course, and still unconscious. It was a long surgery, requiring considerable amounts of anaesthetic. I'll have a nurse let you know. I'd recommend getting some rest. You must all be exhausted."

"You have no idea," Adam said. "Thanks, Brian."

"My pleasure. I'll see you later if anything changes."

Adam knew there was no hope of finding beds or gurneys in the busy hospital, so he pulled Grace aside and suggested offering their home for rotating naps. The bungalow in Buena Vista was perhaps ten minutes away.

"These people need some sleep," he said.

"They've been through hell," Grace agreed. "Let's see if we can persuade them."

Only repeated promises to awaken them and bring them back the moment Jay awakened finally persuaded them to get some rest. Hope held her counsel until James led them away, key duly transferred, then flatly refused to leave.

"I'm going to be here when Jay wakes up," she told Grace.

"I'm staying with you, then," Grace said. "I'm sure James can manage. Unless you're going home, Adam?"

"No. I'll need to talk to him as soon as he's able."

The vigil continued.

*****

Hope and Grace fell asleep for a while, on couches a nurse had found unoccupied in one of the residents' break rooms. Adam prowled and paced, then finally braced himself on two chairs and had a nap himself.

When the nurse came at two in the morning and gently touched his shoulder, he sprung into wakefulness, realizing with surprise that he hadn't had a nightmare. Thank God.

"Is he awake?" Adam asked.

"He is. He's asked for you."

"He has?" Adam found that rather amazing. Why him, and not his parents or Hope? "How is he?"

"Remarkable," said the nurse. "I'll take you to him."

Adam decided that talking to Jay came first; calling his parents and awakening the Rampling women would have to wait. He strode down the hallway after the nurse, feeling an intense desire to see and speak to Jay.

He entered the dim room, momentarily overwhelmed by the beeping equipment, tubes and wires; instantly, it transported him back six and a half years to when he was lying in a similar bed. He gave himself a mental shake and approached the younger man.

"Jay. I'm here. How do you feel?"

"Adam," Jay croaked. "I have to tell you two things."

It sounded like "I havva tellya ta thins," but Adam got it.

"Are you sure you're up to this, man?"

"No. But very important. Names. Cockr'n and Morse."

"Okay, slowly now. The first one. Cochrane? Cock-run?"

"Yes."

"And Morse?"

Jay closed his eyes and tried to shake his head.

"Morris?"

"Uh."

"I'll take that as a yes. And what else?"

"Balan. Dead."

Adam, shocked, wondered if he'd heard correctly, until he saw a tear roll from Jay's eye and slip onto the pillow.

"Livia Balan? She's dead?"

"Uh."

"Hell, Jay, I'm sorry. Where is she? Can you tell me?"

"In the greenhouse."

God damn it, Adam thought. Livia Balan was a piece of work but had likely experienced some terrible things in her short life and absolutely didn't deserve this. He felt a stab of sadness mingled with horror.

"In the apple grove," Jay said. "Tell Deanna. She'll find it, show you."

"How did she die, Jay?"

"Shot. Cockr'n."

Adam experienced a powerful urge to comfort Jay, to hug and hold him around the medical equipment that surrounded him.

"Shit. What can I say? I'm so sorry."

"You were right," Jay said, and passed out.

Blood rushed into Adam's head. He could see it now. Livia had somehow been lured to the greenhouse, or had been kidnapped on campus, and forced to call Jay under threat. Cochrane, whom Adam assumed was Mercury, made her behave as if all was well while pointing a gun at her head. Oldest trick in the book.

Adam left Jay's room in a fury directed partly at himself. He called James as he hurried back to Hope and Grace, told him to bring the Griffins back to the hospital, and briefly explained that a long night awaited them: Livia Balan had been murdered.

"We have to find Deanna Arlington's home number and wake her up," Adam said. "Jay said she'd know how to find this greenhouse."

"I'm on it, Adam. See you in fifteen."

Arriving at the residents' room, Adam gently awakened Grace with a soft touch and a kiss.

"Jay?" she said.

"He was awake for a few minutes but fell asleep again. He's coming out of the anaesthetic. Nothing wrong with his memory," Adam added. "I have to go, Grace. Something's come up. The Griffins are on their way. Tell Hope for me, okay?"

She nodded groggily. "Stay safe, Adam. Please."

"I will, Babe. I don't think there will be any more gunfire tonight. Just something I have to take care of."

"Can you tell me?"

"Yes, but later. I love you."

"I love you."

*****

They crept under the leafless apple and sour cherry trees, Adam and James and Lorne, crime scene investigator Abby Markham following. Deanna Arlington had been startled out of sleep by insistent and persistent phone calls and gave specific instructions to the grove.

"I don't know where the greenhouse is," she had said, "but if Jay says it's in the apple grove, it's got to be more or less there. What's happened? Is Jay all right? I couldn't find him earlier."

"Jay is all right now," James said, trying to tell the truth but not the whole truth. "We'll let you know more in the morning." He thought for a moment about Deanna. Was she safe? "Where are you, Ms. Arlington? Do you live with someone?"

"Yes, with my parents. Boring but cheap. Why?"

"Just didn't want you to be alone. I'll talk to you soon."

He'd hung up before Deanna could ask more questions he couldn't answer, drove the Griffins to the hospital and picked up Adam. Lorne and Abby met them on the little dirt road off Preston Avenue.

Flashlights beamed through the trees, slim and erect compared to the aspens in the Twisted Forest. Finally, Adam caught a glimpse of a small structure and waved his team ahead. Stealthily, they approached, aware that the second man — Morris — was still at large. The officers in the plane had found the black truck. It had been abandoned.

Lorne silently signalled that he would scout the wider perimeter, as Adam and James indicated for Abby to take cover as they walked around the building. It was dead quiet, except for an occasional burst of traffic noise from College Drive.

Lorne returned, shaking his head, and they pried open the door to the growth chamber. Black as hell inside. Adam didn't know if the lights should have been on, or not; how does one grow mushrooms in a greenhouse? Should they be kept in the dark at night? Or had someone disabled the greenhouse systems, making it less easy to find?

The four officers stood stock still and silent in the doorway. There wasn't a sound. Adam found a light switch by feeling around the doorway and flicked it; nothing.

He called out, then, to no response, and they finally beamed flashlights around, looked under the long tables of contained dirt, and saw the body of Livia Balan.

Abby looked at Adam, who nodded, and she approached the body. In the light provided by three flashlights, she quickly checked the body to the extent possible and said, "Gunshot wound to the forehead. Dead maybe twelve hours."

"That's a hell of a shot," Lorne said, bending over. "She might as well have had a target painted on her forehead."

"Looks like Cochrane was a trained assassin," Adam said. "Military or police, do you think, Lorne?"

"Yep. I do."

"So what in hell was he doing here, killing off researchers trying to grow a few mushrooms?"

Chapter Thirty

Adam was taking no more chances. With the man called Morris still on the lam, he arranged for twenty-four-hour coverage on Jay's hospital room. Emmy Petrenko had taken his advice and left town with her daughter. Livia Balan was dead, but no way in hell would the same fate meet Deanna Arlington on his watch.

He reviewed the players over and over in his mind. Taras Petrenko. Jay Griffin, his sister and his parents. Livia Balan. Deanna Arlington. And Emmy. Surely there were no more potential victims related to Gryphon.

Adam returned to the hospital, picked up Grace, had a brief conversation with Hope in which she again refused to leave, and went home.

By the time he fell heavily into his own bed, it was after four in the morning. He pulled Grace into his exhausted body, craving the warmth and comfort, the normalcy of their sleeping routine.

He awakened once to a nightmare as a thin, grey dawn touched the edges of the window; but Grace immediately turned and crooned to him, reminding him that he was safe and only dreaming. Her tactic was working increasingly well, as his semi-conscious brain learned to accept and understand her words. He went back to sleep until ten.

It was only six hours, but he felt adequately refreshed and awake, at least for the time being. Grace had already crawled out of bed and by the aromas greeting his nose, was obviously making breakfast and coffee.

"Good morning, Babe," he greeted her. "Smells amazing. What are we having?"

"Omelette, toast, bacon, coffee, juice and whatever else I can cram into you," she said, kissing him. "When was the last time you had an actual meal?"

"Don't remember. I'm starving."

"No doubt. Get this down you, Adam, then tell me what the hell is going on."

He wolfed the food, drank the orange juice and coffee, and launched into the details of the previous day. When he told Grace about Livia's death, tears spilled down her face.

"Oh, Adam, that poor girl. She must have been terrified, and then . . . oh, no," she said, gulping back a sob. "What will you do now? Do you think you know who's responsible?"

Adam didn't answer; he was thinking of something else.

"Can you access the photo I emailed you from here?" he asked. "I want to see what you're seeing."

"Yes, sure. I can log into my work email. Let me grab my computer."

There had been little time for Adam to contemplate the photo. He'd glanced at it, but then had been called away to multiple interviews and the madness of yesterday. Grace returned with her laptop and quickly opened the email.

"There. You see? It's easier on a bigger screen, like the one our photographer has, but here . . ." Grace enlarged the photo to the extent possible and showed Adam the logo on the hotel. "Hotel Blixen, in Prague. I'm positive."

He peered at the building, then focused on the image of the woman, her face turned to the side, much of her profile in shadow. She was laughing, and had her arm tucked into the van man's. Adam drew in a breath. He knew her, he realized. And he understood.

"I love you, genius," he said, and kissed Grace soundly. "Two more days. I promise."

"You've got it, don't you?"

"I do. I'd better roll, or that two-day window will start closing fast." He jumped up and headed for the shower, then returned to Grace, pulled her to her feet and held her. "Let's go somewhere. Far away. Plan our wedding, our lives together. Think about where you want to go, love."

"Really?"

"Yes. We need some time together, just us, away from work and the potential that either of us will get called in. Okay. I'm off to get clean."

There remained traces of blood on his chest, and Adam scrubbed them off viciously. Even his hair had been daubed, as well as encrusted with bits of leaves and twigs. He watched the faintly red water sluice down the drain and felt a sense of renewal. And excitement.

I'm coming for you, he thought. *You're brilliant, but I have found you.*

*****

Adam vibrated all the way downtown, concepts and connections swirling through his brain. First, though, before he could launch into the final stages of the investigation, he was called into the chief's office.

Not that he was surprised. He hadn't spoken to Dan McIvor in days, although he had arranged for Charlotte to stay in touch with him. By now, he had surely heard about Livia Balan, and wanted an update.

"Chief," Adam said, knocking at the open door.

"Come in, Adam. Have a seat. I hear we have another victim."

"I'm afraid so. She was connected to the project, as I think you know. The hitman we dubbed Mercury, whose real name was apparently Cochrane, either lured her to a well-hidden greenhouse, or kidnapped her and took her there. She was forced to call Jay Griffin, and the rest of the mess played out at Hafford."

"How did you learn his name? And do you have a Christian name?"

"No to the latter. Jay told me his name, the first thing he did after waking from surgery."

"Could it be an alias?"

"It could, but I don't think so. I think he didn't care if Jay knew his name. He expected to kill him."

"Right. Adam, how close are you to solving this case? Let's just say the political voices are screaming in my ear. Daily."

"Very close. I think I know how it was done — Taras's murder, I mean. And if I'm right, I know who."

"Okay. Keep me posted. I understand you have protection on the Griffin kid."

"Yes, and Deanna Arlington. We will not lose any more people, Chief. No damn way."

"Are you still going to become my new inspector?"

That gave Adam pause. He had committed to the promotion, but he'd forgotten about it — pushed it out of his mind — as he focused on the case.

"Chief, I am. I can't think about it right now. This case . . . it's the most complicated and frankly weird one I've ever tackled. Not to mention trying to get my head around all the science involved. Give me a week, and we'll talk again?"

"A week?" The chief's eyebrows flicked upward. "You think this will be wrapped in a week?"

"Sooner, I hope. Just asking for the seven days."

"All right, Adam. Good luck. Will I see an email with details by tomorrow?"

"Guaranteed."

Adam left the chief's office and headed for James's desk, which was empty. He found him in the incident room, backside braced on a table, staring at the photos of the suspects and victims, the notes and other evidence.

"Hey. What are you thinking?" Adam said in greeting.

"I don't know yet. Looking at all these faces, and remembering yesterday, I'm mostly thinking this has been pretty wild."

"No kidding. Do we have the names of the EPPI board and executives?"

"Yep." James handed him a clipboard. "I printed them out."

Adam took the offered list and scanned the names. A CEO, eight other executives, twenty board directors. And there he was.

Cochrane. Dr. Jeffrey L. Cochrane. Vice-president, research. Adam pointed to the name and cocked an eyebrow at James.

"Holy shit," James breathed. "Holy shit."

"Get me a full bio on Cochrane. Age, offspring, spouse, education, every committee and board he's ever sat on, the works. And his financial involvement in EPPI — remuneration, stock options, the number of shares he owns. Let me know the minute you've got it, okay?"

"On it, Adam." James left the room, and after a moment of staring at the photos on the board, Adam went to his office, looked up a number, picked up the phone and dialled.

"College of Dentistry," a crisp voice said. "How can I help you?"

"Detective Sergeant Adam Davis, Saskatoon Police. I need to speak to your dean. As soon as possible."

*****

An hour later, Adam was walking through the college escorted by Dean Kevin Vincent, peering around the corridors.

"Tell me about your security protocols," Adam said, after explaining his reason for the visit.

"We have cameras here and here," Vincent said, pointing, "but of course we need to protect our patients' confidentiality, so they are not recorded during treatment."

The dental college provided education and instruction, but also ran a full clinic accessible to members of the public. Adam knew that, somewhere in the back of his mind, but it had only forced its way to the front a few days ago.

"Right. I'll need to see the footage from the two days before Taras Petrenko died, the Friday and Saturday. Did you know him, Dr. Vincent?"

"Only slightly. Faculty parties and that sort of thing. I always enjoyed his company, though. A tragic loss to the university."

"Yes."

"I'll set you up to view the video with our security personnel. Follow me." Vincent stopped. "You don't really think . . ."

"Yes. I do."

The dean shook his head, his expression one of mingled disappointment and disgust, and continued down the hall. Soon, Adam was ensconced in a dark room with the head of security, who rolled video at great speed. Students and professors came and went all Friday afternoon, darting around like agitated birds, and by five the hallways were relatively clear.

Janitors. Another professor. The dean himself. Then, at about seven in the evening, came a little blip; a tiny, split-second jerk of the tape. The security man jumped; Adam swore.

"It's been tampered with," Adam said.

"Looks that way."

"Hell. Who has access to this room?"

"Obviously the security people, the dean, the associate deans. That's about it."

"Is it staffed twenty-four-seven?"

"No. We do have personnel on the ground at all times, but not actually in this room. It is always locked, though."

"Okay. Thanks for your time and effort."

Adam didn't say that the dental college should improve its security. That wasn't the problem.

He returned to the station and called Charlotte, asking her to file a request for information with Interpol.

Knowing he'd have to wait for the information to come from James and Charlotte, he decided to return to the hospital and check on Jay Griffin. Brian Ashern had not called, so Adam felt reasonably assured that Jay was doing well; but he still wanted to see for himself.

Royal University Hospital sat at the west end of the campus, looming behind a stone gate. Adam used his privilege to park wherever the hell he wanted and was inside the hospital ten minutes later. He checked at the information desk to see if Jay was still in recovery or if he had been moved, and was somewhat surprised to learn he indeed was resting comfortably in his own room.

Adam took the stairs two at a time until he reached the third floor, then found Jay's room — not difficult, considering the officer sitting outside. The door was slightly ajar, and Adam was just about to simultaneously knock and push it open when he heard murmuring. It sounded familiar. Like Grace.

He knew he shouldn't have, but he peeked through the door. Hope lay beside Jay on the bed, half-covering his uninjured side with her body, a hand smoothing the blanket over his chest. Adam had seen this before, when Grace had been in the hospital after being attacked in the early spring. Hope had walked into the curtained room, dropped her coat and purse, ignored everyone gathered around her sister and crawled onto the bed, crooning and hugging. There she had stayed for two days.

Grace had done the same thing the first night Adam and she had made love. He'd awakened to a nightmare, but Grace, undaunted, had loved him from his feet to his head, comforting him and, admittedly, arousing him.

"You're going to be all right," he heard Hope say. "I'm here, Jay, and you're going to be all right. I'm not leaving."

"Hope," Jay said, in a strangled voice. "I may be infirm, but you're making me crazy."

A rich, warm laugh gurgled out of Hope. "Mmm. That's a good sign."

Adam, only marginally to his credit, actually blushed at witnessing the intimate scene and crept backward away from the door. Jay was clearly recovering well. He was in good hands.

Chapter Thirty-One

"Adam, I've got it," James said, bursting into his sergeant's office. "Here's the bio on Jeffrey Cochrane. I've emailed it as well. You're going to love this."

James plunked himself in the chair opposite Adam and beamed as his sergeant grabbed the sheets of paper and started to read.

Jeffrey Leamington Cochrane, age fifty-eight, born in Spokane, Washington; presently residing in Los Angeles, California. Educated at the University of Southern California and Charles University, Prague; PhD in cellular and molecular biology. Married twice, to Adina Novak and Cheryl Clarke. Three children: Davorna, Ronald, Andrea. Vice-president, research, Euro-Pure Pharma International. Ten per cent stake in the company, $900K salary, stock options $1.8 million.

Adam flicked the paper as if he were killing a fly, and a smile quirked the corner of his mouth as he looked up at James.

Prague. Where Andrea Horvath had met Taras Petrenko. Where the photo of van man was taken in front of the Blixen Hotel.

And what had Jay said? "What the hell are you going to do, Adam? Fly to Prague and Los Angeles to arrest the board and CEO of EPPI?"

Well, not quite. But very, very close.

"Get Charlotte, Lorne and Joan into the incident room. I'll meet you there in five. Well done, my friend."

Adam had one more call to make before he joined his team — to Jack McDougall. Then he strode down the hallway, ready to lay out his theory like a banquet for his officers to chew on.

His cellphone rang as he walked in and, giving the gathered detectives a small shrug of apology, he answered.

"Adam Davis."

"Sergeant, it's Kevin Vincent."

"Hello, Dr. Vincent. What's up?"

"I went to speak with her, but she's disappeared. No one has seen her today, as far as I can tell. Her office was locked, and when I found the key and let myself in, it had been partly cleaned out. There's no computer."

"Shit, you're kidding me. Have you tried her at home?"

"Yes. No answer. I haven't had time to go over there, though."

"Okay. I'm on it. Vincent, stay put, all right? Don't go over there. I'll take care of it. Thank you."

Adam hung up and turned to the waiting officers. "Never mind. My glorious theory will have to wait. They're in the wind. Get an APB out on both of them. They've likely found out about Cochrane from Morris, or at least suspect that he's been arrested or killed. Let's move."

As they rushed down the hallway, Adam thought, how would they get away? Plane, train, automobile, other?

"Joan," he called to the rapidly disappearing figure of Karpinski, "check the train station. Lorne, get in touch with the RCMP; get them to watch for their car on the highways. You'll have to find a plate number first. Any chance they'd try a bus?"

James shook his head. "Too slow and too limiting in terms of movement," he said. "Train probably the same. Still."

"Right. You're right. Char, call the airport immediately. Find out if there are any jets, private and commercial, ready to take off, or which ones have in the last few hours. And call NavCanada. Tell them to hold them if they're coming through security; do that first. And get two officers over to their home."

"On it."

"James. Let's go."

"What are the odds we'll find them? That they haven't long since taken off?"

"Slim to none, but we have to try."

Two minutes later, they jumped into a cruiser with James behind the wheel. Adam wanted to be available on radio as they screamed north toward the airport; a relatively short trip at the speed James was pushing on Warman Road.

Adam vibrated with frustration, waiting for news from Charlotte. Finally, the radio crackled.

"Sarge, there are actually five aircraft waiting on the tarmac, one on the runway," she said. "Something to do with the weather in Calgary, Edmonton and Vancouver. It's coming our way; freezing rain. Two of those are charters, one is private."

"I never thought I'd be happy about freezing rain," Adam said. "Bad weather: the great equalizer. Thanks, Char."

"And NavCanada is checking their security lists right now. Obviously, it's been busy, with that many delayed flights. I'll get back to you."

Adam allowed himself a savage smile. They may have flown out earlier, but the weather warnings had at least given him a chance.

"Char, get Lorne and Joan to back us up out here. That's a lot of planes to check. And maybe Jonesy and MacDonald, too."

"Got it. And out."

"Ever stormed a plane, James?" he asked.

"Nope. You?"

"Once. Can't wait to do it again."

James turned onto Fifty-First Street, took the overpass and flew down the final few blocks to the airport. Adam already had his door open when James hit the brakes in front of the terminal, screeching to a stop in front of the first set of doors. They raced in and ran to the security office, showed their badges. Charlotte had called to give airport security warning that several members of the police force would descend upon them within minutes.

"We have to get on those planes," Adam told the officer in charge. "I want to start with the one on the runway, just in case."

"Right. Follow me."

The security man led them through a behind-the-scenes labyrinth and commandeered an air traffic controller's cart from a very surprised employee. Soon they were zipping across the tarmac toward the first plane poised to take off, should the weather allow.

The cart was equipped with a ladder, and soon Adam was climbing up to the door, which had been released and opened by a flight attendant. He scrambled onto the relatively small plane, seating perhaps fifty, and walked down the aisle, scanning frightened faces as James planted himself at the front. The captain came over the sound system, telling his passengers not to worry, but really, why wouldn't they, Adam thought. His invasion of the craft couldn't possibly have been for an innocuous reason.

They weren't there.

"No one in the bathrooms?" Adam asked.

The flight attendant shook his head. Adam gave him a reassuring nod, thanked him for his patience, and told him that all was well.

By the time he and James were back in the cart, driving toward the next plane in line, his cellphone buzzed.

"Adam," said Charlotte when he answered. "No one by that name has gone through security. But we do have a Novak."

"We do?" Adam punched at the sky with a balled fist. "Yes! Which plane?"

"One of the two to Vancouver. Flight 8575, Air Canada."

"You are bloody amazing. Good work to notice that name. Thanks, Charlotte."

"And Lorne and Joan have arrived. They're on their way to you."

"Fantastic. Thanks." He turned to James. "I think we've found one of them. Flight 8575," he told the driver of the cart.

This was a much bigger plane, a full-sized jet that awed Adam slightly as they drove up near its belly. It was one thing to board an aircraft from the terminal, quite another to stand below it.

Lorne and Joan awaited them near the massive wheels. The security chief spoke into his radio, and a moment later the door eased open. Adam crawled up the ladder again, followed by his officers.

This time, the passengers were not silent and agape. They were babbling, moving, twisting in their seats. A commotion near the middle of the plane held everyone's attention. Adam stared down the aisle, momentarily baffled, seeing a distraught flight attendant with her arms thrust out.

Then, as the attendant moved to the side, he saw Andrea "Novak" Cochrane Horvath holding a child against her body. And the needle she held to the little girl's throat.

The emergency door was open.

"Everyone, sit down and be quiet!" he roared. "Andrea Horvath. Let her go. Now."

Adam advanced on her, prowling down the aisle with his hand on his sidearm. He wouldn't put anything past this insane and intelligent murderer.

"Hello, Detective. How lovely to see you again," she said, her voice even. Calm. Crazy, Adam thought. "However, you should leave this plane, and allow me to do the same. With the child. Otherwise . . ." she gave a tiny shrug and tipped her head toward the open door.

Adam saw no point in arguing that she couldn't possibly get away with this hostage ploy. Andrea Horvath was too far gone to care, in his estimation.

"I will stick her," she said. "And you know how well that will go. For her."

The girl suddenly squirmed in fear; she was certainly old enough, perhaps ten or eleven, to understand that something very bad was going on.

Andrea tightened her grip, hard enough to make the child cry out.

Adam signalled to James, who immediately began to walk past the rows of terrified people, telling them to get down.

"I don't want to shoot you," Adam said, in his most menacing tone. "But I will if I have to."

"No, you won't," Andrea said. "You won't fire your weapon in this plane. What if you miss?"

"I don't miss, Dr. Horvath. I didn't miss when I shot your brother at fifty metres. I won't miss you at three."

"Ah. So he is dead. I wondered." An expression of dismissal flitted across her face. "Well, you'd better get on with it. I can stand here all day."

At that, the child's mother, who had been shaking and weeping quietly, began to scream.

"No! Let my daughter go! Please!" And she lurched at Andrea Horvath.

"No!" Adam yelled in turn, lunging to restrain the woman; but Horvath gave her a sharp kick, landing her boot squarely in the woman's face as she came in a crouch out of her seat.

"That's enough," Andrea said.

But she had done Adam a favour. Andrea's position had changed slightly, and with the mother crumpled in the aisle, he had a clear shot. No way in hell was he letting her off the plane, and if he jumped her, who knew where the needle might land? And would he knock her out of the plane with the child in her grasp?

And where was Devon Horvath? Adam realized he didn't know if the dean of pharmacy was on the plane as well. He hadn't seen him, but he had been completely focused on Andrea from the moment he'd stepped into the cabin.

"Where is Devon, Andrea?"

"Somewhere safe. With the samples."

"Samples?"

"Of Gryphon. Oh yes, Detective, we found them at the Light Source. So, even if you shoot me, we have the goodies."

"Perhaps. But that's all you have. You don't know where they grow. I know Ronald Cochrane didn't have time to call you. I was right there. And Morris had disappeared by then."

"Mmm. Maybe we can make a deal. I give you this brat, and you tell me where they are."

"That's not going to happen. Let the child go."

Andrea narrowed her eyes at Adam.

"If that's the way you want it," she said, and snapped her body and the child toward the open door.

Adam had no time to pray that the impact of a bullet wouldn't send her and the child reeling through the opening. He raised his gun in both hands, aimed at the arm furthest away from the little girl, and pulled the trigger.

Adam Davis did not miss. Andrea screamed, let go of the girl, and whirled to the side as she clutched her arm. Adam leaped at the girl, grabbed her around the waist and pushed her into the aisle; James, almost simultaneously, lunged at Andrea, found the needle on the floor where she had dropped it, and pulled her down prone in the wide space beside the emergency exit.

Chaos erupted as people screamed at the gunshot noise and jumped out of their seats. Lorne Fisher bellowed a warning to stay put and shut up. The girl's mother collapsed, and an extremely with-it flight attendant quickly attended to her.

Adam joined James and wrestled Andrea Horvath onto her stomach.

"I need a tourniquet here," Adam yelled. "Do you have one on board?"

"Coming, Sergeant," another attendant called back, and returned with remarkable speed bearing the device.

James grabbed it with a nod of appreciation and tightened it on Andrea's arm.

"Hell of a shot, Sarge," he said to Adam.

"Thanks. This time, I meant to do that."

"I know."

They turned their somewhat subdued perpetrator over, and Adam kneeled in front of her.

"You're under arrest, Andrea Cochrane Horvath, for the murders of Taras Petrenko, Livia Balan and Jon Smyth. As well, I'm arresting you for the attempted murder of Jay Griffin and the kidnapping of a child, name as yet unknown. Get an ambulance," he added to the flight attendant. "Lorne, can you bag up this needle, please. And be very fucking careful."

"Yes, Sarge."

Andrea glared at Adam with fury and hatred sparking in her eyes.

"You may have me," she spat, "but you'll never save Gryphon. This is much bigger than you think."

Chapter Thirty-Two

Forced to relinquish his suspect to the health authorities, although under heavy guard, Adam focused on finding the two people still at large: Dean Devon Horvath and the man called Morris.

Driving the streets of Saskatoon and the highways of Canada would get him nowhere. He released another all-points bulletin for both and called a meeting in the incident room for eight the next morning. Charlotte arrived first, bearing news from Interpol.

"You were right about Ronald Cochrane. He had more aliases than I have flowers in my garden. And passports. Eight that they know of."

"What was his background?"

"He served in the American military for six years. Trained as a sniper, which does not help explain what a lousy shot he was. Although, stationary use of a rifle with a scope is not the same as firing a handgun while you're on the run in a forest."

"Good point, Char. As far as I know from Jay, Cochrane was spraying the universe in his general direction, and he did miss me. Then what?"

"He became a mercenary, essentially, in the interests of industrial espionage. Mostly for his father's firm. I suspect it paid better than the army."

"Guaranteed."

James and Joan entered the room, followed a moment later by Lorne. Adam brought them up to speed on Cochrane's Interpol file, and then asked Charlotte to continue.

"As far as Morris goes," she said, "they think he's just a hired assassin; no ties to the family. But that's if they've got the right guy."

"And van man? Jon Smyth?"

"Nothing so far."

"Okay. Our priorities, of course, are to find Morris and Horvath, and to interview Andrea Horvath as soon as possible."

"How did they kill Petrenko, do you think, Adam?" James asked. "And what really blows my mind is why it was necessary in the first place. Over a mushroom? Really?"

"Seems extreme, doesn't it? But EPPI didn't see it that way. They thought Taras had found a potentially miraculous substance, which they either wanted to eliminate from the face of the Earth, or they wanted to use for their own pharmaceuticals."

"Why would they want to eliminate Gryphon, though?" Charlotte asked. "If they're right, and if Petrenko was right, it could have saved a lot of people a lot of misery. Maybe even lives?"

"Because it would have collapsed the market for many of their drugs. If Gryphon has anti-inflammatory, antibiotic and potentially other properties — especially if it can be delivered in one dose for several disorders — all their research, investment and existing similar drugs would be wasted and useless. We're talking billions. Not to mention Jeffrey Cochrane's reputation."

Four faces gazed back at Adam with jaws open. "Wow," James finally said. "But how did they find out, considering the research was being conducted in as much secrecy as possible?"

"Livia Balan. She let something slip to Devon Horvath when she slept with him in a bid to make Taras jealous. She told us that she said nothing specific, only that the project was going well and she was excited about it. We may never know, but she must have said more: maybe that Gryphon would change the world, or drugs as we knew them. Or let slip a bit of scientific lingo that alerted him. And he told Andrea."

"Okay, wait, Adam. They're both in on it, right? What was his part?"

"Devon extracted the poison from the inky cap mushroom — the poison that isn't a poison until you mix it with alcohol. If someone eats an inky cap — let's say inadvertently, because who really wants to eat that? — and then has a couple of drinks, they might get pretty sick. I believe Devon, the pharma-genius, distilled the coprine down so that Andrea could administer a heavy dose in a small amount of liquid."

"What the hell were they getting out of this? Is it as simple as money?" Joan asked.

"Partly," Adam said. "Mostly, I would think. But there are two other motives in play. One is EPPI's, and Jeffry Cochrane's, reputation, as I said earlier. And revenge. Taras, you'll recall, reported EPPI to the German authorities when he was still a PhD candidate and working for them in Berlin. He had found a potentially life-threatening side effect to the drug they were developing. The German drug administration levied a hefty fine and demanded that they stop creating the drug.

EPPI tried to get rid of Taras then, but he managed to disappear."

"This isn't just about Gryphon," James said, his face lighting up as a revelation hit him. "This was about the potential damage Taras could do to EPPI in the long run. His brilliance was what they wanted to eliminate, since obviously he would never work for EPPI again. It would go against his ethics."

"Exactly."

"That's . . . fucking evil."

"Yes," Adam said vehemently. "It is."

"What I don't get," Lorne said, "is how they found Taras. Also, he would obviously have recognized Andrea, right? They had an affair. So what happened?"

"Andrea and Devon Horvath have been at the University of Saskatchewan for about two years," Adam said. "That's when all of this began. Andrea found and recognized Taras, maybe during a conference, and wondered what he was up to. Both Horvaths then applied to teach and do research here and were hired.

"They had Taras followed, using the van that once belonged to Douglas Brennan. If and when they decided to make a move on Taras and it went sideways, they could always point to him as a suspect. That was a good move; it sure made me wonder if Brennan was our guy."

"Okay, but didn't Taras know that Andrea worked for her father?"

"I don't think he did. When he knew her in Prague, they were both basically kids. Either she wasn't involved at EPPI yet, or she was so savvy even then that she didn't let her affiliations slip to Taras. She had a heavy loyalty to Dad, who could make all her dreams come true."

"It doesn't make sense to me that she became a professor of dentistry, though," Charlotte said. "Why would she enter the dental profession, and not, like her father, cellular biology or something related?"

"Well, first of all, she does have two undergrad degrees, in biology and anatomy. Second, I think she chose dentistry to become one of EPPI's assassins."

"Ohhhh . . . I get it. It's easy to off people in the chair. No big noises from firearms; no stabbings in the alleys; no bludgeoning at the Light Source. Is that what you're getting at, Sarge?" Charlotte asked.

"Yes. But she needed help. So she married Devon Horvath, the big pharmacy brain, and promised him enormous wealth and power."

"Not a love match, then."

"I don't think so. Marriage made in financial heaven. Which brings me to another motive: she wanted Taras and he spurned her. And he had long ago turned his back on EPPI, too. She wanted to either have him back or kill him so no one else could have him. It wasn't just Livia Balan who found Devon Horvath unpalatable. Andrea does too."

"Another thing. Why does EPPI have offices in Prague and in Los Angeles?" Joan asked.

"They also have offices in Berlin and in Egypt. It's a multinational pharma company, and having multiple locations paves the way into various markets. Jeffrey Cochrane is American, but the CEO is Czech."

"It's bizarre to me, how all of this landed here in our little city. Comparatively speaking," Charlotte said.

"I know. I thought at first I was on the wrong track, maybe losing my mind," Adam said with a wry laugh. "It's because of the Canadian Light Source — the only synchrotron in Canada, and it's certainly on the international scientific map. It attracted Taras, and criminal activity or no, it also attracted Horvath. We've hit the big time."

"How'd she do it, Adam? There was no sign of injection or patch or anything else on Petrenko's body, according to the autopsy."

"I think I know, but I'll wait until I interview her. Wouldn't want you guys to think I'm an idiot."

"Hardly, Adam," Charlotte said.

He grinned at his constable. "Well, as you said, she got him in the chair . . ."

The staff sergeant burst into the room at that moment.

"They got Morris," he panted, out of breath.

"Where?" Adam said, jumping to his feet.

"At the hospital. He was coming for Griffin. Big points to Jonesy for taking him down."

"Jones was pulling guard duty?"

"Yeah."

"That'll be the last time he complains about having to do a stakeout," Adam said. "What happened?"

"Guy wearing scrubs came moseying down the hallway, innocent as hell, which made Jones suspicious. Carrying a tray for Jay. Jones followed him into the room, and that woman, you know her, Adam . . ."

"Hope?"

"Sure, whoever. Jay's asleep. Morris drops the tray, probably just a prop to get him in the door. He wasn't expecting a visitor, so he tells Hope to be sure Jay eats something when he wakes up. Hope tells him to leave the room, and Jonesy decides something's definitely off. Then Jay wakes up, kind of squints at this guy, and says, 'Hey, it's you!'

"Before anything else happens, Jonesy gets Morris in a choke-hold. The guy starts fighting, so Jonesy clocks him one and down he goes. He hollers for hospital security, and then calls it in. We've got him. He's on his way down here now."

"I hope they kept the fucking tray. There might be something unhealthy on there, even if it was mainly a prop."

"Yep, Sarge. Jonesy yelled at everyone not to touch it. Including Jay and Hope."

"How the hell did Hope know something wasn't right?"

"She told Jonesy she'd never seen the guy before, and he made her nervous. I guess she'd pretty much seen all the staff on the floor. No guarantee that they wouldn't bring on different staff, but maybe she was just being careful?"

"Or she has incredible intuition and we should recruit her to the force. Thanks, Sergeant. Let us know when Morris and Jonesy get in."

*****

Jones processed Morris and planted his ass in an uncomfortable chair in interview room one. Adam and James watched through the one-way window with interest, wondering how the man they'd glimpsed in the Twisted Forest would behave.

Was he a weak link? He seemed to have played second fiddle to Cochrane, but that didn't necessarily mean he would be easy to break. Still, if Interpol was correct, he had less to lose; he wasn't a member of the family.

Adam felt positive he had solved the case, and he did have Andrea Horvath dead to rights at the very least for threatening the little girl on the plane. Evidence, however, was a different matter.

Who was this guy? Adam tried piecing together possible connections and failed. At this point, he was no one. Just a hitman. With a very swollen nose, thanks to Jay.

"Hello, Mr. Morris," Adam said, entering the room. After telling the tape recorder who was in the room, the date and time, he asked, "First name Robert?"

The man shrugged. Said nothing.

"Or Charlie Emerson?" It was a possible alias that had popped up in Interpol's search.

Nothing.

"Okay, if that's how you want to play it. Tell me what you were doing in the Twisted Forest. Who were you working for?"

Morris gazed over Adam's shoulder, and stayed silent.

"Did Ronald Cochrane hire you? Or his father?"

Nothing.

"It was one or the other, so you might as well tell me." Adam sighed and glared at his suspect. "Come on, Morris. You've been caught. Talk."

"You have nothing on me."

"Ah. So you can speak. You were in the forest with Cochrane; we saw you. So did Jay Griffin. And then you showed up at the hospital. I don't think it was a coincidence."

"I didn't hurt anyone."

That might be true, actually, Adam thought, although he was certainly complicit and definitely a kidnapper.

"If that's the case, why don't you tell me what the hell went down and get yourself out of here?"

"Nope."

"A little scared, maybe, of the big guys?"

No answer to that, either, but the eyes narrowed. Adam pulled out a print of the photo taken in Prague, featuring Jon Smyth and Andrea Horvath. He still didn't know who the man was, nor his real name. Adam pushed the photo toward Morris.

"Who is this, Morris? Your dead colleague. Who is he?"

To Adam's surprise, Morris's head snapped up.

"What are you talking about?"

Holy hell, Adam thought. He doesn't know.

"The guy in the van. This guy, whose fake identification read Jon Smyth. Found under one of our bridges, stabbed to death. Who is he?"

"What the fuck? You're fucking lying to me."

"No, I'm not. I can bring you proof, if necessary. It would only take a minute. We believe Cochrane killed him after he almost gave the game away, in front of Jay Griffin's apartment. He's dead, Morris. Believe me."

"Oh, shit," the man breathed. "No. No way." He surprised Adam again: his eyes misted over, and his hands shook.

"Why does this matter to you? Tell me, Morris."

A long delay ensued, as Morris clearly wrestled with himself over what to say, if anything. Adam waited, quietly, patiently. Finally, the prisoner gave his head a massive shake.

"Those fucking bastards. They killed him? What the fuck for?"

"Because I saw him, and the van. Then he pulled out in the vehicle and we got the plate number. We think Cochrane was pissed. What do you think?"

"Cochrane was always pissed about something. Hair trigger temper. That asshole."

Morris paused again.

"Okay. Fine. I'll tell you what I know. Jon Smyth was Colin Sheridan, and he was like my baby brother. We came up in the army together, did a stint overseas. That's where he met Andrea Cochrane, when she was studying in Prague and we were on leave. And he fell in love. Little idiot."

Chapter Thirty-Three

The Vancouver Police found Devon Horvath the next morning and discovered the molecular Gryphon samples during a strip search. For now, he would remain in custody in that coastal city, at least until a decision was made about where he would be accused and stand trial. Los Angeles? Prague? Or Saskatoon?

The previous afternoon, Andrea Horvath underwent successful surgery for the wound in her arm, which proved to be a relatively simple patch-up; the bullet had gone through, leaving her without significant damage.

Adam vibrated throughout the day, waiting for word from RUH on when he could interview her. At ten, Brian Ashern told him it shouldn't be too long, but she was still in recovery.

Adam didn't want to release any information to the public until he'd spoken to her, but he also didn't want to wait much longer. The citizenry deserved to know the case had been solved, and the police force, especially its chief, couldn't wait to get city council and the university president off their backs.

Too agitated to sit in his office and with little left to investigate, Adam headed to RUH to visit Jay, wondering if Hope would still be at his side.

She wasn't, but there were two men in the room: Douglas Brennan, Light Source CEO, and someone Adam didn't recognize.

"Hey, Adam," Jay greeted him. "Good to see you. You know Doug Brennan, right? And this is Eaton Walter, vice-president, research, of NSERC."

Adam greeted Brennan and held out his hand to Walter.

"It's good to meet you. You gave us a big break in the case. I'm glad to be able to thank you in person."

"I did?" asked Walter. "Well, I'm happy to have helped, but I can't imagine . . ."

"As we always say, every little thing helps. And it's true. Your evidence about the faculty club lunch was exactly what we needed. So thanks."

"We were just talking about Gryphon," Brennan put in. "Obviously, we don't want the project to collapse, despite losing Taras. We thought we'd test the waters with Jay, here."

"What did he say? Forget it, this mushroom is way too dangerous?" Adam quipped.

Walter laughed. "No, I think we'll be able to come to an agreement. Assuming, of course, that you've arrested the bad guys?"

"We're getting close. The top bad guy is up to Interpol, but I think they're on it. I'll let you talk and come back later."

"No, that's fine, Detective. We'll be on our way. I think we have an agreement in principle. Right, Jay?"

"Absolutely."

"Take care, Griffin," Brennan said. "We'll see you when you're back in action. Goodbye, Detective."

Nods and handshakes duly given, the two scientists left, leaving Adam and Jay alone. Jay's eyes were bright with excitement.

"Does this mean you'll take over the project?" Adam asked, pulling up a chair.

"Looks that way. Man, I can't believe it. I'll still need to find an advisor, but it'll be my baby." His face clouded, then. "I do, and I will, miss Taras, though. Without him, it will be a much tougher go. But we'll make it. We have to, in his memory if for no other reason."

"I'm really happy for you, Jay. You can't let this mushroom go to waste. Has Hope been by today?"

"She's here somewhere; she made herself scarce when Brennan showed up with Walter. I think she went down to get something to eat."

"That's going well, then?"

Jay's face changed entirely. The soft look in his hazel eyes told Adam everything.

"She's . . . absolutely incredible," Jay said. "Funny, sharp, a bit motherly . . ." he paused as Adam laughed at the understatement. "And beautiful. So beautiful."

"Just like her sister," Adam said. "Welcome to being in the thrall of a Rampling woman."

"No kidding. That's the word, all right. Listen, Adam . . . I don't know how to thank you for saving my life. And my parents' lives. God, if you hadn't been looking for us . . ."

"Had a little help from Hope and your sister, you know. Without them, I wouldn't have known what to do."

"Still."

"What happened that day, Jay? Did Livia call you? Why did you go to meet her?"

"She called to say my mushrooms were growing in the greenhouse. I was so excited, I guess I wasn't thinking clearly. But I did ask her, Adam, if everything was okay, and she said it was. I was very careful; I looked around me every step of the way, and I did a circuit around the building. And I was thinking, well, I wouldn't be alone, right? Livia was there. As long as no one followed me, it would be okay. It didn't occur to me that she'd been taken hostage. Oh, God. Poor Livia. I feel so guilty, Adam."

"I know, Jay. But it's not your fault, and you'll come to that. I don't feel very good about it, either."

"What don't you feel good about, Adam?" Hope asked, coming into the room. "You saved Jay's life." She put her arms around Adam and hugged him tightly.

"Yes, thank God, and thanks to you and Christina," Adam mumbled, his face partly obscured by Hope's hair. "We were talking about Livia Balan."

"Oh." Hope's face fell. "That was terrible. I'm so sorry. But it's not your fault. Either of you."

"That's what I told Jay."

"For once, you're right." And Hope smiled up at her brother-in-law-to-be.

*****

Halfway down the hallway, Adam's phone buzzed, and he pulled it from his pocket to see Dr. Ashern's name on the screen. Andrea Horvath was awake and doing fine. Did Adam want to pop by?

"I'm actually in the hospital," Adam told the doctor. "Which room? I'll be there in seconds."

Ashern gave him the number, and Adam took the stairs up a floor; Ashern awaited him at the nursing desk.

"You're not going to tell me to go easy on her, Brian, right? She killed Taras, not to mention threatened the life of a little girl."

"It was actually Andrea who murdered Taras?"

"Yes, it was. I'll tell you how and why later. Show me to her room."

Ashern led Adam to the end of the hallway, where two police officers in full uniform stood at attention. Adam greeted them and went into the antiseptic room to conduct the final interview in the Gryphon case.

He could see immediately that Andrea Horvath was alert and furious. Adam restrained himself from calling her an insane murderous bitch, and mildly said, "Hello, Andrea. How are you feeling?"

"Great, thanks to you, you bastard."

"Don't thank me. You were the one ready to throw an innocent child to the tarmac. Or inject her with poison." Adam realized he hadn't yet received the report on what the needle contained, but it didn't really matter now.

"I have updates for you, Andrea," he continued. "We found Morris, who told us the identity of Jon Smyth. Poor bugger, he really fell for you, didn't he? Enough to risk, and lose, his life for your crimes, not to mention bring his buddy into the conspiracy. And Devon is in police custody in Vancouver." Her eyebrows shot up. "Oh yes. And they found the samples, disgusting as they were."

Andrea shrugged, but couldn't entirely mask her shock.

"What I need to establish is how you killed Taras," Adam said. "Would you like to tell me, or should I tell you?"

"Why don't you tell me, if you're so fucking smart?"

"Okay. You can confirm as I go along. At the lunch at the faculty club, Devon seeded Taras's food with something. Something hard. Pebbles, maybe? It doesn't matter. It wasn't a guarantee, but it worked. He broke a tooth, or a filling; Eaton Walter noticed the crunch, and Taras excused himself from the table, holding his face.

"He tried to gut it out, but by late Friday afternoon it hurt him a lot, didn't it? You were on campus and made sure you bumped into him. You talked him into coming to the clinic, where you would give him pain relief. He agreed.

"Your brother, Ronald Cochrane, was here, too. You let him into the security room after making sure no one was in there. As a vice-dean, you have a key. He obliterated the piece of video that showed you and Taras in the hallway.

"After that, it was easy. You filled a dental syringe with procaine and coprine, expertly distilled by Devon, and injected the mixture to both relieve his pain and to poison him.

"It was the perfect weekend for it. Plans had been made for dinner at the Stocktons. You didn't know if Taras would have wine, or how much; but if he was going to accept a glass or two, that would be the time. And he did. Stockton helped you out by refilling his glass.

"Three hours after the dinner, Taras was purging the contents of his body on the Light Source floor. No one had to be there. He did it all for you, all alone. The security in the CLS building would not be so easily hacked as the dental clinic's, so you couldn't get him there. And it was the perfect murder scene for an absent murderer.

"It would've been better if the alcohol had hit him at home — and it did — but he braved it out, thinking he was finished vomiting and went to conduct his experiment. He even did you the favour of starting the laundry with his soiled shirt in it.

"You knew Emmy was away. No one would have found Taras until potentially Monday sometime, or even later, had he collapsed at home. That would have opened the door to a different set of suspects, wouldn't it?"

Andrea's mouth had long since fallen open. Now she closed it with a snap.

"Go ahead and prove it, asshole," she said.

"Your face told me everything I need to know. With Morris's evidence, you're going to jail. Forever. And so is your father."

Adam paused, and grinned widely.

"And Gryphon," he added, "will continue. Doug Brennan and Eaton Walter have made sure of that."

*****

Lorne Fisher arranged for Ioan and Sofia Griffin, who remained in Saskatoon to be with their children, to take a peek at Robert Morris in a lineup. They had spent the largest part of thirty-six hours with the man, and Adam wanted to cross his Ts by ensuring he was the same person lurking in the Twisted Forest. Sofia trembled a little, but Ioan stood like a statue and supported his wife. They both identified him as one of their two captors.

Charlotte and Joan, armed with a warrant, went to Andrea and Devon Horvath's offices, as well as Devon's lab and Andrea's cubby in the dental clinic, to gather whatever evidence they might have left behind. Adam still suspected that an additional dose of coprine, or perhaps some other strange substance, had been delivered to Taras by patch, possibly on Friday in the guise of painkiller.

James got back in touch with Interpol to update the force on what they had learned in the last two days. The issue remaining was linking Andrea's actions with her father, so James connected Emmy Petrenko, still in France, with the international cops. Her evidence regarding what happened with EPPI in Taras's younger days would support the involvement of Jeffrey Cochrane.

Adam, returning to the station from the hospital, attended a briefing with Chief Dan McIvor, Doug Brennan, University President Ellen MacKenzie, the science deans and Mayor David Wolfe. Such briefings were rare. In fact, Adam couldn't recall a similar event, and hadn't personally been involved in one; that was usually inspector rank territory.

It had already begun.

"Adam, come in," said the chief after Adam knocked on the boardroom door. "You know everyone here, I think?"

"We haven't met," said MacKenzie, standing and offering Adam her hand. "If it were not an embarrassing breach of protocol or behaviour, I would hug you instead. Thank you, Sergeant Davis. Not just for solving these terrible crimes, but for saving the university's reputation — to the extent possible. We're still guilty of having hired two criminal minds. And perhaps for poor security in some of our colleges?"

"Thank you, Dr. MacKenzie," Adam said. "I'm honoured. And your security is generally quite appropriate. I might suggest that fewer people be given access to the systems."

"We're looking at that. Normally, we do not have professors murdering each other. We view the systems as a means of preventing theft or assault. It's hard for me to accept that some highly-trained expert slipped in and was able to alter our video."

"Any suggestions for the CLS, Adam?" Brennan asked. "We thought, or rather think, we have an excellent system."

"No. Yours is rock solid, Doug. But what I've learned from this case is the significance of having the Canadian Light Source in our city. It's obviously put us on the international map, which has had some, ah, unintentional consequences. I've also learned a lot about mushrooms," he added. "And poison."

"When will the news break, Sergeant?" the mayor asked. "Are you ready to tell the public?"

"We are. I was hoping to hear back from Interpol first, but we'll arrange a news conference and press release for tomorrow at the latest."

"I want to say, Davis," Wolfe continued, "that we are all very grateful you've solved this case."

Adam looked down for a moment, remembering the murder of Livia Balan, the horrific captivity endured by the Griffin parents, the forced departure of Emmy Petrenko, the near death of an innocent child, and particularly the attempted murder of Jay Griffin.

He thought of Taras Petrenko, the great mind and human who had lost his life to the passions of greed and desire. Adam knew he could hardly have prevented Tara's death, but wondered if he indeed deserved gratitude considering the other victims.

"Adam?" the chief prompted. "Are you all right? What are you thinking?"

Adam raised his head and simply said, "That I'm sorry."

Chapter Thirty-Four

The StarPhoenix
November 2, 200_
Page One

Police capture suspects in deaths of university scientist, grad student

By Grace Rampling
and Lacey McPhail

Saskatoon Police have arrested two university professors and another man for the murders of biology professor Taras Petrenko and graduate student Livia Balan.

Dentistry professor and vice-dean Andrea Cochrane Horvath and pharmacy dean Devon Quince Horvath, a married couple, face first-degree murder charges in both deaths, as well as three kidnapping charges. Another first-degree murder charge has been laid against them in the death of a man found stabbed under the Victoria Bridge, who has been identified as Colin Sheridan, alias Jon Smyth, an American citizen.

Police captured Andrea Horvath in an intense standoff on an Air Canada plane at the Saskatoon airport.

She had opened the emergency exit door and kidnapped a ten-year-old girl, threatening to stab her with a needle that contained poison. Detective Sergeant Adam Davis, the lead officer on the case, shot Horvath in the arm. She is in hospital recovering under heavy guard.

Devon Horvath had tried to flee the country via Vancouver on a separate flight but was apprehended by police in that city.

The tendrils of this case reach to a multinational pharmaceutical company, Euro-Pure Pharma International (EPPI), for which Andrea Horvath's father, Jeffrey L. Cochrane, is vice-president of research. Saskatoon Police worked closely with Interpol to identify the senior Cochrane as the leader of the complex murder case. He was arrested in Los Angeles Thursday.

Another man, Ronald Cochrane, Andrea's brother, was killed by Davis in a chase west of Saskatoon near Hafford, in the area known by locals as the Twisted Forest or Crooked Bush. Cochrane shot Jay Griffin, a member of Petrenko's research team. Griffin was seriously injured but is recovering.

The case revolved around a project known as Gryphon, named for Jay Griffin, which was in progress at the Canadian Light Source. Gryphon is a unique mushroom that appears to hold remarkable anti-inflammatory, antibiotic and potentially other healing properties.

"We understand that EPPI, once Cochrane learned of Gryphon through the Horvaths, either wanted to develop drugs based on the mushroom, or wanted to destroy it," said Detective Constable James Weatherall in an interview. "Gryphon could potentially replace a large number of EPPI's pharmaceuticals. The company couldn't risk it."

Mayor David Wolfe expressed relief that the case had been solved.

"I've spent countless hours on the phone speaking to concerned citizens," he said. "I would also like to express my condolences to the families, colleagues and friends of Taras Petrenko and Livia Balan."

University President Ellen MacKenzie echoed Wolfe's sentiments, and added that the U of S would immediately embark on a security audit, as well as review faculty hiring protocols.

"The Horvaths came to us with the best of references," she said. "They were well-trained professionals with impressive resumés, and indeed Devon Horvath conducted excellent research. However, they still were not what they seemed to be."

Continued on page 3 . . .

*****

"How," Grace asked Adam that night, "did you figure out the method of coprine delivery?"

"Who said, when you've eliminated the impossible, whatever remains must be the truth?"

"Sherlock Holmes, smarty. That's not the whole quote, but you're close. It was that toothache that kept nagging at you."

"Yeah. It kept coming up. Finally, James reached Eaton Walter, who heard the crunch of Taras's tooth at the faculty club lunch. It had to be related, I thought. Then I called Jack McDougall and asked if he thought that could be the solution. He said, as usual, 'Aye, Adam, you may be onto something.' Which means yes.

"And, they may also have slapped a patch on him, telling him it was a painkiller, to ratchet up the poison in his system. Jack said if it was administered briefly on Friday, the mark may have been gone by Monday, when they started the autopsy. So props to your osmosis theory."

"I must echo the voices of the rest of the city and say, thank God this case is over. I've missed you. Very much."

"I've missed you, too. Have you thought about where we should go on a trip yet?"

"No. It hasn't exactly been quiet at my shop, either. Today was very, very long. But it was worth it. What a story. Want to eat?"

"Yes. I'm starving. What are we having? And by the way, I'm sorry you've been doing all the cooking lately. I'll do better. I promise."

"I got some chicken out of the freezer this morning . . ." Grace said and stopped as the doorbell rang. "Who could that be? Gah, I'm too tired for company. Are you expecting anyone?"

"No. I'll get it, Grace."

Adam heaved himself out of his chair and went to the door, as Grace theorized it must be someone canvassing for charity. But it was not. It was James and Bruce.

"Hey, James. And Bruce! What's up? Come in. Everything okay?"

"We won't stay long, Adam," James said, stepping in. "We have some news."

The light in his friend's eyes, the smile creeping crookedly up one side of his face, told Adam what was coming.

"Come in anyway," Adam said.

The two men kicked off their shoes and shambled into the kitchen, heads ducked shyly. Their body language confirmed it for Adam.

Grace turned from the stove, saw who it was, and launched herself at Bruce. Lately, there had been little time for socializing, and she hadn't seen either man since her engagement party. She was delighted to see Bruce, who had saved her life in the spring. She loved him for it, as well as for himself.

"Honey!" she cried. "Good to see you," she said, and hugged James, as well. "But this is a surprise."

She glanced at Adam, standing behind the visitors beaming, and her left eyebrow went up.

"What?" she asked. "Adam looks like he's eaten a canary. Proverbially speaking."

Bruce took a step away from Grace, grinned and held up his left hand, wiggling the fingers. A golden band gleamed on one of them, a diamond spraying light from the middle with elegant engraving surrounding it.

"Ohhhhh," Grace breathed. "It's beautiful. This has to have been made by the same goldsmith who did mine. Isn't it? Does this mean what I think it means?"

"Yes!" James yelled, and punched the air.

"Yes," Bruce agreed. "He proposed. Last night. I said yes."

"Finally," James put in. "It only took three tries, damn him."

"What made this time the charm?"

"Well, Adam helped. Which is why we're here. You're the first we've told, apart from our parents."

"What did you say, lovely man?" Grace asked.

"Some garble about life being short. You know me, always there to help with some original and genius comment."

"Ha," James said.

But Bruce's face became still and very serious. He turned, walked over to Adam and firmly put his arms around him. Grace's heart gave a thump. The two men were very similar in height, size and colouring; a more beautiful embrace she couldn't imagine — apart from her own, with Adam.

"Thank you," Bruce said, backing away and looking Adam in the eyes. "I needed to hear what you said to James. I was so caught up in legalization, so angry that it hadn't happened long ago, that I thought to hell with the institution of marriage. I love James, and I know he loves me, and I thought that was enough. But it wasn't, for James. I needed to honour that. And now I'm . . . beside myself. Happy. So thank you."

Grace could see Adam misting up, swallowing hard around a lump in his throat, and wanted to fling her own arms around him; but she waited for the interaction with Bruce to play out.

"You're welcome," Adam managed to say.

"Group hug," Grace suggested.

They gathered in the middle of the kitchen floor until Grace finally broke it up and suggested a glass of wine might be in order. And the four friends toasted each other, first seriously, then with teasing and laughter.

*****

After finally eating a very late dinner, Grace and Adam were doing the dishes when she turned to him.

"Seriously. What did you say to James, that he apparently shared with Bruce, that made him say yes?"

"It really was, more or less, that life is short," Adam said. "It wasn't some huge revelation. It was Jay who got me thinking about it. I told James I was always aware of how much I love you. That I would do anything to protect you, and to be with you forever. To me, that involves marriage — maybe not for everyone, but for me.

"The protection, and devotion, is physical, financial and emotional. They are bound up in law. And I said that if James felt the same way about Bruce, he should ask him again to marry him. That's about it. Come to think of it, it's even more important with gay couples. I'm not sure if it's still this way, but in the past, gay couples were simply roommates under financial law, while hetero couples were considered common-law spouses."

"You said that?"

"Um, yes. The first part. I'm extrapolating a bit."

"Will you marry me?"

"I thought we'd already established that."

"You asked me, and I said yes. But I want to ask you too, so that you know I love you, that I would do anything to protect you and to be with you forever. Will you marry me?"

"You are serious."

"Very."

"Yes. I will marry you, Grace Rampling," Adam said, quietly, his voice shaking.

He kissed her, then, madly, fingers in her hair to steady her face as full lips met fuller ones, tongues entwined, Grace making moaning noises deep in her throat. Adam, not ending the kiss, unbuttoned her blouse, unclasped her bra and tore open his own shirt, wanting to feel her breasts against him, naked and soft.

After a moment, though, Grace backed away, almost unable to breathe, and stood bare to the waist before him.

"There's one more thing," she panted.

"What, Babe? God, please, make it fast."

She laughed and reached over to the kitchen counter, around and behind a canister, and drew out a small box. With a nervous smile, she handed it to Adam.

Opening it, he found a wide gold band set with a cushion-shaped diamond. Turning it so that the inside caught the light, he could see two coats of arms engraved inside: MacAlister, his mother's clan, and Rampling.

Tiny words read, "Yours forever. Grace."

Chapter Thirty-Five

One week later

Lawan sat in Auntie Grace's lap in Auntie Grace's living room. Hope had dropped her off on her way to pick up Jay.

"Could you . . . could you keep her for a few hours, Grace?" Hope had asked, nervously.

"Even eight or nine," Grace had said, her face soft with understanding. "Don't rush back, my sister. We'll be fine."

But Grace wasn't, at least not quite, fine. Experiencing much of a day with her beautiful, sweet little niece was evoking powerful feelings Grace was not ready for. Nor had she really expected them.

By the time Adam returned from work — early in the afternoon, since it was Saturday — he found Grace gently weeping over Lawan's sleeping form.

"Honey," he said, racing over. "What's wrong? Are you all right? Is Lawan?"

Grace flicked away a tear and smiled tremulously at Adam, in an effort to pretend she had not been crying. Adam was not so easily fooled. He knelt before the woman and the child.

"Babe. You have been crying. Tell me."

"I don't know why, Adam. She's so lovely, so adorable. I'm a little overwhelmed, I guess. I'm happy, too, for Hope and for Jay and for . . ." Grace gulped. The tears were threatening to overflow again.

"Aw, sweet love. Here. Let me take her and put her down. I'll be right back."

Adam carefully lifted Lawan in his arms and carried her to the second bedroom, managing not to awaken her. He grabbed a box of tissues and hurried back to Grace.

"Here, let me mop you up," he said, dabbing at Grace's cheeks. "Now. Talk to me."

"Can we just make love?" Grace whispered. "I want you, Adam."

"And I want you. Always. First, though, talk."

Grace looked down at her hands, busy shredding a damp tissue.

"I'm thirty, Adam."

"I know, Grace. I'm thirty-two."

"Can we, do you think . . . just do it? Get married, get on with our lives? Like, today?"

Adam laughed. "Well, maybe not today. Maybe very soon, though? And then try for babies?"

She nodded, speechless for the moment. He always knew what she was thinking. Always. She'd have to get a mask or something, to prevent him from reading her mind all the time.

"Yes, please," she finally got out. "Every night. Let's try every night."

"And every afternoon."

Adam scooped up his trembling love, kissed her deeply, and carried her off toward the bedroom.

"What if Lawan wakes up?" Grace asked breathlessly, halfway down the hall.

"We'll manage. Just don't scream my name too loudly."

"I don't know if I can do that."

"There are pillows and shoulders to bite."

"We could save the trip for our honeymoon," Grace put in, incongruously.

"Yes. We could."

"Will we need a bigger house, do you think?"

"Possibly. How many babes do you want, love?"

"Two? Four? I don't know. How many do you want, Adam?"

"As many as you like. Hush, Grace. Let me love you now."

*****

Jay was so ready to leave the hospital, he was showered, dressed and sitting on his bed vibrating by eight in the morning.

The doctor arrived an hour later for the final check, and by that time, Jay could have flung himself out the window just to be gone.

"You're doing very well, Jay," said Dr. Ashern. "Remarkably well, in fact. You're good to go, as soon as someone comes to collect you. I want to see you in a week. Without fail. We want to check your nerve responses, tendons, all those things. Promise."

"I promise."

"Take care, now. See you soon."

Jay didn't mention to Brian Ashern that his healing process had a little outside help. Once his mother had gathered herself together after her own ordeal, she had slipped home to the Hafford farm and picked up her kit of crazy poultices and shit-tasting tonics. Jay did not, of course, object. He swallowed the murk and acquiesced to midnight applications of Gryphon, mixed with other magical flora, on his injured arm. Hope would sneak in to remove them before morning.

He had another hour to vibrate. At ten, Hope appeared, charging in with dark-brown-and-auburn hair wild about her face, eyes snapping with something fiery. She wore a flattering and fairly snug T-shirt under a voluminous sweater.

"Hello, beautiful," Jay said. "You look amazing."

Hope blushed. "Are you ready to go? Your mom's expecting us for lunch, right?"

"I'm so ready I can hardly stand it."

"I thought you might be. Here, get in the wheelchair."

"No way. I'm walking out."

"That's not hospital protocol, you know."

"I know."

Hope rolled her eyes, shrugged, and picked up Jay's bag.

"You dropped Lawan off at Grace's?" he asked. "She's okay with that?"

"More than okay. I think she's been dying to spend some time alone with her."

No one stopped them as they strode together down the hallway and out the door. Sofia, craving normal family time, had invited them to the farm for the afternoon, and Jay had agreed, if Hope was also welcome. Besides, he was not yet allowed to drive. His mother had smiled and said, of course.

On the way to Hafford, Jay detected a slight nervousness in Hope, who was uncharacteristically quiet as she drove the familiar highway. He had to admit a few nerves of his own. Their relationship was new and had developed under extreme circumstances; what would happen next?

When they pulled up in the farmyard, Sofia — who had clearly been watching for them — rushed out to greet them.

"Jay. Hope. I'm so glad to see you both," Sofia said, hugging them. "Come in, come in."

"I've brought a couple of side dishes," said Hope. "I hope you don't mind?"

"That's so sweet. Thank you, dear," said Sofia.

"I'll just get them. I'll be right back." Hope returned, slowly, to the truck, giving Jay a moment alone with his mother.

"My baby, my son, my Jay," Sofia crooned, hugging him again. "My God. How did this all go so wrong? And it was my very own mushroom that started it all."

"Mom, you're not taking any responsibility for any of this, right? It's my fault. I brought it to the attention of my professor. I am guilty of starting all this, if anyone is."

"Of course you're not," Sofia objected, totally abandoning logic. "It was those greedy awful Horvaths and Cochranes. It's not your fault at all. You were trying to do something wonderful."

Jay laughed. "You do know that doesn't make sense, Mom. If I'm not at fault, how could you be?"

She laughed, too. "Yes. I suppose I do know that. Another thing I know is that you're going to drink this, right now," she added, handing him yet another potion.

He downed it as Sofia held half of him tightly, avoiding the injured arm.

"I love you so much. You are an amazing human and I am proud to say I made you. With your father's help, of course."

"Mom. If there is any good in me, it's because of you." Jay's voice broke. "I love you, too. Thank God you're all right. Thank God."

Hope returned, then, dishes in her hands, and the two turned to her.

"Right," Sofia said briskly. "Ready for lunch? I'll just call Ioan."

After the meal, Jay asked Hope if she would like to take a short walk, maybe to visit the animals, see the rest of the farmyard. He didn't think he could wait another minute to be alone with her; he had to break the tension, open the conversation, ask her how she felt.

They wandered toward the barn, and as soon as they were out of sight and out of earshot, Jay stopped and turned to her. Yet she spoke first, her cheeks on fire, her voice unsteady; but she held his gaze.

"I want you to come home with me, Jay," she said softly. "Today."

"Hope. My God. Are you sure? You know what will happen. At least, what I want to have happen. Are you ready? Are you sure you want me in your home?"

"Yes. I'm sure. I do."

"Hope. Do you . . . want me?"

She gave him a slightly worried look, which in turn worried Jay. He couldn't be misreading her, could he?

"Are you okay, do you think? Does it hurt?" she asked.

"Does what hurt?"

"Your arm, for God's sake, man."

"No. It's a little stiff, you know. The tendons and such aren't quite there yet. But no, it doesn't really hurt. Mom's magic helped." He gently placed his hands around her face. "I'm fine. And I can't wait another minute."

Hope looked up at him looming over her and began to tremble. "Ohh, Jay, not . . ."

"Here? Oh yes. Here. And now."

He pulled her against him, softly at first, then tightly, absorbing the sensation of finally, fully holding Hope against his body. He gently turned her head to cradle it against his chest, feeling her heartbeat racing in tandem with his own.

After several moments of standing together, Hope pulled her head back.

"If you don't kiss me soon, I may lose my mind."

Jay smiled down at her, as much in relief as with humour. No, he hadn't misinterpreted.

Taking a massive breath, he whispered, "Now, then." And lowered his lips to hers.

Acknowledgements

Griffin's Cure is a slightly more speculative novel than the others in the Adam and Grace series. Nonetheless, after considerable research and conversation, editing and proofreading, and the occasional surge of fury, I trust the concepts are reasonable and applicable to one of many challenges facing humankind.

I must thank my husband, Ken Paulson, for his hours of research assistance, support and the occasional wonderful ideas that led to some of the scenes in this book.

Thank you to the Canadian Light Source, which offered me an in-depth tour of the facility and its security systems. It was incredibly helpful and ever so kind.

Many thanks to my beta readers and editors, whose invaluable advice and helpful comments were taken to heart. Love you all.

About the Author

J.C. Paulson is the author of the Adam and Grace mystery series. A long-time journalist, she never intended to write novels until a dark insomniac night when the plot of Adam's Witness, the first book, came to her fevered brain. The hook was set.

Originally intended to be a trilogy, the series has expanded to four books with a fifth coming next year; and Adam and Grace have become part of the household.

The Adam and Grace Series

Adam's Witness

When newspaper reporter Grace Rampling literally stumbles over the body of a Catholic bishop, she abruptly finds herself at the centre of a police investigation — not only as a key witness, but a suspect and even potential victim.

Lead investigator Detective Sergeant Adam Davis is thrown by the fierce attraction he feels toward Grace that, if acted upon, could throw the entire case into jeopardy.

With Grace at risk and off limits, Adam races to unravel an increasingly disturbing mystery, while he struggles to both protect and resist the woman of his dreams.

Broken Through

A dead dog. A smashed car. A wild storm . . . and then, a violent death.

The quiet streets of a Prairie city have rarely seen such brutality. Tough crime reporter Grace Rampling is covering the case until it suddenly becomes very personal: a close friend is on the front line of danger.

Grace's lover, Detective Sgt. Adam Davis, is forced to return home from a conference, confront his PTSD and find a murderer before he, or she, kills again. And as Adam knows, a psychopath never commits just one crime.

Fire Lake

Grace Rampling and her lover, Sgt. Adam Davis, escape for a weekend to a remote Northern Canadian lake, in the pristine wilderness. What should be a peaceful holiday suddenly erupts into chaos, when in the middle of the night, an arsonist's fire shocks them out of their love nest.

They rush across the dark water to make a hideous discovery: an Indigenous veteran is dead. He had once protected Grace, and she is devastated to find him murdered in the forest.

But soon, Grace and Adam's attention is diverted by a terrifying realization. Someone is lurking in the dark, and they might be next.

Finding the author

J.C. Paulson

https://www.jcpaulsonwriter.com/
https://twitter.com/joanne_paulson
https://www.facebook.com/jcpaulsonauthor/

Join her mailing list for updates on future publications, sales and cool stuff by getting in touch on any of these sites, or find her on Amazon at:

https://www.amazon.com/J-C-Paulson/e/B071GVF9N4

Made in the USA
Middletown, DE
13 September 2020